I0718983

Also by Phyllis Wachob

Teachers Abroad Mysteries

#1 Revolution Revenge
#2 Oasis Assassin
#3 Turkish Delight Gone Sour
#4 Singapore Fling

Kern Kapers Mysteries

#1 Body in the Orchard
#2 Killer Kern
#3 Hot Tub Homicide
#4 Cuyama Cold Case

Cuyama Cold Case

Phyllis Wachob

Dedication

This novel is dedicated to my brothers Jim, Pete and Willie, the kids who grew up wandering the streets of New Cuyama including Lyn, Janice, Eddie, Martie, Luann, Patty, Timmy, Cynthia, Nancy and all the rest.

Acknowledgements

This series of mysteries would have been impossible to write and bring to fruition without the help of many friends and family members. The critique and change of cover design, contents, flow, and characters would not have been enjoyable, in fact, agonizing and slow, without their help. So, thanks to my many friends who listened to the tellings and retellings, my long-time cover designer Doug Thompson, my photographer Francisco Montesinos, my proofreaders Diane Rowles and Larry Harman. A special thanks goes to all my fellow members of the Writers of Kern, who keep the encouragement coming.

Preface

Some of the places in this novel are real, for example the restaurants Bill Lee's Bamboo Chopsticks, the Sugar Mill, Dewar's, and the Buckhorn's cafe. These places of Bakersfield and Kern and Santa Barbara Counties are easily found in histories, maps, guides and on the web. However, Darrell Pitt's office and the community where Very lives are fictional. In its essence, this is a work of fiction. Names, characters, places and incidents are either the product of the author's imagination or are used fictitiously, and any resemblance to actual persons, living or dead, businesses or establishments, events or locales is coincidental.

Cast of Characters

Vermilion Blew: retired school librarian and teacher
Bradley Parker: AKA the White Stetson, friend of the
    Sanchez's and former lawman
Darrell Pitts: Private Investigator, Very's business
    partner
Olivia Grainger: Darrell's new secretary/helper
AnnaRose Bullitt: murdered girl
Glen Bullitt: half-brother of AnnaRose
Eugene Bullitt: father of AnnaRose
Cynthia Bullitt: sister of AnnaRose
Betty Jean Bullitt: mother of AnnaRose
Mickey Kenton: neighbor of the Bullitt's
Raymond Kenton: father of Mickey and neighbor
Wayne Gordon: friend of Mickey Kenton's
Joey Sanchez: Very's best friend
Deputy Bobby Sanchez: Joey's husband
Cleopatra: Very's cat
Gabriela (Gabby) Hernandez: young friend of Very's
Father Sullivan: parish priest well-known in Bakersfield
Frankie Monroe: Very's fiancé

A Note about Cuyama

Cuyama is a Chumash (Native American) word meaning clam. Indeed, clam and oyster shell deposits have been found there. The Chumash were hunter-gatherers that traveled seasonally in the Cuyama Valley and left cave and rock paintings in the area. At the beginning of the nineteenth century, the Spanish arrived and the Chumash were forced into the mission system. Two large land grants were given in the Valley. Settlers raised cattle and some wheat, but water was always an issue.

In 1948, oil was discovered and Richfield Oil Company built the town of New Cuyama to house and support the oil workers. Young families moved in and soon facilities sprouted. Schools, churches, a shopping center, and a community hall were built. And in 1952, the Cuyama Buckhorn made its debut.

If you go to Cuyama in 2024, you will find little changed. The oil is running out. Agriculture, driven by the usage of well water, has taken over. But that water, too, is running out. The air is still clean, the hills are still barren, still gleam golden in the setting sun and there is still little for teenagers to do…

Chapter One: Introduction to the Cold Case

"A cold case?" Very said. "A Cuyama case?"

Darrell, her partner in the Private Investigation firm, smiled at her. Very looked at the three other people in the room. She knew Olivia, the new secretary and she suspected, Darrell's new girlfriend. Olivia was wedged in the corner in the tiny office on the second floor of the nondescript building on 17th Street. Being wedged was an easy task for her as she was slender to the point of anorexia and could fit herself into any space with ease. An unfamiliar man, somewhere in the middle age of life, stood next to Olivia. He too was thin, which was convenient as he was also forced to crowd into a small space just behind the second computer and desk. He had a nervous tic that had seemingly attacked his upper body. He looked very, very nervous, as if he couldn't make up his mind whether he wanted to be here. An obligation, to be here? And presumably, the new client.

The fourth person, she knew, or rather, she had seen him before. The first two times she had encountered him, he was wearing a white Stetson, an affectation she found amusing, anachronistic and arrogant. Today, he was without it, or rather, not wearing it. After all, men's hats were not worn inside, a rule her mother rigorously enforced in her home. All those Bakersfield men with no manners were told to take the 'filthy things' off their heads when they came in the door. The 'White Stetson' would have won the approval of her mother. On that point, at least. His craggy face was solemn and he turned his eyes towards Very. Gray, shades of gray. They matched his hair color. Everyone else wore summer casual clothes, but the White Stetson was more formally dressed in clean, new jeans and a white shirt, long-sleeved and buttoned up to the top. A smile of recognition flitted across his face. Vermilion Blew nodded her head to him in the faintest of acknowledgments. Why was he here?

The room was stuffy with the late spring, or was it early summer, heat. Summer arrived earlier and earlier and today, the office was more than crowded, waaay beyond its capacity. It had been a small office for one P.I., Darrell Pitts, whose name came first on the stencil on the door. More furniture had been added when Very joined the firm, part-time only, but it was 'cozy' when both showed up at the same time to work. The recent addition of Olivia had made the space cramped, crowded, confined. The analogy of a lemon popped up; squeeze a lemon and the seeds shoot out, followed by stinging juice. Who was going to be the first to be ejected?

Darrell cleared his throat, preparatory to speaking. A new-found confidence emerged that Very could only wonder at. When she had first met Darrell, he was solitary, shy, uncomfortable with anything but numbers. He had fallen into the PI game because he had worked for an accountancy agency, doing research for investigators who looked for fraud in companies. Gradually, he had taken on more and more of this kind of work, until he decided to open his own office. He worked best alone, or so he thought. He had earned his license and shortly afterwards, Very had tried to hire him. He couldn't have been much of a businessman, because instead of taking Very's money, he had trained her to look for the man who ruined her life. And then she had started working on other cases. The second name on the door to the office was hers. They had forged a relationship that veered from brother and sister, mentor and mentee, friends, and finally a person to call when threatened by a gunman.

Darrell explained, "You lived there and you know the place, or knew the place. This is Glen, and he has come to us with a request, he's going to hire us. And you know Bradley, don't you? Bradley Parker. I asked if he would join us, pro bono, for obvious reasons. But he knows the case. And you're here because you have special talents."

Very wanted to roll her eyes, but she only closed and opened them. She looked hard at Darrell. "So, I lived there…"

"But you're also very good at finding out things from people," Darrell continued.

"Yeah, you can make people confess," Olivia added. "Maybe it's because you're a woman, with that touch."

Very had always suspected that Olivia wasn't a feminist and also that the drivel that came out of her mouth was good intentioned. She bit her tongue.

"So," she turned to the client, now visibly shaking. "What's your name? And what is this about?"

"My name is Glen and I'm here because of my father. It's for my father. He wants to clear his name. He was never arrested, never accused, but everyone thought he did it. He wants to make sure. You know, JonBenet Ramsey."

They all fell silent at the mention of the infamous case.

"Don't you remember? The mother and the father, the older brother, just a kid at the time. The cops thought that one of them had done it. Years and years of harassing the family. They finally moved out of state, I think just to get away from all the publicity and gossip. The press hounded them, law enforcement, newspapers, all of them condemned them, pointed fingers. In the end, there was no evidence, but it ruined their lives."

"So what does this have to do with JonBenet Ramsey?" Very's question was met with silence.

She turned to Bradley, "So I lived there, for a while, a long time ago, but what is your connection?"

"I was a new hire at the sheriff's department. One of my first assignments was this cold case. I didn't do a good job. I was frustrated not to be able to question the witnesses like they should have been. But I agree with Glen here. It's time to finish this off, put it all into the past. Maybe we can find who really did it."

"So, you think I can get someone to confess?" Very demanded.

"You know what we mean, you talk with people, they tell you things. You are really, really good at that." Darrell looked around the room to find confirmation.

"I'm doing it out of atonement. I failed this family years ago, I didn't pursue what I should have. And I've checked, the cold case files are still there, the evidence seems to be intact. It would be invaluable to have another set of eyes on the case." Bradley paused and looked at Very. "Joey and Bobby, good friends of yours, although Bobby is frustrated with you, speak highly of your abilities."

"To get into trouble? I'll bet that's what Sheriff Bobby has said about me." Very put on a 'try to convince me' look, or what she thought was the look.

"Trouble, but also that you have tenacity, inquisitiveness…"

"Gullibility?" Very questioned.

"That wasn't mentioned, but 'brave' was bandied about."

"Gullible and brave, two halves of the same coin?"

Brad opened his mouth to speak, but closed it.

"Ohh," Very said, leaning forward to confront Brad, "Cat got your tongue?"

Darrell broke in, "Very, please. We're not here to argue about what someone else thinks of you. I know you, you solve cases, you collect evidence. You are just really good at what you do. We need you."

"Well, if you haven't forgotten, I am working on a case right now. My plane leaves at noon." Very gritted her teeth. How dare these people come at her right now, just a few hours before she was scheduled to fly to Canada to look for Frankie Monroe. He had left her at the altar, really it was her parents decorated back yard, almost 40 years before. Two years ago, when a corpse showed up in the orchard with a stub of a movie ticket from the last time she had seen him, she had plunged herself into the mystery. But the body in the orchard was the beginning of a search for where Frankie had disappeared to. She thought she had put it all behind her and had gone on to a different life. But just a few weeks before, Darrell had gotten a lead. It was the first good lead in the last few years, but the man in question had avoided her. Now, the only option she felt she had left, was to confront him directly. She had bought a plane ticket to Sudbury, Ontario. Her plans were vague, but part of it was the idea of knocking on the door of the address Darrell had found. Crazy? Misguided? The thing a wacky old maid would do?

"We just want to make sure you are with us, that you will work on this case with us." Darrell's voice came with a slight whine. "How long will this take, in Canada?"

"Darrell, how do I know? You know how long I've been looking for Frankie; it isn't going to happen overnight. I don't think; I don't know. I have a return ticket for a week from now. But looking for a missing person that has been missing for forty years? Who knows?"

Bradley's deep voice spoke up. "I heard about your quest."

Very turned to him. "My quest? My Quest. It sounds like some Don Quixote thing. Next, you'll have me jousting at windmills, huh? You think I'm as nutty as everyone else does? I'm the one who digs up the past, trying to find answers to life's unanswerable questions. Why did he leave me, where is he now, did he ever love me? If he's dead, why can't I find him? I know all the questions, thank you, but I don't have any answers." Very pouted and defied the members of the small gathering to deny her this one last gasp of the journey to find answers.

"I don't think you're crazy. Everyone says I'm crazy, my dad's crazy," Glen said quietly. "I understand your 'quest' to find answers. It's been 50 years, I wasn't even around. But this has hung over my head ever since I was born. As long as I can remember, I was her younger brother, she was my only sister, my real half-sister. The closest thing to a blood sibling I was ever going to have. But, maybe you are right, it's all too much, too long ago, not worth it. Just forget it. We can't do this."

"But your dad?" Olivia asked. "How is this going to make him feel?"

Glen hung his head; a look of resignation clouded his face.

Very stood and tried to look defiant.

"You used to live in Cuyama, right?" Darrell asked. "You told me that. You told me about what a great little place it was to be a child in."

"I left a very long time ago. I only lived there for six years or so. I left when I was eight. My dad worked for the oil company and we moved back to Bakersfield, which is where my family was from. And so, what does this have to do with anything?"

"Insights, that's what. This happened there," Darrell answered. "She lived there."

"Who is she?"

"The little girl whose case we want to reopen. Not JonBenet Ramsey, but sort of," Darrell tried to explain.

"My sister, my older sister. We have the same father. But she died before I was born, I told you," Glen tried to explain

"In Cuyama?" Very's face began to lose color.

"Yeah, 54 years ago, to be exact."

"Her name?" Very asked.

But just as Glen said it; Very mouthed the name as well.

"AnnaRose Bullitt," they said together.

Very's face lost even more color and she reached out her hand, placing it firmly on the nearest shoulder, which belonged to Bradley Parker. Her knees buckled and she slowly began to sink downwards. Brad reached out his arms and gently caught Very as she fell towards the floor, easing her fall and at the same time, enveloping her in his strong embrace.

Chapter 2: Postponing the Trip to Canada

Strong arms held her as she tried to control her slump towards the floor. The power to speak had deserted her, even as she mouthed, "Oh dear." Very struggled to lift her head, breathe air, regain her place as an upright observer of the small gathering.

Her body was squeezed as a large vise pulled up and then pushed her into a chair. She deliberately kept her eyes closed so she wouldn't see what was happening. A method of control she had learned as a child. If you can't see it happening, it must not be happening to you. Pretend it was someone else.

The vise gradually left her and she breathed, trying to bring her eyeballs into the light. It better not have been the White Stetson, Bradley Parker, who had fondled her into the chair. No, not fondled, just taken way too many liberties with her bare arms and light clothed body. She noticed that the heat of his body had gone and that she was free to move herself.

She felt a glass being pressed to her lips and she gratefully sipped, then lightly pushed it away. "I'm okay."

Darrell's face loomed into her view. "You say you're okay, but I know you. You only faint if there is a good reason."

"It's warm in here, there are too many people, I didn't get a good night's sleep. What do you want me to say?" Very retorted. Too harsh, he was only being kind and concerned.

The group looked at her as she recovered.

Glen was the first to speak. "So, you remember the case. AnnaRose?"

Darrell said, "Wow, it must have been important. Newspapers and all?"

Glen looked at him sideways, "Newspapers every day for weeks."

Bradley continued. "TV. If you lived here, it must of have been hard to ignore or forget. Even if you were a kid, you would have heard something."

"I felt traumatized, I couldn't shut it out. Besides…" Very stopped. How could she describe what had happened? Not just to AnnaRose, but to every young girl in Bakersfield. The nightmares, the fear of strangers, the not wanting to be alone in the house, not wanting to even hear about Cuyama.

"But you told me you left in 1959. This was later, more than a year later." Darrell shook his head.

"I knew her. I knew AnnaRose." Very stopped, trying to push the lump in her throat back into her chest. She reached for the glass of water and took another sip. "I was her friend, her big sister. Her babysitter, of sorts. I lived just down the street."

They waited for Very to tell her story, the story of how Vermilion Blew and Anna Rose Bullitt had played together, been older sister and younger sister all those years ago.

"Mrs. Bullitt was pregnant and then she had a baby. She didn't always have time to keep AnnaRose occupied. She was a very excitable little girl. We might call her hyperactive or ADHD or some such term these days. But she loved to spin around, twirl, happy and laughing. She would grab things and throw them in the air. I was old enough to keep her company, happy, out of harm's way and not being destructive. I protected her, I kept her busy. Her mom needed the rest. And I was old enough to call her if something went wrong, or if someone got hurt. We had lots of lunches together." Very stopped and let images run through her head. She had forgotten, or deliberately pushed from her memory, scenes of a squealing child, twirling herself around until she became dizzy and fell on the grass in the backyard. A contest of ugly faces, making mush balls of the insides of the white bread on sandwiches, snorting red Kool-Aid out her nose. Laughing, shrieking, screeching and squawking through her short life.

Very inhaled and continued. "It was hard to say goodbye when I left. My mom was about to have a new baby by then, but AnnaRose was my first sister. And I never saw her again. Never had a chance to say goodbye. My parents tried to keep the news from me, but it was everywhere. All my friends at school were talking about it. It was on the TV news, and in the newspaper. I could read, I could see the headlines. I really couldn't talk about it with my friends; I never told them I knew her. I was…"

Olivia leaned forward, "How did you cope?

"I didn't. I started sleepwalking, although I don't think my parents knew, or if they knew, they never said anything. I think they thought it was best not to talk about it. Just to pretend it never happened. I don't think they knew how to bring the topic up. The fact that I never wanted to talk about Cuyama and my life there didn't clue them in, I guess. But I was a mess for awhile. They tried to keep me away from the newspapers and never, ever talked about it in front of me. My dad would jump up and turn off the news when it came on, but I heard enough from my friends. And then, we were all shocked by it. It's hard to quantify the distress, and others were undoubtedly not hit as hard with it as I was, understandably. But they knew my connection with AnnaRose. Maybe my mother said once, 'if you want to talk about it…' But the happenings on that day were buried deep and smothered with heaps of neglect and forgetfulness."

Everyone was quiet, acknowledging the raw pain of Very's recollections.

"Once," she began again, "we took a trip to the coast and went via Hwy 166, through the Cuyama Valley. We stopped at the Buckhorn to eat, but I said I wasn't feeling well and stayed in the car. We went by the house where we had lived. My sister had never lived there, so she was kind of excited to see the house. They took photos standing on the doorstep. I stayed in the car, with a stomachache I said. I had my eyes closed all the way there and beyond. As soon as we got to the coast, I immediately felt better. This was years later, and I think my parents still hadn't understood the shock it had caused me. And to this day, I've never returned to Cuyama."

"But you talked about living there," Darrell protested. "Fondly."

"I couldn't exactly deny that I lived there and if I talked about it, briefly, I conjured up some good memories to fill the conversation with. There were good times. I just didn't want to remember the bad, so of course I never talked about what happened to AnnaRose."

"I had no idea," Darrell hung his head.

"Why should you? How could you have known? I would never have talked casually about the little girl I knew who was raped and murdered."

Glen spoke up, his voice a quavering whisper. "But will you help?"

"What can I do?" Very whined. "The police, the sheriff's department spent weeks, and months looking into it years ago. And now you tell me that you," she turned to Bradley, "were involved in a cold case investigation years later. What can I do, any of us do, that wasn't done the first and the second time?"

"My dad didn't do it. Oh, he may be keeping secrets. I'm sure he's lying about a lot of things. About Cindy, about that day, about Betty Jean, about his marriage and his divorce. But one thing I do know, he would never strangle and rape his own daughter!"

Bradley cleared his throat. "Very's right. What can she do? We thought we'd ask because she's smart, she's inquisitive, she looks at things with a keen eye for detail, and she's a dogged researcher."

Very looked at the man who had just moments before held her in his arms. She had a look of surprise, incredulity even, on her face.

"So I've been told. No personal knowledge, I admit." Brad's smile was a thin line on his lips. "Empathetic, non-threatening, can put the puzzle together."

"Because I always finish the jigsaw puzzles? Who filled your head with this stuff?" Very felt crowded out in the room where she was being discussed.

"The woman's touch," Darrell added. "That was my contribution."

Olivia smiled over Darrell's shoulder.

"And exactly why are you on the case?" Very turned to Bradley.

"Old cop with an ax to grind. I failed once, but I won't fail again. I'm committed to this investigation. Let's put it this way, we would like you on the case, but you are NOT indispensable. Go to Canada."

"No," Very said, standing. "I'll cancel the flight, go in a couple of weeks. Until then, I'll help. Can't let the woman's intuition thing go to waste."

A collective sigh of relief swept the room. Very reached for her purse with her phone and stepped out into the corridor. She closed the door behind her and breathed in the cooler air in the corridor. She called the number on her ticket.

This trip to Canada had meant that she had already cancelled any other appointments or commitments she had. She had freed up the next ten days in case. Now, she was liberated from that quest, at least for a while. As she dealt with the airlines, she mulled over her decision to go and what she had hoped to achieve. She had hoped to catch Frankie off-guard, that was one reason to simply go and not advertise her presence.

Frankie was the first, not the only, but the first that she had felt that strong physical attraction to. He was good-looking without being really handsome, with a ready smile and a sense of fun. She had thrown caution to the winds and indulged herself, never expecting to get pregnant. She had been surprised when she had told him of her condition that he had suggested marriage. It was 1973 and lots of girls were having their babies by themselves. If the guy stuck around, better, but the gold ring on the finger was not the most important thing. Of course, her mother was happier to know that the quick decision to get married was a joint choice and a resolution that she herself had chosen, as did her grandmother. What could her mother say, but congratulations and I'll help you buy a dress. The backyard had been prepared, the simple invitations sent out, all had gathered. And the groom did not make an appearance.

Very was not the first, nor the last, to be left dangling. Within the week, she had had a miscarriage. Then in the depths of her depression, a friend suggested moving out of Bakersfield, away from memories, the storms, the uncertainties of the future. She needed a new future, somewhere else. She had contacted Frankie's mother, but she had no clue where her son had gone. She had shrugged off his disappearance with a cryptic comment that linked Frankie's bolt to the same one that Frankie's father had done, years before. For two years, Very had lived a fulfilling life in the Bay Area, getting a Library qualification and then a job.

Unfortunately, the job was in Bakersfield. But her parents had been happy to have her at home and treated her as more of a boarder than a young child. Then her father became ill and died, and her mother didn't want Very to leave. By that time, Very had a life, friends, activities and every summer off to travel and explore. She liked her life, she liked her job, a mix of English teacher and high school librarian, and she couldn't think why she needed to make any move. Her mother grew more and more frail and finally she, too, passed away, leaving Very her parents' house. It was a house that was almost 50 years old, had not been modernized, had begun to fail at the seams, the seams that had warped and stretched at the intersection of the 20th and the 21st centuries. When Very suggested solar panels, her mother scoffed. The water pipes leaked, they needed to be replaced. The electrical system had begun to fail, one outlet, one light at a time. Very longed for renewal of the house, but her mother clung to the old adage, 'if it ain't broke, don't fix it.' Very's wails of, 'it is broke,' fell on closed, deaf ears. When Very's mother died, Very felt as though it was her duty to keep the house as a memorial to her parents, especially her mother, who had spent years gardening and caring for the place.

It was after Very had begun the search for Frankie Monroe, when she realized that she needed to have a home of her own. The furniture, the pots and pans, the paintings or whatever on the walls, needed to be her own, not her mother's. Oh, if she liked it, she could keep it, but the ugly orange pot that held bacon grease, out it went. And then the new house she had bought had begun to take on the shape of Very's house. The body that she had found in the hot tub had only been a blip on the way of Very embracing the active retirement lifestyle of Five Points.

Finding Frankie, if he was out there, had been important for the last few years. She needed to know if he had fled Very, their unborn baby, the commitment of marriage or if he had fled because of the low-life characters he had been associating with. Very had thought it important to find out, to comprehend his actions, but now, the search on behalf of AnnaRose seemed more important. It demanded a piece of her heart. She was old enough now to know that the only important things in life were the people who are in it – or have been in it. Family, friends, acquaintances, the connections to other people. The gold nuggets of life, nothing else was important. That long-ago connection to AnnaRose pulled her.

She headed back into the stuffy room, pausing at the sign on the door. Pitts and Blew, Private Detectives. It reminded her of the first day she had visited, as a customer of Darrell. She had thought of herself as Bridget O'Shaunessy, coming to hire Sam Spade. What a hoot!

The hum stopped as she stepped in the door.

"You have me for three weeks. I was lucky, someone was at the airport trying to find a seat on that plane. I gave up the place to someone on standby. I've done one good deed today. What else do we have? Where do we start?"

Bradley stood as Very plopped into his chair. Her face broke into a mass of emotion, disappointment, memories, pain. Tears welled at the corners of her eyes.

Bradley struggled in his pocket and produced a handkerchief. He thrust it into Very's hand. "It's clean."

Very looked, unfolded it and daubed at her tears. White, large, masculine, smelled of laundry soap. "I'll return it, clean, later."

Darrell leaned forward, "Okay, where do we start?"

Chapter Three: Planning the Investigation

"How are we going to do this investigation? What are the plans?" Darrell took control of the conversation. It was his office, his company; the rest of the people there were employees, clients, hangers-on and Very.

Bradley's strong baritone rumble started them off, "I'll get as much information as I can on the old cases. They are part of the public record at this point. We may not be able to get the original coroner's report. It was pretty gruesome as I recall, and we might not really want to see the details. I will make a short precis of what I remember. I will also see whatever may still be around from the crime scene kit. Also, I can access the second investigation, the cold case that I was involved in."

"When was that?" Very asked.

"Eleven years after the incident." Brad refused to look directly at Very.

"And why?"

"Why? Well, periodically…"

"But why then? What happened to make someone decide to reopen the case?"

"I don't know that there was anything in particular, just periodic review."

"No one asked? Sometimes you hear about someone who had been in prison and their cellmate talks and then years later, they decide they can use the information to get their own sentence lighter or parole or something. No one confessed in prison?"

Brad looked at Very. Tentatively he answered. "No, not that I was aware of. I don't really know where the impetus came from. I long had suspicions that someone needed some Brownie points to make a promotion. You know the thing, solve an old unsolvable case and everyone applauds. I was just a very, very junior guy."

"Maps, we need maps," Olivia chimed in, "they always have maps on TV."

"Maps of the valley, Old Cuyama, New Cuyama, make sure you have one of the streets in New Cuyama. The layout of the streets, the houses, who lived where. The distances, how long would it take to drive, walk. We need to see a recreation of the place on the wall. We could do it here." Very approached the wall that had a poster of the one and only concert Darrell had been to since coming to Bakersfield. "Put everything here."

Olivia caught the infection. "Timelines, timelines for everybody. Who was where, when and then we leave space to fill in whatever."

Brad spoke, "A lot of that is in the notes from the case, and the cold case."

Olivia smiled with pleasure, "We have lots to put up here. We could do a recreation of who was at home, or at work, where they were during the time frames."

"There was a lot of lying going on," Brad said softly. "If we can't be sure the information was correct, then what good is it?"

All attention turned to Brad. "I took statements from lots of people. A lot was pure repetition from the original case. Some was inaccurate, some was different, but it was impossible to tell if it was important or not. I wasn't allowed to probe too deep. Not possible to ask certain questions, just take statements like the original case. I was held back."

Very, anger rising in her voice, "Who stopped you?"

"I was intimidated by my boss. I wasn't allowed to take the time. I was always being assigned to other duties and then when I was pressed to come up with the interviews or reinterviews, I had no time to do it properly. I was young, stupid, afraid of my bosses. Frankly, I was so new to it all, I wasn't sure what it was that I should be asking, what it was I was investigating."

The room was silent. They all remembered a first job, a new hire who had no idea what they should be doing. The fear of asking 'stupid' questions, the trembling in the limbs at writing or giving a report. The confusion, the inadequacy of training, or orientation to the task. Being new, being a trainee is never fun. Never.

"The one thing I was sure of was that a whole lot of people weren't telling the truth." Brad crossed his arms in defiance of anyone contradicting him. "They didn't tell the truth the first time, then they lied about it all and made up some more falsehoods the second time around." He looked directly at Glen, "Including your old man."

Glen hung his head, "I know. Even as he tries to say he wants his name cleared, he still lies. He knows it looks bad for him. But he wants this, he wants to go to his grave with a clean name. He didn't do this. Not to AnnaRose."

"Okay," Brad countered, "but we still need to hear the real facts, not what sounds good to his ears. And then there are people who can no longer be truthful. Betty Jean Bullitt for example. I think she lied, but I can't prove it. There are certain things that just don't ring with an accurate sound. But we can't go back and ask the questions again. Their lies and truths are buried with them."

"Maybe not. Did you ever talk with Cynthia, my half-sister? She lived with her mom. Maybe she knows something, stories, fables, gossip."

Very added, "Glen's right. Sometimes the narratives of our lives are based on myths, on imaginary events, on history that isn't explained in one telling. When we tell, we only give part of the story. 'Make it short' my friends say. But that can't always dig deep enough. There's always more, from a different angle, from a different version."

Silence gave assent to the truth of Very's words, even as the thought ruffled through the possibilities of never finding the simple, unrefined facts.

Brad sat and spoke quietly. "Even Betty Jean. Perhaps she lied as well. It would help her deal with herself, her own failings as a mother, if she was prevaricating about where she was when AnnaRose was taken. But we can't go back and ask again. She's gone."

"Ask Cindy," Glen said again.

"We need a list of people to interview again, those that are still alive. Glen, is your dad up to talking with us?" Very asked. "And Cindy," she turned to Brad, "Did you talk with her?"

"No, she was a minor and a baby when AnnaRose…disappeared. She would have had to have her mother there, or her father. It wasn't important at the time. But now…?"

Very looked around. "Who is writing this all down?" She looked pointedly at Olivia.

"Sure, I can do that." Olivia grabbed a pen and a notebook.

"And we need a chief, someone in charge." Very looked around as they all looked at her. "No, you don't, I'm emotionally involved. I'm too close to all of it. And maybe you are too?" she turned to Brad.

"Well, I consider my involvement to be a colossal failure. And yes, I'm too involved to be dispassionate. In some ways, it needs to be an outsider."

Heads swiveled to Darrell. His eyes opened wide and he opened his mouth. Nothing came out.

"Your name is on the door. C'mon Darrell, you can do this. This isn't any different than the other cases you've done," Very said.

"Murder, I've never done murder. No, no, I don't do unnatural death. And I don't do cold cases, I don't know what to do."

"Frankie Monroe is a cold case and I think you did very well on that one." Very tried to smile and reassure. "You know, we can all help you, especially Olivia."

Olivia looked gooey-eyed at Darrell and smiled at him. Darrell's face did not register the intended compliment. When was he going to get it? He brought her in, so he must have had some interest in her. Or was he now rethinking his hire? Or perhaps this is the time to bond over a case?

"There, that is settled, Darrell is the lead on this investigation. Does he have everyone's contact information? Olivia, are you going to coordinate the notes, the stuff on the wall, like maps and timelines? Good," Very said without pausing.

"Unfortunately, it's Saturday, so some of this stuff can't be done until Monday." Darrell looked downcast.

"The internet," Brad said, "we can always start with the addresses, phone numbers, work history, anything we can get from web sources."

"And you know, of course, that Darrell has the most amazing access to websites. Because he's a PI and works a lot of skip tracing cases, he's paid for access to a lot of awesome information. I'll bet he can find anyone we might be looking for, alive or dead." Very smiled to everyone. She had worked with some of the 'pay only' sites and knew what kind of information was available, for a price. "Frankie Monroe looked to be truly lost, and see what he did?"

"You haven't found him yet," Darrell said.

Olivia had found three sheets of paper and had tacked them to the wall. She had taken a black marker and written in bold letters on each one. "People to interview" read one, "Documents to get" read a second. She hesitated at the third and decided to start filling in what she could on the others. She had a smaller pen and began to fill in people and documents and who was going to get what.

Very slumped in a chair, "Coffee, I could just kill for a cup of coffee."

Brad leaned over from his chair a few inches away. He whispered, "Poor choice of words." Louder he said, "I could use some coffee too."

The ensuing search for cups and coffee, the coffee maker, sugar, stirrers reduced Very to laughter. "That Marx Brothers movie."

"The stateroom scene, on the ship." Brad smiled broadly.

They looked at each other and snickered, just shy of giggling. The other three stopped and looked questioningly.

"It's a scene where a whole bunch of people try to crowd into a ship's cabin and they all get into each other's way. The Marx Brothers." Brad explained.

Question marks still sat on the faces of the three younger people.

"You've never seen it?" Very asked.

"Old movie, from the 1930's." Brad prompted.

"That's before you were born. When did you see it?" Darrell looked askance at the two.

"Saturday afternoon movies. Didn't everybody watch old black and white movies on Saturdays?" Very asked. She was met with vacant stares. She turned to Bradley, "What was your favorite? Mine was 'King Kong.'"

"The Maltese Falcon was right up there, but I'm not sure if I could pick just one…"

"Stop," Darrell said. "We'll never get anywhere if you two don't stop…"

Glen spoke up softly from the corner he stood in. "I'll go to Starbucks or somewhere and get coffee. What does everyone want?"

"How about some sandwiches?" Very suggested.

"Hamburgers," Darrell piped up. "Sandwiches won't cover it. I'm hungry!"

Calls for what kind of sandwiches, then for pizza were bandied about. Brad, in the midst of all the confusion, pulled out his phone and punched in a number, then proceeded to punch in more information. "And five really hot coffees?" he asked.

The others looked at him, "You didn't ask what I wanted," whined Darrell.

"I'm trying to go vegan," Olivia volunteered.

"Enough to go around, and it will be delivered." Brad stood firm.

"And what happens when the door opens?" Very and Brad laughed at the inside joke.

Soon, they were all gathered around a huge platter of various sandwiches, packages of chips and sipping hot coffee. Brad had paid, and no one dared to complain.

As soon as the immediate hunger pangs had been satiated, they got back to work. Brad filled them in on the details as far as he remembered them, not giving exact times and places, which he insisted needed to be verified when he got the files. Olivia filled in the blanks on the three papers on the wall.

By two, they had finished all they could without more precise information, or more comprehensive computer work. They looked at the papers on the wall. Olivia was busy drawing tiny hearts on one page, cute kitties on another, while she listened to the conversation.

"Monday morning? Everyone? How about you, Glen, do you think you need to be here?" Very turned to the client.

"How about if I come after I finish my work in the morning? One or two in the afternoon? And you can call if you need to. I don't see that I have any work here, and it's too crowded in any case."

All agreed and then Very began to pack up to leave. "Anyone want these extra sandwiches? Darrell, you always liked to take things home? Did you like Brad's choice, by the way?" Very smiled slyly.

"Sure, I'll wrap them up for you," Olivia said, with a chirp and a broad smile to Darrell.

Very and Brad happened to try to exit the office at the same time and tangled at the door.

"After you, madam," Brad said in a deep voice with a Southern gloss.

Very went in front, but waited for him to close the door and they walked down the stairs together. At the street, Very turned to go to her car.

"See you tomorrow," Brad said.

"Sunday, I don't work on Sunday," Very retorted. "It's my day of rest."

"I meant at the Sanchez's house, dinner."

"Oh gosh, I've not been invited. Remember, I was supposed to be on my way to Canada, looking for… Never mind."

"I'm sure you'd be welcome, you know the Sanchez's, none of their friends would be turned away." Brad smiled, dimples on his cheeks, a hint of teeth and a rogue glint in his eye.

"And you'll be there?"

"Why of course."

"On time, for dinner and conversation?" Very teased.

"And alone," he said.

Chapter Four: Reliving the Past

Very went home. As soon as she got in, she called her cat sitter and cancelled. She looked in her fridge to see what food might be there. She had deliberately eaten up or thrown out fruit, vegetables and milk. She checked the freezer. A number of plastic containers revealed leftovers that would make a meal until she got to the store. Clever Very, making sure there was food just in case.

"Meow," sang Cleopatra, rubbing her ankles.

"Oh, kitty. I didn't really want to leave you, but there were important things to do. Hmph, important? Maybe not."

Very checked the cat bowl where kibbles sat in the bottom. Not hungry, then, just wanted attention.

She flopped on the couch, craving solitude, time alone with her thoughts. Cleopatra jumped on the couch and tried to find a place to nap. Very stroked her back and the cat settled to purr. As ideas flitted in and out of Very's consciousness, she petted harder and harder, stroking the cat with increasing intensity. Suddenly, Cleopatra turned and bit, hard, on her hand.

"Ouch!" Very screamed. She reached out and smacked her cat, hard, on her backside as the naughty animal scampered away. "What was that for? I don't pet you, you scream at me, I do pet you and you bite me."

She looked at her hand; three puncture wounds showed bright red spots of blood. Very got up and washed her wounds. Cleopatra was nowhere to be found. Maybe under the bed, licking paws and belly to comfort herself. Why do pets bite? Out-of-the-blue bites? What vibes do they pick up from their owners? What kind of vibes was Very giving off that caused her cat to bite?

The day's events had overwhelmed Very. She was overwrought because of the impending trip to Canada, but the added revelations of AnnaRose, way too much for one day. Maybe she should go swimming? Was it late enough for the kids to be out of the pool?

She found Cleopatra under the bed. She reached under and stroked her tail, apologizing for the outsized reaction. "It was just a nip, but we mustn't be too hard on human skin. It's delicate and wounds get infected really easily."

Dressed in a bright red muumuu she had found in the back of her mother's closet, she took to the street, strolling slowly towards the clubhouse and pool. She heard a whine just to her rear and she turned. MaryAnne, in her golf cart, slowed just to Very's left.

"Wanna ride?" she chirped.

Very hesitated. She walked because she wanted the exercise, to save fuel, to experience the solitude. But it would be polite to say yes and build rapport with her fellow citizens of Five Points. She opened her mouth to answer.

"Oh, no, maybe you want and need the exercise. You know what they say, 'A mile a day keeps the doctor away." MaryAnne beamed.

Very bit her lip and looked sideways.

"Oh, you know, like an apple a day? Or better yet, 'Go the extra mile, it's never crowded.' We all need our exercise. Haven't you joined the morning aerobics group? You need to, it's so much fun. 'The body achieves what the mind believes.' That's our motto. Don't you think that's cute?"

Very smiled, hoping that the gesture would count as a response. She heard the whine of the golf cart starting to pull away and she sighed. Not today, MaryAnne. Solitary laps, that was going to fill the bill.

MaryAnne slowly accelerated and as she did, she called back over her shoulder, "'Good things come to those who sweat!'"

Very lifted her hand in a wave.

The rest of her exercise routine went smoothly and when she arrived back home, Cleopatra seemed to have recovered from her trauma of being hit for, what to her mind, was no good reason.

Emotion, too much of it, had affected Very's behavior, and by extension, that of her pet. What can trauma do to us? Cause us to abuse ourselves, our pets, our children, our friends? The ones who loved us, the only ones capable of curing us. Very showered, hung up her wet suit and, dressing in summer clothes, went outside to sit. The sun had dipped below the shade trees and the air was still. Distant sounds of cars and dogs barking were the only noise to disturb her. The air was still spring like, and Very breathed deeply, an attempt to calm herself.

Trauma, a blow, a collapse, a shock. How does this affect us? Very thought of the feelings of fear, wanting to know, and yet, afraid of the knowledge. Her parents had not understood how she felt. It wasn't that they were insensitive, not at all, but they had no coping mechanisms for that kind of hurt. A scabbed knee can be kissed and bandaged, a knock on the head soothed with an icepack. Have a headache? Take an aspirin. Where was the aspirin for a wound that was only to the psyche?

The man who had so brutally injured AnnaRose could not touch her, but Very had feared his appearance. She, and her friends as well, had felt the angst, the horror, the dread of the reappearance of the monster who had so brutally slain the innocent girl. A girl like them, a child who should only have been able to trust adults, not one to be suspicious of every big person around. And then, they all felt the terror left in AnnaRose's wake.

Did they understand, her parents? Did they know why she had refused to come out of the car that day in Cuyama? It was an action that was unlike the inquisitive, happy-go-lucky Very. Now, looking back, which she hadn't done in scores of years, she thought maybe they had realized something was amiss. They never spoke of it to her, and even that day, there was no drama, just gentle urging and a 'belief' in her made-up lies. It was not done, in her home, to talk of past tragedy. It was not polite, not what civilized people did. Her mother had standards, Very was not always sure about which standards, or even exactly what they were. But she did know that the discussion of the murder of a person one knew, was not talked about. One buried the thoughts and did not speak of them. They surely would go away.

And it was probably the same with the day Frankie left. Of course, they were upset and unhappy, but they knew that Very was much more. They never assigned blame. And then, when Very lost the baby, there was less, not more, language in the household. And Very had done a good job of forgetting and going on, excising those few months of her life. But then, the body in the orchard turned up. And digging up the body also excavated Very's past encounters with Frankie. Ever since that day, the thoughts had swirled in her head. Did she really love Frankie, or were they getting married solely for the baby? Certainly, they would never have married so soon, or so informally, but was that wedding only for the baby?

And which was worse, being left by Frankie, or losing the baby? If she were honest, neither was what she would have chosen, marriage or child, at that time. If that were the case, why the trauma? Did it lessen the pain to honestly admit that she would never have chosen to marry Frankie and have his baby?

Years later, the discovery of the body, and finding that it wasn't his body dumped in the orchard, had unearthed feelings, questions and an uprooting of the anguish of that time. But then, she began to discover more about him, his life, his background, his personality that had not been revealed to her at the time. She had begun to comprehend the depths of his personality and history that had created a Frankie Monroe that she did not recognize.

Now, she was searching in Canada. Why? What was the purpose of the Quest? Was it to find Frankie? Was it to stamp out the blow, the damage that had been caused? It had changed her course, forced her to create new goals, new visions of her future. Had that been a bad thing? She now admitted that she had been drifting when she met Frankie. With a newly earned BA, she had been applying for jobs, half-heartedly; losing herself in a whirl of social events, purposeless, and living with her parents in a throwback to her childhood. Meeting Frankie threw up new possibilities, a different turn to her life, and she had embraced it. At the time, she had not done any self-reflection. Was it too late now?

What if this Marvin Franks is Frankie? It was quite likely to be, based on the name, the only slighted altered birth date and that photo. So much like him, what he would look like today. Very had not stopped to think what a reunion would be like. She hadn't thought that it was likely to be awkward. She neglected to create a scenario of what she was going to say. Was she angry, and would she admit that? Accuse Frankie of abandonment? Did she want a reunion? Was she willing to fantasize about a rekindling a lifelong love affair?

But what if he were married, with kids? A wife by his side?

No, he owed her an explanation. Wife, kids, grandkids, wonderful job, lovely home, wonderful life? He still was beholden to give her some sort of answers. She knew that he had become mixed up with drug dealers, but the depth of that involvement was not clear. Should she ask? Or worse, what if that was what he had turned out to be, a crazed drug dealer? A decayed nonperformer? A person that she could never respect?

Very felt herself begin to shake; she felt her anger rising, a white-hot boiling from within. Steady girl, she told herself. She had always been prone to quick flashes of emotion, but she had taught herself to push them down, to talk to herself to manage and control her fervor. Her mother had chided her and reminded her that others did not like a wrathful person. She had cultivated placidity and harmony. She had also learned to channel flashes of anger and disappointment into galvanizing action. And a way for her to return to equilibrium. Now was the time to rethink the Frankie thing.

If he had run away, what traumas may still haunt him? What suffering had he endured? Very thought of the 'click' of the phone being hung up. He knew who she was. Was he not willing to face the wounds he had caused? Did he not want to engage with her, on any level? It appeared as though that was the case. But, Very felt acutely that it was his responsibility to tell her. He owed it to her to disclose why he left. She needed closure, even if he didn't.

She glanced at the sky, at the beginnings of a spectacular sunset. This time of year, with moisture left in the atmosphere, before the desiccation of the summer set in, the end of the day could be so beautiful. A puff of a breeze blew across her, and stirred the leaves of the bushes that bordered the back yard. She let out her breath, emptying her soul of the thoughts about Frankie.

AnnaRose. A true trauma, the agony of her disappearance and then the discovery of her murdered body. Compared to the runaway Frankie, this was a tragedy of first magnitude. What kind of shock and damage had been visited upon AnnaRose's mother? What did it mean for her family? For the infant sister, even for the brother she had met this morning. He said that he had never met her, that he only knew her through photos and stories. How had this affected his life? How had he coped with the anguish of the lost sibling? What do multiple blows mean for children? The younger sister, Cindy, had subsequently lost her mother. What do multiple traumas have on people, especially young ones? Very shivered to think.

Glen had characterized his sister as a bit strange. After her mother died, she went to live with her aunt, so she grew up with family. What had that relationship been like? She could have been accepted as a daughter and treated as such, or she could have had a fraught relationship. Cindy Bullitt was on Very's list of people to interview. The woman's touch thing, she figured. Of course, Cindy had been too young to remember anything of that time, but maybe she could give some insight into what Betty Jean Bullitt might have thought, or knew. Maybe there was something she could add. But what possibly could be new?

The sun set and Very went inside, calling to Cleopatra who had started to learn to 'stray' in the evenings. She had learned that she had some cat neighbors two doors down across the fence and had started visiting in the evenings. Was it wise to let your pet make friends with unknown animals? What if they turned out to be unsuitable companions? Very laughed at her thoughts; a mother's worst fear, that her child will consort with unacceptable playmates!

Later that evening, Very sat down at the computer and looked up 'trauma' on Google. At first she read about physical trauma and first aid. Then she fell into the darker stories of inherited suffering from Holocaust survivors. Many of those, who had immigrated to America or England after their ordeals in the concentration camps of Hitler, had created lives that appeared to be successful and fulfilling. But they had passed their stress onto their children and even grandchildren. Like physical diseases that are inherited, diseases of the mind can be visited on the next generations. The absence of discussion does not always lead to forgetfulness and healing.

Very stopped looking at the computer. She needed to clear her head, and revisiting topics like this were not helping. Cleopatra appeared and jumped up on the big desk that had belonged to her grandfather. Room enough for the computer, printer, stacks of papers and a cat. Very stoked her soft fur and felt better. Cleo began to purr and Very let the moment carry her to softer thoughts.

Trauma does not need to truncate or to define a life. People live on; they are productive, have jobs, marriages, families, hobbies, friends. It was not our job to judge anyone else, or predict what a blow or a shock will do.

We all have trauma in our lives.

Chapter Five: Sunday Dinner at the Sanchez House

By Sunday afternoon, Very had settled into a routine of exercise, house cleaning, laundry, answering emails and then she began to prepare for the evening dinner. This outfit didn't fit very well, never had, but it was a gorgeous color on her. That blouse was great, but wasn't she going to wear a skirt, and would the blouse go with the flouncy blue with pink flowers? No, she needed a plain color. Oh, what did it matter? It was only dinner, just a regular evening with the Sanchez family, not a sit down in the dining room with three forks, two spoons and a plethora of knives. The White Stetson, now known as Bradley Parker, would wear jeans, a pressed shirt, probably white, it being Sunday, and his Stetson. His uniform. But what was her uniform? What she had worn in the classroom and the library for 35 years? And what was that? Yes, the skirt and a casual, plain colored blouse. With jewelry? Maybe change her earrings for something interesting? The reticulated crocodiles from Australia? The Indian head pennies from a century ago? Stop, stop, or being late was a possibility, just put on clothes.

She had carefully made a tray of nibbles and placed them artistically on her mother's silver tray. Normally she simply snatched whatever was at hand and slapped it on a plastic tray from some previous potluck. Non-breakable. But today, she had boiled eggs and now carefully arranged the eggs around the outside, shimmering mounded golden halves and with red pimentos and green pickle pieces shyly peeking out. Long spears of green dill pickles slithered between the eggs. Very opened a can of black pitted olives and artfully placed them, half-hidden under the edges of the eggs and around the green spears. Was it too much to put some home-made potato salad in the center? She had made it at the same time as the eggs, not wanting to decide which to take. Now, she thought that both could go. She foraged for a few springs of parsley and stuck them in at what she hoped looked like a random and artful display.

Half of a can of black olives remained on the counter. She knew she had bought them for Joey and Bobby's granddaughter Clara and the child would be delighted to adorn her fingers with the edible treats. No, wait, maybe Clara was too old for olive on fingers? Perhaps this time her mother would point out that this was a baby trick and Clara had outgrown this display. Food should be eaten on plates, with utensils. Very put the remainder of the olives into a small plastic container and put it into the cool bag. Clara could decide if she wanted more olives or not.

When it came time to dress, Very chose a white eyelet blouse, the floaty flowery skirt, and she carefully applied make-up. She stuck a clip in her hair to keep her bangs from drifting into her eyes. Throwing her head back, or raking her hand through her errant wisps; which was worse? Neither was appropriate for a woman of her age. Not a teenager with a swagger anymore.

She looked at herself in the mirror and took stock. Need to dump the bright red lipstick. Maybe aging celebrities can get away with it, but not Very. She wiped fiercely, then reapplied in a warm apricot shade.

Very knew who she was dressing for, but was she happy with it? Content with what she had chosen from her wardrobe? The day before, she had been on her way to dig up her old flame, the man she was prepared to marry, and now she was dressing for another man. Maybe just as inappropriate? Oh hell, she was just going to go, go to dinner at her friends' house.

When she arrived, the street was lined with a number of cars. She was not one to check out other's vehicles of choice. The one she drove was the one that mattered to her. Therefore, she was unable to ascertain who was already in attendance. She saw a number of family vans. Joey and Bobby's kids, as they had families to cart around. But Bradley must, oh he must drive a pickup truck. No self-respecting man in Bakersfield drove an effete sedan. But there was no macho looking pickup on the street. Therefore, she had arrived before him. He could make an entrance and she could watch.

Very entered and soon was surrounded by the large Sanchez family. There were only three boys, but each had married and had produced the next generation, so the backyard was buzzing. Cousins gravitated towards cousins, sisters-in-law gathered in a circle, and the men stood around the barbecue. The family functioned as it was meant to. Quarrels happened, and they were resolved, jealousies reared their heads, and they were talked down, sorrows were shared. Dramas and disappointments fed the atmosphere, but were parceled out among the members. No one had more than their share and no one had more than they could cope with. Very felt as though she were familiar with all, shared with all, but never pulled into the depths, or basked in the heights. She was a friend.

As soon as she entered the back yard, she was spotted by Clara, who came running for a hug from her 'Aunt Berry.' She shyly asked after the olives. They went to the kitchen together and Very popped open the plastic container. She helped Clara decorate her fingers, while finishing off the remainder of the salty black orbs, by putting them on and then sucking them off her own fingers.

Just as she was beginning the bite/suck on her final olive, she saw the White Stetson enter the kitchen. Clara laughed with a high-pitched squeal of delight and Bradley Parker smiled.

Very began to open her mouth to say hello, when the olive raced to the back of her tongue and began to lodge in her throat. Clara laughed again, and Very felt the olive slowly moving down to the narrower part of her throat. She tried to breathe in, choked, and then exhaled violently, spitting the olive out. She reached out her hand and caught the offending projectile before it traveled too far beyond her reach. She breathed in again, while contemplating the aborted trajectory. It had been aimed directly at Brad's sparkling white shirt.

Very threw the olive into her mouth, knowing that there were only two places it could go, and not wanting to waste food. She chewed and then carefully swallowed. "Hi," she said slowly, meeting his gaze.

He answered by touching his hat, and with a faint smile, backed outside.

Clara, her fingers still decorated with black olives, saw him leave. "You said, 'hi', but he didn't say anything back. Isn't he supposed to say 'hi' back? I don't think he was being nice." Her face screwed up into a grimace.

"Oh, I think he was being very polite. I think he was trying very hard not to laugh at us."

"Oh, but we're the best," Clara said, a fresh series of giggles threatening to emerge.

Very took the salad plate outside, to place on the sides table.

The weather had become hotter as the day unfolded, and the boys were positioning a large fan in the corner, as well as coaxing the overhead fan on the covered patio to twirl appropriately. The air moved sluggishly. The oldest of the Sanchez boys, Bobby Jr., was bent over spraying the exposed legs of all the shorts wearers. As he approached Very, she demurely lifted her skirt and asked for a spritz on her ankles. A gang of young boys marauded, fly swatters at the ready, hoping to rid the world of the pests.

Joey grabbed Very and pulled her into a corner, near the fan. They had a good view of the whole party, the food preparation, the barbecue. Joey was the matriarch and the glue of the family. Her husband teased her that all three sons had married their mother, and Joey got along with all of them. At the moment, they were taken up with the food tables or catering to the young children. Even though the young boys were noisy and wielded instruments of destruction, they knew the eyes of a dad or mom were on them. At the moment, they were safe.

Very eyed the barbecue. It was a massive affair, with a monster hood, two preparation counters and a side table piled with meat, sauces and vegetables to grill. It was the center of the men's part of the yard and all the adult males had gathered around, beer cans in hand. One budding young man approached tentatively, coke can clutched in his hand, body held in casual stiffness. An uncle moved back and allowed him a space in the circle. Joining the men, a rite of passage? They talked sports, which Very didn't follow, so there was nothing for her there.

But with Joey, and eventually the daughters-in-law, the talk turned to children, another topic that Very wasn't fond of. Babies were not on her radar, as adolescents were, but she had had over thirty years of teaching and was keen to exit the talk on teenagers. But she stayed. They also talked food logistics.

Very leaned over and whispered to Joey, "I'm so glad you have this family."

"There are headaches, but I, too, am glad to have this family." Joey leaned back in her chair and closed her eyes for a moment, resting from the hullabaloo of preparation. She opened her eyes and leaned towards Very. "I've heard that you and Bradley are working on a case together."

Very looked towards the barbecue area, "Yes. And how come I've not met him before? Isn't he a good friend of Bobby's?"

"Yes," Joey said, "but more of a work friend. They lost touch for a while, and then recently… If you want the real lowdown, you need to talk with Bobby Jr."

"Not Bobby Sr.? If they worked together, it would seem that he would know more than your son. True?"

"My husband is quite reluctant to talk about him. If you've known someone for a while, it's hard to watch their life spiral out of control. Lately, it's as though he is treated more as an acquaintance than a life-long friend."

"So, what's with the white Stetson? I mean, it's not unlike a Bakersfield thing to do, but it is a bit…extreme? Or affected. It makes him stand out."

Joey laughed. "You'd have to ask him. But I think the hat belonged to a family member. What nicer way to honor your ancestry that to sport an article of clothing that belonged to one of them."

"Yeah, I have been known to wear my mother's old red muumuu. Something like that?" Very laughed.

"So, tell me about this latest case, the Cuyama Cold Case."

Very filled in Joey on the outlines and where they had gotten so far. "Nothing new, nothing to report, really. Do you remember the case? You lived here then, didn't you?"

"I remember a little bit. I remember feeling scared, horrified, a bit panicky. I mean, even though she was younger, it was an anxious time. And the fact that no one was arrested. After a while, it died down and as there was no suspect, no one reported on it again. And the cold case, years ago, wasn't reported, as there was no conclusion. So we just forgot about it. Better, I think, than worrying ourselves into a tizzy."

"For me, of course, it was a different. You do know that I knew her?"

"No, Very, oh no, I didn't. How terrible for you."

"I'd moved away by then, so there was no direct connection any more. But hearing about it again, and being asked to help, created a fainting fit. And guess whose arms I fell into?" Very smiled.

"Nooooooo. Very, that was shameless flirting."

"It was not. It was genuine resurfacing of the trauma I felt. And yesterday, I began to think hard, ruminate if you will, on the concept of trauma, the blow to our psyche, from something horrible, unfathomable. It can't be easy, to relive, or try not to relive, the wounds from our past."

"And what about your trip? What's happening with the search in Canada?"

"Put off for three weeks. I'll go eventually. It's something I need to do for myself. And if Frankie has been there for almost 40 years, a few weeks won't make a difference. I need to make my mind work on this cold case now, while everyone else is here, to work alongside."

Joey smiled a sad smile at Very. "You are busy."

Bobby Jr. strolled over and greeted Very. Joey got up and offered her seat to her eldest son.

"Ah, the matriarch's throne, I am a lucky one." He turned to Very. "So, what are you up to? Private investigating, huh?"

"Yeah, and you can tell me about one of my fellow sleuths. Your mom said to ask you about Bradley, aka the White Stetson."

Bobby laughed, "That Stetson, an affectation, definitely. Well, you have noticed a sadness about him? His wife died of cancer, long and awful. And then his son started not doing well. I knew his son from school, we played sports together. And I kind of kept in touch. I didn't know his dad, much, just a dad, you know? And then the son had a car accident, a drunk driver plowed into him, but he had been drinking too, so it became complicated. Brad gritted his teeth and supported his son, but it was hard on him. Dad can tell you more. It was about then that he quit law enforcement altogether."

"Gosh, that sounds like trauma."

"He moved away for a while. And when he came back, he was wearing the white Stetson all the time. If someone called him on it, he made a joke, but he didn't laugh. I don't know that I have ever seen him laugh. Smile sadly, kind of a sorrowful smile, but to give a big belly laugh…" Bobby shook his head. "So, it is good to know that he is back working on something."

A shifting and moving appeared at the barbecue station, a preparation for declaring grilled meat to be available.

"Bang!" came a loud explosion from the street.

Everything stopped. A silence spread over the group. Very rolled her eyes and said quietly, "Backfiring. A car backfiring."

But the three men formerly or currently involved in law enforcement ducked into a crouch.

Bobby Sr. shouted, "Take cover everyone! Get down!"

A woman screamed. Children squealed and ran.

Three men, running in a crouch, headed for the side yard entrance. Very noticed the White Stetson bobbing awkwardly in the rear.

Chapter Six: Gathering Information

Bradley appeared in the doorway. Very and Darrell looked down guiltily trying to hide the snarky grins on their faces, but Olivia could not suppress her laughter. She tried to close her mouth, then a large burble bubble burst out. Darrell also tried to quash the glee, but giggles struggled in his throat.

"What is so funny?" Brad asked, not sure he wanted to come into the tiny room.

"Oh, I was just telling them a funny story, about cars backfiring and it being mistaken for gunfire." Very smiled sweetly, but her lips curled into a moue of suppressed hilarity. A look at Brad's face, showing annoyance at the telling of the previous night's misadventure, made Very back off. "Listen, it is funny after the fact, but of course, not at the time." She pasted on a diplomatic grin.

Brad hesitated. It was obvious that he didn't like being the butt of a joke, but he didn't know these people well enough to read the situation. Ignore, or defend himself; treat it like a serious case of defending the women and children, or a huge joke on him, and the other men? Pretend it didn't happen, or join in their silly guffaws?

He heaved a large sigh. "I brought coffee. I made it myself. You need to choose your color."

In a large cardboard carrier were five metallic cups of different colors. The mugs were sleek designer thermos mugs of the best quality, with a tight lid on top. Brad held up a bag, "Stuff to go in."

Olivia put her head down and graciously took the sack and extracted cream and sugar packets, stirrers and napkins.

Very looked directly at Brad, "How thoughtful of you." As soon as it came out, she wanted to take it back. Hokey and insincere? Could she have chosen better phrasing? It was her telling of the backfiring being mistaken for gunshots story that had set them all laughing – at him. He must know that she had embroidered the story, milked it for all it was worth. The rescue by three brave law enforcement dudes from someone with a gun, only it was an old car with intestinal problems.

Very chose a dark blue masculine-looking mug and handed it to Glen, who slithered from his corner. "Cream, sugar?"

"Both, please," said Glen, unspiraling himself into the central space. "No one had to do this. It's more than enough. And because I'm here earlier than I said I'd be, much appreciated."

"Hey," Very chirped. "Don't look a gift horse in the mouth."

Olivia looked at the bright pink cup she had chosen. "So we just get one cup, just this?"

Brad smiled. "There's a thermos, a big one, in the car. I'll go get it now, if you want."

Darrell looked at the coffee maker on the crowded countertop. "We already have a coffee maker," he whined.

They all looked at the cheap coffee maker. The carafe was dirty, and the bottom looked as if the last pot had burned a ring on the bottom. It said 'four cups' on the side, but they all knew that the maximum was a scant one and a half mugfuls. For one person, Darrell, and with the occasional addition of Very, it had been adequate, barely. But with four and more on this investigation, Brad's solution was better.

Very looked slyly at Brad, "Did you remember the doughnuts?"

"I've got this," Darrell announced, reaching up to the top of a cupboard. Two packages of chocolate covered cookies fell into his hands.

Brad took a package, "All right!" He pulled and the sealed end split neatly. He held it out for everyone.

Olivia jumped up and pulled a folding TV tray from behind the second desk. It was one of those wooden and metal ones that threatened to collapse at any moment. She unfolded it and placed in squarely in the middle of the room, making the space even less than before.

Five dedicated coffee drinkers set to work erasing their caffeine cravings. Silence was maintained while slurps and munches made inroads into the refreshments.

Very waited until looks of satisfaction appeared on everyone's faces. "Okay. Saturday, we talked about dividing up the tasks, who would see whom, interview whom, what each person's job was to be. Glen," she turned to their client. "You don't have to be here. We can report to you, or phone you and ask questions. What do you think?"

Glen looked startled. Perhaps he thought he should be in the center of things, or that nothing could be done without him. Now, it seemed up to him whether to attend the office meetings or not. He looked around the tight space, not enough chairs or tables, desks or even a place for him to stand. "Maybe, I should…ah…take off? Now?"

"More coffee?" Brad said standing. "I'll get the thermos from the car." He left, creating a bit of elbow room.

Very turned to Glen. "Have another cup of coffee and then decide. It would be helpful to have your input, but it's not always necessary for you to be, like BE here all the time. I mean, we won't be here ALL the time."

More coffee arrived and mugs refilled.

"Map," Very declared. "We need a map of New Cuyama township. It's just one neighborhood, really. Just those very few streets, but we need to see where it happened, or at least where it started. Then…"

Brad interrupted. "We need a map of the Valley that needs to include Old Cuyama and more, up to and including where she was found."

"Here's a Google map of the township," said Olivia at the computer. I can print it out, but it's only this big."

Very bent over Olivia's shoulder. The street names jumped out at her; Caliente Avenue, Morales St. There was Sisquoc Street where she had lived. Meantime, the printer was spewing out a few copies.

"Can we make this bigger, to put on the wall?" Very asked.

"I can do that," Glen volunteered. "Architectural Drawing is one thing I can do. How big?"

They all looked at the wall. A three by five foot one would be good, but then, where would the other information go? Olivia spoke, "Not too big, it has to fit."

Glen took a copy of the town plan and stuck it into the small folder he carried. "Any other maps?"

Brad answered. "The Valley. Olivia, can you just zoom out a bit from that map?"

They waited as Olivia found the exact breadth of the map Brad wanted. "You see, here, it's the Kern County line. There was an enormous fuss, during the first few days, about whose county would take the case. New Cuyama, where AnnaRose lived and from where she had disappeared, is in Santa Barbara County. In fact, so is Old Cuyama, the two schools, the services, library, fire department etc. They are also all in Santa Barbara. Come to think of it, most of the farmland and grazing is also in the county. At first, they were on it. They called out the search parties, they organized everything. I think they thought she would be found a few blocks from home. But the place where she was found was just over the line in Kern County. And that's what began the dispute between the two departments."

"So, exactly what happened? Who got the case? I thought you worked for Kern County," Very asked.

"Yeah, and as far as I'm concerned that's the reason why this is still a cold case." Brad leaned back in his chair. He took off his hat, put it in his lap and ran his hand through his thick graying hair. "When the search really got going, the day after she disappeared, the Kern County law enforcement was brought in. Calling on your neighbor to help is often done in locations like this. There's a place where San Luis Obispo, Santa Barbara and Kern Counties all converge. So, all of those county people were asked to help. The person who found the body, on the afternoon after she went missing, was a Kern County Sheriff's deputy. He claimed the case. Really, Santa Barbara should have had it, and should never have let Kern County take any of the evidence away. It was all unclear, everything. Back in the day, this petty squabbling hindered the whole thing, the search, the investigation, everything was tainted with the egos of small-minded men. And even to this very day, the jurisdictional disputes hamper everything." Brad stopped.

Looking at his hat in his hands, he cleared his throat. "I think there is more to be found. If any of you doubted Glen's questioning, I want you to stop right now. This is not a vanity search, this is real. I know there is more to be found. And the first place I will start is with the Santa Barbara Sheriff's department. I think they never shared all they knew. I believe information was held back. Oh, maybe it was perception of someone's alibi, or some piece of information they knew about a person's background, or their viewpoint about evidence, what was good, bad, or inconsequential. Did they really interview everybody they should have? Did they follow up? We know that memories are funny things. Time is crucial. We forget, we remember differently every single time we recall something. It's a basic tenet of investigation. This was not done in the case of the Santa Barbara bunch, and it wasn't done here."

Very looked around at the faces of those who had signed up for the return investigation. With Brad's assessment, they all must know there was more to be found, but could they? Could they re-interview suspects or witnesses? It had been so long, and so many had died, moved away or perhaps, had forgotten anything they ever did know. What could they discover that two experienced, dedicated departments had missed? Everyone's face reflected these same questions. It was a lark on Saturday, 'yeah, we'll take on this cold case,' but the realities had begun to sink in.

Very turned to Glen. It was his money, or maybe his father's money, and how much was he willing to spend? Very had retired, she had a pension, this was only a little pick-up job. Brad was similarly placed, but Darrell and Olivia were working. They couldn't afford to do this pro bono. Did Glen realize how much of this search depended on whims? The ability or willingness of witnesses to go back over what had happened? The hard-to-find breaks in this case did not match those on the TV shows, this was for real.

But…what about her own quixotic search? Couldn't she say that all these questions were ones that she needed to answer for herself in the lonely, wacky business of trying to find Frankie Monroe? For two and a half years, she had been searching for a person who didn't want to be found. It was analogous to this case. Physician, heal thyself. More appropriately, Private Investigator, look in your own backyard. She sighed. AnnaRose WAS her backyard; she was her big sister.

Very went back to the job at hand. "So, the first job is maps. We have covered that."

Olivia piped up. "Time line, we need a time line."

"Where do we start?" asked Darrell. "AnnaRose's birth? That morning?"

"Not just for AnnaRose, but for all connected. We need Betty Jean Bullitt's time line. Where she was, when, with whom. And then all the other major players," Brad put in.

"Calendars? Like appointment calendars?" Darrell asked.

"Minute by minute for some. Lots of space. And a list of everyone we need to track, like a list of speakers or a cast of characters. We need to know where everyone was, what everyone's alibi was. Everyone." Darrell shuffled on his desk for more blank pages.

"A lot of that we can get from the reports, the original and the cold case reports. We can find out where they said they were. We need to look for discrepancies." Brad added. "And for that, first, cold case and maybe a re-interview, we need lots of space. Lots of calendars."

"Well, the license is supposed to be displayed in a prominent place, but I guess for the duration, I can take it down. And then we can have this wall too." Darrell gestured to the only other wall available. The lone window took up the third wall, and the door the fourth.

"Okay," said Olivia, "that wall is the timeline, lots of room for everyone involved. When do I start? When do I stop the timeline? When she, the victim, I mean…"

"AnnaRose. Her name is AnnaRose," Glen said. "I never met her. But my dad always drilled into me that you keep someone alive by remembering them, and by using their name. Call her AnnaRose."

"Do you have a photo of her?" Olivia asked.

"Yeah, we have one. It was taken just a few days before she disappeared. It's not the best, but it's a good likeness. I have others, baby pictures. I think Cindy has more. But here it is." Glen opened the folder he had and looked for the black and white brownie snapshot. It had little frilled edges and was square. The contrast wasn't good and it had faded. But they all saw the little girl's face with a wistful gaze.

Very stood and put her hand out to touch it. "It does look like her, like I remember her." She looked closer. She saw the girl standing on the doorstep of a house, three steps up from the front sidewalk. Very's hand shook as she reached behind her for the arm of her chair. "I remember the house and the floor plan. It was exactly like our house, just three doors down the street, on Sisquoc Street."

"Cindy still lives there." Glen said.

Brad broke in, "We should go there, look at the lay of the land. Remember what we can." He turned to Very.

She looked up, "You mean today, now?" Very sat and tried to breathe evenly, attempting to cover up the beginnings of a panic attack. "You want me to go back to the scene of the crime, just like that?"

"Yeah. Are you okay? Look a little white in the face, green around the gills." He waited for Very's answer.

"Listen we can go now and be there in just a little over an hour. We can pick up some lunch at the Buckhorn," he prodded.

"It's still there?"

"Of course, where would it go?"

Very's head filled with the splash of water in a small swimming pool where she was trying to swim from one side to the other. The clink of ice in a glass of red, red liquid, the fondly remembered Shirley Temple. Deer heads, the whole things, leering at her from the wall.

Suddenly, Brad's strong arms were around her again and a sound from far away pleaded with her, "No, not again. Don't faint on me now."

Chapter Seven: Visit to Cuyama I

After Very recovered, Bradley got copies of the maps from Olivia and information from Glen about Cindy's phone number and address.

"I'm not going to call," Brad said. "If she's home, she's home and if she's not, well, we will do this again some time. I just don't want to have her prepare too much, or have the opportunity to put us off."

Darrell looked at Very. He opened his mouth. Was he going to protest at not being invited? After all, this was Darrell's investigation. Now, Very had taken over as Chief Investigator and Brad had started calling the shots, even deciding who to interview and how. Very read Darrell's body language. She needed to say something.

"Darrell, this is just a short preliminary part of this investigation. I think Brad wants to get me out there, diffuse the panic maybe. Next time, you get to go. Right now, we need you here, to hold down the fort, to gather the important information. You and Olivia need to get the background all laid out. The maps on the wall, the timelines worked on."

Darrell looked defeated, but shrugged his shoulders in resignation. Olivia quickly took over. "Look Darrell, is this what we want?" She held up a sheaf of papers. With the other hand, she waved a mini bye-bye to Very and Brad. She turned back to Darrell. "Bigger, what do you think?"

Brad rolled his eyes at Very, who grabbed his arm and marched him out of the office. In the hallway, after the door had firmly shut, Very turned to Brad. "I don't know what it is with you men. We women spend so much time trying to keep you guys from getting your feelings hurt. And you men spend so much time trying to undo our work. I think Olivia has a good handle on that man's fragile ego. You need to try a little harder." The last pronouncement was said in Very's teacher cum counselor voice.

"What about your fainting fit, what would you call that?" Brad hit back.

"That was anguish of my own making, not some made up slight from someone else. I'll explain that later. The Buckhorn, huh?" Very said, inviting Brad to tell her more about the Cuyama institution.

The drive to Cuyama was smooth. They went out Highway 99 to 166, made a right turn and headed for the coast range of hills. In some parts of the country, these elevations might be called mountains, but here in California, they were only hills. Very sat quietly watching the scenery go by. When she was young, the edge of Bakersfield was at Valley Plaza, the first mall in Bakersfield. Beyond that to the south and west, were fields, mostly dry expanses of scrub. Now, lines of citrus trees, pistachios and almonds marched back from the two-lane road. Where did all of this come from? Where did the water come from, to water all these plants? Then she began to understand why there was panic in the last few years about drought and saving water. She had known years where the winter rainfall was less than the average six inches a year, and she recalled the Sundays when she was young when they were all charged to pray for rain. Rain in August or September was unlikely and actually not good for the cotton crop, but pray they did. But why was she now being asked to limit her flushes, and abbreviate her already very short showers? So these acres of commercial crops could grow where God had not meant them to grow? She frowned.

Soon, they passed all the trees and emerged into more familiar landscape. Western San Joaquin Valley desert. Then they arrived on the outskirts of Maricopa. Very sat up and stared at the scattered houses, the dry grass where nothing else could grow. The soil had been strewn with the detritus of the oil industry. She scanned the front yards, the back yards, the side yards, so devoid of the lush green grass and trees of Bakersfield. She strained her eyes, trying to find a bull wheel. When she was young, many of the massive wooden wheels lay strewn around the landscape here in Maricopa, abandoned symbols of the oil industry of yesteryear. Gradually, all the wheels which had been left to rot by the oil companies, had been claimed by the inhabitants, to sit in their front yards, to capture a bit of the old historic feelings of the town. The town had been sparsely populated until the discovery of oil in the early years of the twentieth century, when the town grew, slightly. It had never had a big population; perhaps it had fewer inhabitants now than fifty or a hundred years ago.

They drove down the main street of town, a block and a half of sad, outdated store fronts. Oil. It had always been big in this part of California. It still was. Very's dad worked for the oil company, and had gotten a job in Cuyama when oil was found there. Very's friends' dads also worked in the oil fields. They smelled when they came home from work. And scrubbing the hands and fingernails only cleared out a little of the odor. Very's dad had a better job, he worked as an engineer. And while he, too, went out to the fields, he didn't get oily dirt under his fingernails every day. Very's mother never let her forget this, they were an engineer's family.

Then, the speed limit changed and they headed out of Maricopa. On the right, Very turned to stare. It was still there, the little café, now just a long low wooden house. Unpainted, the boards on the sides of the house had weathered into brown boards of some more primitive time. She remembered. On the way back from Bakersfield, never going to, her dad would stop at this café, the Bull Wheel Café, if she remembered correctly. Inside, she would head to the soda pop refrigerator in the corner. It was old-fashioned, and she had never known another place to have one like that. It was a massive cold water bath, and the soda bottles were lined up like soldiers, shoulder deep in cold water. She always chose a Dr. Pepper. Funny, she hadn't had a Dr. Pepper in years, but the sight of the old café, now a private home, made her taste buds tingle. And did they have a bull wheel out in front? Was it her memory or was it the wanting to see one of the old symbols of her youth, the time before the disappearance? She turned her face away.

Within minutes, they came to the hill. Ahead, slicing a shelf onto the hillside, was the roadway. Soon they were on it, with signs warning of passing, a grade of 7%, and to watch out for trucks. The grade was long and steep, causing the engine of the truck to roar with the effort. She had forgotten this barrier to Cuyama, the slow and steep uphill slog, but then she remembered the scary downhill. Her dad had cursed the ice on the grade as they took the road to Bakersfield. Christmas Eve, it must have been, just after the short twilight, and they were desperate to join family for the Christmas celebration, always held on the Eve. She was old enough to feel the fear as he gripped the steering wheel and worked the brakes, muttering curses under his breath. This was the divider, between the San Joaquin Valley, Bakersfield, and the small Cuyama Valley. Once you had passed this short section, the rest was straight forward.

When they had reached the top, Very turned in her seat to view the distant valley and the brown hills. It was a barren road and was surrounded by barren hills. She could never remember any of it ever being green, although low bushes grew here and there.

Very swayed with the next few miles of long curves and slow ups and downs. The two-lane road was almost empty. The Cuyama Valley appeared suddenly. In the distance, Very saw green fields, interspersed with dry sections. They passed a few farmhouses off to either side, a sign that read 'San Luis Obispo County' and then the elementary school. She had attended there for a few years and as one always does, she remembered the kindergarten, and the first grade, and the second grade classrooms, the office, the nurse's tiny cubbyhole. It went by in a blink. Then there was Old Cuyama, a few buildings and rows of small rooms, that had been a simple motel. The high school, loomed suddenly like the other buildings, to the south of the road. There was a sign at the entrance to the parking lot, now populated with a few cars. Then the civic buildings, consisting of the fire station, the library, the Health Service.

Less than a minute later, they were in New Cuyama. A niggling feeling crept up her spine. There was the oval park, where she had played with her dolls, the church just across the road and small houses, with simple front yards. The C & H Market was there, and the Post Office. The large vacant lot was still vacant. It looked the same. It had not changed. Like some old movie, where the characters were taken back in time, she knew exactly where she was. She knew what these people would say and do. She could hear the creepy music that would play in the background.

Brad slowed and pulled off the highway, parking his truck just opposite the entrance to the Buckhorn. It too, looked the same. She saw it with the eyes of an adult, the Buckhorn sign, the big plate glass windows, the highway and across the highway, fields and then the hills. The hills to the north were shining, a light, bright glare on their sterile surfaces. They were folded like the smooth claws of some giant animal. She knew that later in the day, the shadows would grow in the cracks, and the hills would be multi-hued and menacing. This was the view out of the kitchen window of their house. Her mother looked at those hills every day as she prepared dinner and washed the dishes. What did she think of this view? Had she liked it, found it interesting, or was it a symbol of the desolation of Cuyama? Did she feel stuck out here in the back of beyond, the nowhere land, or did she like the comfort of the view of nature? Very had never asked her, and now it was too late.

They entered the Buckhorn's café. She had last been here more than fifty years ago. The countertops must have been renovated, the seats given new covers, but again, she felt as if she had walked out of the future into the past. As she walked by, she took a peek into the bar. On the north side of the wall were heads of deer, bucks with huge racks of antlers. The antlers looked dusty, but they were all impressive, big brown glass eyes staring straight ahead, huge magnificent specimens of their species. California mule deer. She had vague memories of the bar. Of course, she was far too young to go into the place, but if she came with her father, she would have had to stick close. And she had been fascinated with the deer heads.

They sat in the booth, close to the big window that looked out on the hills to the north, the Caliente Range of mountains. Beyond the hills was the Carrizo Plain, with a soda lake and California Indian remains, petroglyphs and campsites. The scene was a timeless one, seemingly undisturbed by man. Very looked and looked, resting her chin on her hand, taking in the feel and the sight of the familiar land.

"Penny for your thoughts?" Brad said after the waitress had left them with menus.

"Nothing has changed. Nothing. It's like an old horror movie, black and white, creepy music. I'm an adult, this is the twenty-first century, but this place is still back in the 50's and 60's."

They finished their lunch and drove the few blocks to Sisquoc Street. The houses, for the most part, looked like they could use paint, new windows, new roofs, new front yards. The ones that seemed okay were only slightly better. They were all small, two bedrooms and one bath. Some garages had obviously been made into bedrooms, which increased the capacity. But none were roomy, only the yards were large and spacious.

Brad stopped in front of a house. "This is it?" Very asked. "I know Glen told us she still lived here, but I had no idea it was the very same house. I lived up the street in a house with the identical floor plan. I can still draw it."

They walked to the front door. Very hung back, unwilling to approach the house, letting Brad do it. He knocked.

A woman opened the door. She was casually dressed in crop pants and comfortable tee shirt. Flip-flops hung loosely on her feet. Her light brown hair had started to gray. Very gasped as she looked into her face;

the heart-shaped face with the pointed chin she remembered as AnnaRose's. Sisters.

"Cynthia?" Brad asked.

"Yeah, yeah, come in, Glen said you were coming. Why did you come all the way here? I can't tell you anything." Cynthia held open the door which led directly into the front room.

Very, startled, said, "Did Glen call you? This morning?" She looked at Brad with an annoyed glance. Rattled, she stood uncertainly.

"Yeah, he called. He thought it was unfair to me to have you guys just come in on wings…" Cindy gestured to come in further to the house.

She pointed to a couch and a couple of matching arm chairs. They were newer than the house, but of the style as the ones Very remembered. The room dimensions fitted Very's memory.

"You guys want a Coke or something?" Cindy turned to the dining room and disappeared into the kitchen.

"No thanks," shouted Very.

Cindy reemerged with a tall glass in her hand and an accompanying Coke can. "Suit yourself. She sprawled on the couch, which left the chairs to Very and Brad. They sat.

Very started. "We just wanted you to tell us anything you can about AnnaRose and her…"

"Death? Not really. I was too young; I don't even remember the details myself. I can tell you what my mother told me about her. My mom always kept a picture on her bedside table. I still have it, somewhere. But she didn't talk too much about it. I think he knew it wouldn't be the best conversation for a little kid to hear the gruesome details.

"Dad, Mr. Bullitt, has been so good to me. Glen is the closest thing I'll have to a brother. But Eugene Bullitt isn't my father, my real father, my biological father, I guess they call it these days. But his name is on my Birth Certificate, so, he was my father."

"How do you know he isn't your father?" Very asked.

"My mom told me, when I was about thirteen. I guess she thought it was about time to give me that information. But he was always like a dad, so I let him be my dad. It's better than being an orphan."

"When did your mom die?"

Cindy hesitated, letting the silence buffer the awkward question. "When I was thirteen. Yeah, a car accident. Wham, gone. I left here and lived with my aunt in Santa Maria. Then I got married young, a mistake. But this was my house, my mother left it to me. And Dad kept it for me. He rented it out, so I always had a little of my own money to spend. He'd give me money when I was a teenager and say that it was my inheritance. Wow, do you know what it's like to be given $100 when you're fifteen? Like a millionaire. I always had money, never went on welfare or anything. Always a little of my own money. But after I divorced husband number three, I came here. It's my house. And I've been here ever since. Sorry, I can't tell you anymore. Kind of a sad life, huh?"

"Not really, no." Very looked around the room. "Funny, I lived in a house, just down the street. It was the same house, same floor plan. When I came here to play with your sister, I knew where everything was. It brings back memories."

Cindy rose, setting her glass on the wooden coffee table, etched with years of round stains from glasses without coasters. "Good luck," she said. "Sorry I couldn't be of more help."

Very and Brad found themselves on the way out the door. Very turned to say goodbye, when Cindy said in a detached and unemotional voice. "It wasn't an accident, my mother. In the car. No accident."

Chapter Eight: The Place Where AnnaRose Was Found

Although Very and Brad lingered on the front stoop, no more information was forthcoming from Cynthia. When asked why she thought it wasn't an accident, she simply shrugged. She reiterated, but did not add more. "It wasn't an accident." When Very suggested suicide or murder, run off the road, poisoned, Cindy clammed up. Finally, she shut the door in their faces.

When they got into the car, Very pointed down the street. "That's where I lived." They drove by, slowly, and Very recalled the sidewalk from the front door to the street where she had learned to roller skate. They stopped. The house now had a cement fence, and a well-kept front yard. Very got out and walked closer. She stared, then got out her phone and took a photo.

Back in the car, Very instructed Brad to drive slowly, and she pointed out where her childhood friend Patty had lived, where Susie had lived. She instructed him to drive to the end of the street, only one block long. They drove around the rest of the township. Very pointed out the churches, the vacant lot where the wading pool for kids had been. There was a new community pool near the baseball field. It took five minutes for the sightseeing tour. At the end of Sisquoc street sat a row of new houses, added since Very left. They were bigger, and nicer, but they were still in Cuyama.

"Let's go. Up the highway. We can stop at the school."

They went past the oval park and turned onto 166. They drove out of town, crossing the Cuyama River just before the cluster of civic buildings. Very laughed. "There's a pedestrian bridge. When I was a kid, you either came out and walked along the highway, not safe or pleasant, or you walked, balanced, on the big pipe. The pipe's still there, but now there's a cute little bridge. Ah, progress."

"More fields planted with something. When I was here, working on the cold case, it was still a desert. Now, look at all the produce." Brad scanned the fields to the north of the highway, now green with foliage and littered with cars among the rows of irrigated crops.

When they passed the high school, Very started the reminiscing again. "The high school. Although I learned to swim at the Buckhorn's pool, it was just a few years later that they built the high school pool, which then became the community pool. They even had a diving pool and a high board. I was too afraid to go off it. Still am, as a matter of fact. But it was a much bigger pool. I did notice the new community pool."

When they got to the elementary school, Very demanded that they turn in and look. Brad parked and Very got out, gazing through the chain link fence that surrounded the school site.

"What do you see? From your adult perspective, or your girlhood one?" Brad asked.

"The same, it's the same. I'm sure they still use that classroom for kindergarten. It has toilets in the classroom, so it's really good for that. And those others, I'm sure that is still first and second and third grade.

They had added some more classrooms just about the time I left. The baby boomers, you know, those born in 1947 and 1948 and 1949. Each class pushed the number of students. So they needed more classrooms." She looked again. A new coat of paint, but the same.

They got into the truck and headed out towards Bakersfield. The shadows were beginning to lengthen and a purple haze to develop. Very's head swiveled from left to right, drinking in the scenery.

Suddenly Brad slowed and then pulled off and road and stopped. He took out his phone and then accelerated until he reached a small dirt road. He turned right and headed slowly into the farmland. At a split, he turned left. Ahead loomed a large gate. Wrought iron, brown with rust, but it still maintained its high frame over the road. The two large metal arms were flung open. Brad turned cautiously. Ahead lay a farmhouse and outbuildings. The wood had never had paint or had lost it completely. Farm equipment sat among weeds and the carcass of an old car lay rusting in the front. Brad drove by the house, watching for any movement, barking of dogs, a person to challenge him. As soon as they had passed, he breathed out and his shoulders relaxed.

He drove guardedly ahead, slowing at each clump of dry desert scrub. Soon he headed off on a faint track. He stopped at one clump and turned off the engine. He pulled the brake and got out, leaving his door open.

Very followed. She wanted to ask why they were here, but she thought she knew. She let him talk, let him tell her.

"Back there, just a mile, is the Kern County Line. This," he indicated the dry bit of dirt on the back side of the clump, "is where they found her. Because this is Kern County, and the body was here, that's how we got involved. Not the whole reason, but it was an excuse.

And the other was that a Kern County sheriff's dog actually found the body. Now, here's the story. They had been looking all day, this is the day after she was reported missing. They called in all the law enforcement they could reach. You understand, a kid, a young girl, everyone knew they needed to find her fast. They collected her clothes to use for scent for the dogs. So this sheriff's dog had been working all day and was familiar with the scent of the little girl's clothes. Just out there on the highway, late in the day as they were heading home, the dog went crazy. Out there on 166, right on the highway, the dog went berserk. He was barking, trying to get out of the truck through the window. So the guy pulled over, he thought the dog needed a bush right away. Didn't want a mess in his car.

"He let the dog go, and waited. The dog took off, straight in this direction. Then he got out and called. The dog started howling, but didn't come back. So, the deputy started driving. There were tracks out here, someone owned this land and ran cattle, I guess. He followed the road, but also the howls of the dog. If there were any tire tracks, he obliterated them. He didn't know what was up with the dog. Finally, he found him.

"The dog, a big German Shepherd, was standing over the body, howling like a primitive wolf. The dog, according to the statement, was crying in misery. The deputy had never heard his dog sound like that. The radio was out, so he couldn't call anyone. And this was before mobile phones, so there was no way to let anyone know. He tried to get the dog back into the truck, but he wouldn't go. He snarled and lunged at his owner, his handler. The dog just sat in the dust, near the body and refused to leave.

"The deputy, finally, left the dog there. It was getting dark, and you know how it gets out here, fast and deep. He drove like a maniac back to Cuyama. They had set up a temporary headquarters at the Buckhorn, but there was nobody there. They had all gone home. Someone made a phone call and a few law enforcement type people were collected to go out to the site. But you can imagine the scene. Dark, cars and trucks, people walking around everywhere, putting their big boot prints over anything and everything. There couldn't have been much to find after all the tramping around.

"I saw the photo. She was sprawled, face down. She had been raped. Dress pulled up, panties ripped. Her head bashed in. Blood and flies. The image is seared into my memory." He looked at Very. "And now, it is seared into yours as well."

"I guess I knew what it must have been like. But standing here, so close, so intimate." Very shivered and clutched her arms across her chest. "Someday we will all die. My father was in the hospital, my mother in her own bed. A friend died in a car crash, another had a stroke in the prime of her life. How will I end?

"But this? This is so personal. Murder. The worst possible way to die." Very stood silently looking at the dusty ground. The blood was long gone, the imprint of the small frail body had been blown away by years of dust storms.

"You haven't changed your mind?" Brad asked. "You will still help us?"

"I said I would. And now, what makes you doubt it? Why should I change my mind?" Very let a tiny sneer enter her voice.

"Do you really care who did it?" Brad waited a beat for her reply. "I know that Glen wants to clear his Dad's name. He wants to do it for his dad. But you? You have other things on your mind."

"Where do you get off questioning me about my motives? Do you really have any doubt that I am serious about this?" Very stood in the dust, looking around at the desolate place.

"Sorry, I didn't mean that the way it sounded. For you, she was a friend, there was a very personal connection. But I have a reason too. Maybe even more compelling than yours." He sighed and scuffed the dirt, like a little boy who needed to confess, but knew how to use delaying tactics. "I didn't want to talk about it in front of the others. You do know that I was on the cold case investigation eleven years after it happened?"

"And that went nowhere," Very filled in for him.

"I had troubles. I tried, but I couldn't try too hard. First of all, I was new to the force, a rookie. And I got a lot of ribbing because I came in with a Bachelor's degree in Pre-Law. Not Criminal Justice, but in Law. It was if I was on the other side of the equation, not on the side of the police force, but on the side of the criminals. That wasn't true, but I was treated as if it was. And labeled an 'intellectual,' not one of the guys. But also I was teased about 'not making it into law school,' being a cop was second best, as if my heart wasn't in it and theirs was.

"The real reason I joined was because I thought I could make a difference. You know, cops are the first line of the law. I thought that there were too many lawyers and not enough good cops, smart ones, to make it better on the ground. I wasn't there but three months when they assigned me this. At the time, I was excited, but I quickly learned that they did it to bring me down a notch. Next, the lead investigator on the case was a total idiot. He had been assigned to the case in the first instance and I believe he blew it then. He had no idea how to make it right this time, so he took it out on me, and the others involved, but especially me. He knew he couldn't solve it, so he pretended that the rest of us were idiots as well. He held me back, as he did the others. I wanted to talk to Cindy. But she was underage, so no go. We did talk with her mother, Betty Jean. But I had to take a female who was more inexperienced than me, if there was such a thing, and also gun-toting aggressive male. Well, we got no more information.

"And then, I wanted to interview others, for example, Eugene Bullitt. He was AnnaRose's father. He had been around the house, knew the people who lived around there. He might have had insights. He had been questioned during the first investigation, but he had an 'alibi' and that was all there was to it. And then there were the neighbors. If they had moved away, well, they were not available. But no attempt was made to find new addresses for them. There was a man who had been having a relationship with Betty Jean at the time. And his teenage son. We found an address for them, but that was blocked as well. It was just a pro forma investigation, just for the show. I felt frustrated and disappointed, angry, really. But everyone just said, 'That's the way it is.' So, I had to leave it at that."

Very looked around at the scene and it imprinted onto her mind. There was no dead child at her feet, but she knew that once there had been. "And now, you want to do it properly?"

"I need to find out as much as I can. I need to go over and over all of the testimony, all of the alibis, I need to re-interview all the neighbors, the family. I need all of the testimony. Maybe Eugene Bullitt did it. I don't know. But I will find out." Brad looked at the bushes, the hills, the sky.

"Don't let this get too personal! As if I should talk." Very whispered, more to herself than to Brad.

"It's already too personal. Let's go." Brad headed to the truck.

As they climbed into the cab, Brad said, "You know what Cindy said, about her mother and the accident not being an accident? That was just two or three weeks after I interviewed her. The car accident. Now, I don't know what to think."

Very sat very still as Brad started the truck. "If it wasn't an accident, what was it?" she asked.

Brad drove the truck slowly back down the dirt road towards 166 and home.

Chapter Nine: Darrell and Olivia Report

At nine the next morning, all four investigators seemed to meet at the door to the office. Brad carried his large thermos and Olivia squirmed her way in first to snag the coffee cups. She then maneuvered her way out and down the hall to the shared restroom to wash them. Very produced two packages of chocolate cookies and placed them on the TV tray.

"I want to hear your report," Very said before Olivia returned with the cups.

"Well, here we have maps," Darrell pointed out the two maps on the wall. One was of just New Cuyama township and the other was of the Cuyama Valley.

Before anything else, Brad carefully consulted the map on his phone and plotted the coordinates. He asked for a red pen or marker, "It's to put an 'X' in the place where she was found. We went there yesterday. I did take a quick snapshot, but there is nothing there now, of course. And we may have been ten or fifteen feet off in any case. But, it will give us an idea of distances, time frames."

Darrell produced a red pen. Brad marked the spot with a tiny 'x'. He also drew in a faint line with a pencil of the county line divisions. The small red 'x' was in a section where the three counties came together.

The other map, of New Cuyama, had houses marked, specifically the house where AnnaRose had disappeared from. Very took a pencil and drew in a little rectangle and labeled it, 'Very's house.' It was just a few doors up the street. When she finished, she turned and looked at the others, who had watched her carefully. "It may not be necessary for this investigation, but it is important for me."

After they poured coffee, they turned to the other wall. It was covered with sheets of paper. At the center was one that was labeled, 'Betty Jean's timeline.'

"Why Betty Jean's timeline? Why not AnnaRose's timeline?" Very asked.

"Because we don't know AnnaRose's time frames. The only things we know are those that intersect with her mother's. What her mother did and where she went that day are known by others, but AnnaRose just…" Darrell tried to keep the annoyance out of his voice. "We went through the original statements and also the cold case ones, thanks to Brad, who obtained them for us. Now, there may be more evidence in closed files. What do you think, Brad?"

"Could be, but what you have looks pretty thorough. Did you see the photos of the body? The coroner's report?" Brad stood to look at all the papers on the wall.

"Well, we didn't see the photos, but there was a description, which was graphic enough, I think. The coroner's report was redacted, a bit. But I think we have enough for now. Should we try to get the original?"

Brad turned to speak to all, "I think we need to go forward as far as we can go with this. There were people who weren't interviewed or re-interviewed at the time of the cold case investigation. We might try looking further with them before we try to get any sealed information.

That is, if they are still alive and within interview distance."

Darrell stood and spoke, "From what reports are available, here is the timeline for Betty Jean and by extension, what we absolutely know about AnnaRose's whereabouts and the times. So, here it is. Day One: AnnaRose complained about not feeling well and didn't want to go to school. Betty Jean said that she coughed and sounded hoarse. So, her mother said she could stay at home that day. She made a quick phone call to the school and just said she was sick. But that wasn't confirmed, as far as we know. But there doesn't seem to be a reason to lie about whether she phoned or not. No one ever came forward and accused Betty Jean of keeping her kid home from school and not telling anybody." Darrell paused. A pregnant pause, a chance to ask questions, an opportunity to disagree, to bring up objections to the conclusion that it wasn't important. Was it? Did anyone need to go back to check to see if Betty Jean had called her child in sick? Could they verify that with anyone at this distance in time in any case?

"Go on, Darrell. We can deal with that later if it is important. What else?" Very asked. She had never known any of the details. These things may have been in the paper, but she had not been allowed to see the minutiae. It was important now.

"At about ten in the morning, Sarah dropped by. Sarah lived around the corner, just up the street. She was a friend of Betty Jean's and they often had coffee together, so this wasn't unusual or unexpected. They chatted for a while and then Betty Jean said she needed to go to the store. Sarah said that she would go with her. They checked on AnnaRose, who was in bed. Sarah stated that AnnaRose was there and answered her mother. Betty Jean told AnnaRose that they were going to the store and taking Cindy in the stroller. It was only five minutes away and Betty Jean said that it was okay, they'd only be ten or fifteen minutes. And AnnaRose replied that it was fine, she was okay. Sarah confirmed this. So, at eleven in the morning, AnnaRose was confirmed to be in her bed at her house."

"Was this the last time she was seen?" Very asked.

"Well, it depends on what evidence you look at," Brad said. He stood and looked carefully at the sheet of paper that Darrell was referring to. "Yeah, there is more. Maybe or maybe not the last time. Let him go on."

Darrell continued. "At about 11:15, the two women, and Cindy in the stroller, walked this way to the market." Darrell pointed to the map and traced a path that seemingly went between the houses. "They arrived at the market shortly thereafter. Betty Jean bought some groceries, things like milk and bread. This was confirmed by the store clerk. He, of course, knew everybody in town and it was easy to confirm. Now, it gets a bit murky. The two women returned to the Bullitt home and Betty Jean put away the groceries. Sarah invited Betty Jean to come to her house, so Sarah could show her some new material for a dress. This was about 11:30 or 11:45. Betty Jean again checked on AnnaRose. Sarah apparently didn't go into the bedroom, just stood in the hallway, where she heard Betty Jean talking to AnnaRose. She didn't hear a reply, but… Betty Jean put a glass of orange juice on the small table near the bed. She told Sarah that AnnaRose was sleeping and that she would be okay.

"Off they went to Sarah's house and 'lost track of time.' They had some lunch, and maybe something to drink. At about 2pm, Betty Jean wheeled Cindy, who apparently was being 'good as gold,' back home. She found AnnaRose missing."

"Between 10, or maybe 11:30ish, and 2, AnnaRose is kidnapped. The disappearance isn't discovered until 2, but could have happened any time between those hours?" Very confirmed.

The silence was confirmation. "So, what happened next?" Very asked.

"At about 2:25, Sarah got a phone call from Betty Jean. It was still a party line in those days, and a neighbor mistakenly picked up the phone. At least that person heard Betty Jean telling Sarah that AnnaRose wasn't in her bed, and as far as she knew, wasn't anywhere in the house or the yard. Betty Jean asked Sarah what to do. Sarah told her to call the sheriff and begged off, as she needed to meet her kids at the school bus stop. Then she hung up. As soon as she collected her two kids, Sarah and the kids showed up at Betty Jean's house. The sheriff hadn't been called yet for some unknown reason. But, by 3 or 3:30, there was a general hullabaloo." Darrell had started referring to notes in front of him. "Starting at 3, the neighbors were rousted out, and before it was dark, everyone in New Cuyama was looking. First in their yards, in garages, calling her name, checking the fields that surrounded the town. By the end of that day, Day 1 I'm calling it, the neighbors had thoroughly searched in and near the town."

"Could I ask a question?" Olivia interrupted. "I just don't get why Betty Jean left AnnaRose home alone. She was only six years old. Surely, she would have taken her with her or tried to find someone to watch her. It looks like she was a bad mother, but no one has said that. And then, she went to her friend Sarah's house and they 'lost track of time.' How can a responsible mother do that?"

Very leapt in before anyone else could speak. "Times have changed. My mother left me alone when we lived in Cuyama. I remember going to the park by myself. I took a sandwich and a little bottle of water or juice. I played by myself. I wasn't afraid, and neither was she. We never locked our doors. If Betty Jean had checked on AnnaRose and told her where she was going, then she didn't worry. Everyone in town knew everyone else, including their children. If AnnaRose was hungry, or in trouble, all she had to do was to go and knock on anyone's door. Anyone would have helped her. She was safe, at least in the eyes of her mother, and the whole township." Very sighed. "Oh, times have changed."

"It wasn't the mother, she had nothing to do with this, as she had an alibi. Also, Sarah, her friend. Unless, they did it together?" Olivia looked around.

Darrell continued. "Are you ready to hear about the finding of the body, the police interrogations and the suspects? And no one thought Betty Jean had done it. It was a man. So?"

A knock on the door heralded the entry of Glen. He was already clutching a cup of coffee. "Sorry, I meant to be here earlier. Things at home…"

"You have things to do, don't worry about it. We've just been going over the time lines. It was a part of the puzzle that I didn't know. They're up here, in case you need to look." Very said.

Olivia jumped up and indicated another sheet labeled Day 2. "Day 1 ends at 8pm. It was when the search was suspended for the night and everyone went home. The sheriff seems to have gotten involved sometime late in the afternoon. When is not clear, but before the end of the day."

"Did Betty Jean go back to her own home? Alone?" Very asked.

"There was a neighbor. Betty Jean stated that she wanted to be there in case AnnaRose came back. Maybe AnnaRose just ran away and her mother was afraid to not be there in case she returned. That sounds odd, actually. A little girl, by herself, coming back home in the middle of the night."

"You didn't know AnnaRose. I can imagine Betty Jean doing that, saying that. 'Oh, she's just run away and she'll be back. I need to be here.' AnnaRose was that kind of child, headstrong, independent, willing to do anything to get back at her mother if she felt wronged. So, I understand." Very shrank into herself. Talking too much, trying to justify everyone's actions. Did she need to explain about leaving kids to fend for themselves? That even six-year-olds were masters of deception and knew the meaning of duplicity, even if they didn't know the word. Betty Jean was not a bad mother, and no different from the other mothers in the small, seemingly safe town.

"Here we have the timeline for Day 2," Olivia continued. "Basically, nothing happens until the afternoon. But what may be important is that the initial search was conducted by the Santa Barbara Sheriff's department. Now, Cuyama Valley is tricky, as the county lines are weird and come together here. On this map, you can see it. Brad has put in Kern County, but San Luis Obispo is just on the other side of the river, not even a mile from the town. So, they got called in as well. Would it be fair to say, that most people looked towards Bakersfield and Taft, rather than Santa Barbara or any towns in that direction?" Olivia looked at Brad.

"We always went east when we left town. We went to Bakersfield to go to the doctor, and we went to Taft to go to church at the Catholic Church there. I only knew it was Santa Barbara County because it says so on some of the signs, the school, the library, the fire station. It just makes a lot of sense to call in Kern County people to help." Very broke in.

"And it makes sense to think that if she were kidnapped, that she had been taken east towards Bakersfield." Brad added.

"I don't see anything on the Day 2 timeline before 6pm. Kind of blank there."

"Well, we can put in the searches, where everyone looked, who looked, who was questioned, but it doesn't make sense to do that here. The most important thing is this, 'Finding the body.' And that's really interesting," Olivia continued.

"I can tell you. I talked to the deputy who found the body, and he told me in really great detail. It was the same as the story he gave the first time. Very specific, and believable, even if the dog bit is far-fetched." Brad proceeded to tell everyone else the story that he had told Very the day before.

"Contaminating the crime scene," Very blurted out.

Darrell took over. "The body was covered with dust and the surrounding soil had been disturbed by the dog as well as the humans. Let's not blame it all on the 'rescuers.' The time of death, according to the coroner's report was at least 24 hours before, quite possibly more."

"So, this extends our time frame for the kidnapping. We have no real, concrete, good evidence except from Betty Jean and Sarah, that AnnaRose was alive at eleven the day before. And dead by no later than eight maybe even six or seven, that evening. That's a large window. We are looking for someone, or ones, who took AnnaRose from her home, from the street, wherever, between eleven and six. Who was it?" Very's voice showed her anger. "One more question, was she raped? Did they collect any evidence?"

Brad said quietly, "She had been penetrated, but there was no semen, or at least none collected. Probably not a completed act."

"Definitely a man?"

"Most likely. But remember, it could have been more than one person."

"Blood?"

"A little, remember she had been hit on the head. But there is no sure evidence that they had collected AnnaRose's blood. Probably hers."

"And nothing else to identify this person? No fibers, no saliva…?"

Brad showed his irritation. "Very, you saw the place. Out in the middle of nowhere, dust, dirt, disturbed by everyone. A little lackadaisical in those days."

"Photos," Darrell said, handing one to Very.

It was a large eight by ten black and white, taken with a flash. Very looked and then passed it on to Glen.

Darrell tried to hand her another. She leapt up and dashed out the door. She banged the door as she entered the small bathroom at the end of the hall.

Brad found her trying to empty her stomach into the small commode. Finally, Very pulled herself up and washed her mouth out in the sink. As she turned to leave, she found Brad waiting for her at the door.

"Sorry, I didn't mean to make this so difficult," Brad apologized.

"No, you didn't do this. I didn't have very much for breakfast and then, too much coffee. It's my fault, not yours or anyone else's. Let's go back, I'm fine."

"Lunch is on me, you need to eat properly," he said.

With her head held high, Very walked carefully back to the office. The heat from Brad's hand could be felt, even though there was no contact. A security thing. Very allowed it, even while resenting the need for it. She was being way too emotional. She needed to get a hold on her feelings; this agitation was not being good for the case. If she couldn't get a grip on her despair, she needed to drop out of this. If she couldn't control herself in this case, how was she going to be during the search for Frankie? That case was personal, intimate even, but this case of AnnaRose was just very unpleasant.

As they reentered the office, Very said, "DNA, what about DNA analysis?"

"Very, no one even knew about DNA in those days," Darrell answered.

"Now, what about now?"

Brad answered, "There isn't anything left."

Chapter Ten: The Suspects

"None? Nothing? Blood? Anybody's? Fibers?" Very asked.

They looked at her in silence, mute. They all were thinking what a difficult thing this was, a cold case with almost no information.

Olivia put up another paper. At the top she had labeled it, 'Suspects.'

"What we need to do with this is to link or match all of these suspects with the timeline. I know this must have been done before, the first time and then again at the time of the cold case. But seeing it again might generate more ideas, throw up other possibilities. Maybe it will help us add more suspects. Accomplices? Any other actors that we need to know about? What we really need is thoroughness." Olivia looked around at everyone, daring them to contradict her. Olivia had taken the lead on the maps, the timelines, and now the suspects. Was she becoming a real PI, or was she channeling too many mystery TV shows? Time might tell. At least now this was becoming a real organized knowledge collection.

Glen said quietly. "I know my dad should be up there in the suspects group. But can we make him the first one and get it out of the way? Get it done and over with? Let's do the alibi, do it on the timeline. And then, maybe we need more answers."

"You okay with this?" Olivia asked. She waited for only a few seconds before going on. "Okey-dokey, here goes. Eugene Bullitt. Gene is the biological father of AnnaRose, married Betty Jean just before AnnaRose was born. No one ever questioned his paternity. Glen, do you have anything to add?"

"Not on that point. I'm sure he was her father. He always accepted it. Cindy, on the other hand, is another story. He always denied being her father. Even though they were married and had been living together, by the time she was conceived, they had separated. He never accepted that Cindy was his, even though his name was on the birth certificate. But he always told me Cindy was 'his' little girl, even if not biologically. And he said that I should always treat her as a sister. So, I did. And he always made sure she was taken care of. He visited her, gave her money, presents on her birthday. He saved that house for her. He didn't let anyone get hold of it and sell it out from under Cindy. He organized the rental of it when Cindy was young, and did the repairs himself. He collected the rent for it, for years. Cindy was a bit…confused when she was young. Well, you can't blame her for that. But my dad wouldn't let her get rid of the house, told her it was her steady income, and that he would look out for it. She didn't have to do anything, just accept the money every month. Later, he got her to open a bank account and manage her savings. He was really happy when she decided to move back there. It's her house. He wanted her to feel the home part of it. Even though there was tragedy associated with it, it was where she lived for years with her mother. It was always 'her' house. But he was not her father. However, he was AnnaRose's. And I can't imagine that he would do anything like rape and murder her." Glen looked at the floor and shook his head.

How myopic or in denial some children could be towards their parents. Glen just acknowledged that his father's relationship with Betty Jean was married, but the normal order of marriage, children, acceptance of those children, seemed to have gone awry in this family. Glen could acknowledge that, and seemed to be forgiving of his other peccadilloes. Sometimes parents are hated, but even then, children seem only to see one side.

"Why was he a suspect? What is his alibi? Where was he? Did he have a motive?" Very asked.

"Oh, there's a problem there." Glen looked down. "I guess I know I can't believe him, but he must be innocent, he wants his name cleared. You'd think that if he were so determined to clear his name, that he must be innocent?"

"How old is your father? Do you think he might, just possibly, be suffering from dementia? Is he confused? Does he really know what he is asking of you?" Very asked. "I know that sounds kind of snarky of me, but if we are going to continue with this, we need some real answers. A reality check?"

Glen sighed deeply. "Oh, I know there's a problem here."

"You've said that. Maybe you should tell us exactly what the problem is." Brad's voice held an edgy sound.

Olivia put up a photo of Glen Bullitt. She struck a pose, pencil in hand, next to the timeline.

"So, here's the story," Glen started. "There is a gap, maybe a lie. But this is what he maintains, even now. He called Betty Jean the night before. Said he was coming to visit, not going to work. I guess Betty Jean pointed out that AnnaRose would be at school and suggested he come later. Not in the morning. But he said he had already asked for the day off, so this was when he was going to come and see her. At the time, he was living in a rented house in Maricopa. By himself, I think."

Olivia quickly penciled in at the top of the page labeled Day 1. She wrote in a tiny hand, 'Father Eugene called. Said he was coming the next day.' "Is that okay, can everyone understand that this is the evening before?"

"We'll remember," Very assured her. "Okay Glen, go on with the story."

"He drove an old Plymouth, he couldn't afford anything else. He didn't always have a job, even when I was a kid. It was my mom that made sure food was on the table. Anyway, this is what he said then, and he says now. He left home about ten or maybe ten-thirty. And he drove to Cuyama. It takes about forty-five minutes. He said he stopped along the road and drank some coffee from a thermos. He found a little road and pulled off. He said he had made some sandwiches, and he ate those. And he said that he just sat there. He was feeling sad and he wanted to have a little time alone."

"Did anyone corroborate this? Did he see anyone?" Very asked.

"You've been out there. He doesn't even remember exactly where he pulled off. It's deserted, there's nobody there. And if you went just a couple of hundred yards off the road, nobody would notice. People on the highway would just whizz on by. And if it was a field where something was growing, you might encounter a farmer or a field hand. But back then, nothing much grew out there. That was before the time of fields everywhere. Anyway, after a while, he drove into Cuyama. He drove to Betty Jean's house. But when he got there, nobody was at home. He knocked on the door and went in, expecting to find Betty Jean and the kids. But there was no one."

"What time was this?" Very asked.

"He thought it must have been three-thirty or four in the afternoon. He said he knocked on the door. There was no answer, so he just went in. Nobody locked their doors and he thought maybe they were in the back bedroom, or maybe in the yard and didn't hear him knock. But he looked everywhere, and no one was at home. Then, Betty Jean came screaming into the house, carrying Cindy, who was also screaming. Everyone was screaming. Betty Jean wanted him to do something. The baby was hungry. She needed him to call the sheriff, or change the baby's diaper or something. She said that AnnaRose was missing.

"Anyway, instead of calling the sheriff, he went next door and got the neighbors to search. I think he probably felt like Very said. That AnnaRose just walked off by herself and she had gone to the neighbor's house or gone for a walk. I guess everyone knew she would do that. They all searched, and eventually the whole town was out searching and calling for her. No one called the sheriff until about six, I think. It was all chaos." Glen sighed and stopped speaking.

Olivia had been writing all of this down on the timeline. She was using a different color for Eugene and everyone could begin to see the different people involved, and what they were doing. "I'm going to need more paper, more space. There are too many actors in this drama."

Very stood next to the timeline. "Let me get this right. He left home in Maricopa about ten or ten-thirty. Then he drives to Cuyama and sits around in his car until four? Then he goes to the house. What does that mean?" Very turned to Glen with a wide-eyed look.

"I think it means he doesn't have an alibi." Glen leaned against the wall. "No one saw him, no one to vouch for him."

Brad broke in. "No alibi, so he has opportunity, but no motive. Would he have done something to AnnaRose to get back at Betty Jean? How was their relationship? Was he angry about the baby, Cindy, not being his, but having his name? Could that be a reason to murder his daughter?"

"I don't know," Glen said hanging his head. "I only know what he tells me."

"We can't exclude him, you understand that, don't you?" Very said. "But, frankly we don't expect it to be him. Even if he did this years ago, why would he try to clear his name now? Doesn't make sense. We may need to interview him again, probe for misremembered or unremembered items. Maybe he knows something that he doesn't know that he knows. What did he have to say about all the other people in this?" Very turned to Brad. She silently asked for his take on this.

Brad nodded slowly, assenting to Very's assumptions. The silence in the small room lengthened as no one wanted to say anything more. Their client wanted to clear his name, but he wasn't willing to give them much.

"I did interview Eugene Bullitt during the cold case. I felt it was weird that he said he just parked off the road and sat there. He didn't seem to be the contemplative type. He didn't say that he had a quart of whiskey and drank it. That, I might have believed, but just thinking? I also felt as though he didn't know who did this. He didn't seem to have a motive, although the opportunity. He's there, on the board… But." Brad leaned back in his chair, causing it to squeak alarmingly.

"Well, was it just some random stranger that we don't know?" Very asked.

"Could have been," echoed Darrell. "Nobody in the first case, or in the cold case had any real ideas. One minute AnnaRose was there, the next she wasn't. Or rather, a few hours later. It was never established that she was taken from the house. Could she have gone outside? Was she kidnapped from outside the house? How could she have gotten outside? She was only six years old."

"Don't forget," Very interjected. "No one ever locked their doors and a six-year-old is capable of turning the door handle. I think the idea that Eugene had, to alert the neighbors first of all, was a sound one. She could have gotten outside and gone to a neighbor's house. Everyone's doors were unlocked. I mean, if you went on vacation, you might lock them. Maybe some people did at night, yeah, at night. But we never feared intruders."

"Oh, I lock my doors all the time!" Olivia said, her voice quavering. "I can't imagine leaving doors hanging open, for just anyone to come in."

"Oh, Olivia, times have changed. I lock my doors too." Very sat forward, her brows wrinkling in thought. "Maybe that was when my parents started to lock our doors. It was at some point, when I was a kid. We were living in Bakersfield, but all of a sudden, it seeme there was a fuss about the doors. I had to carry a key in case I came home early from school. But then again, I wasn't allowed to be by myself at home, or come home early from school. But in Cuyama, I remember going outside by myself, coming home by myself. I felt so safe, so free. No worries.

"But then, if no one locked their doors, anyone could have gotten in, or she could have gotten out. And maybe unnoticed."

Darrell spoke. "So, what is our outside time frame? When was she last seen? And then, when…"

Brad said, "Eleven am. That was when Betty Jean said she talked with her. The alarm was raised at two. And she was dead by eight that evening."

Chapter Eleven: Revisiting the Cold Case

"We need to revisit the cold case files. We need to see what we do know." Brad squeaked in his chair again.

Darrell spoke. "I have what's available. To the public, I mean. Brad, you can get the rest of the stuff? Have you applied?

"Yeah, I've done the paperwork. I knew there was a reason to make sure my bar membership was up to date. I can be the lawyer for the case, and ask for the sealed records."

"You're a lawyer?" Very asked in a startled one.

Brad smiled slyly. "And you thought I was just a cowboy.?"

"I didn't know. So, you're able to get sealed records? Are there any? What are they?" Very asked.

"I'm not sure what's open and what's not. If there is anything left. There should be some physical evidence, more graphic photos, reports, medical details. It's been a long time. Some of this stuff gets lost, you understand."

Very shivered, visibly, and licked her lips.

"I'll sift through everything, make sure it's relevant. What do we have for now?" Brad turned to Darrell and Olivia.

"Files," said Darrell.

"Cold case files. People's interviews, you know the transcriptions of the interviews." Olivia offered. "Mostly the neighbors, what they saw, where they were. Really, I guess, alibis. Or telling us what they didn't see."

"The coroner's report," said Darrell. "With some redactions. Do we need the redactions? Because they're not part of the cold case or the original case that we were able to see."

Olivia said, "Newspaper reports. We weren't able to get any TV reports because they were really difficult to find. I mean, I'm sure this was on TV."

"Oh, yes, it was, a lot. All three channels. But why can't we get the news from fifty years ago?" Very asked.

"Maybe they didn't record it, if it was live, maybe they just did the show and that was it. Local news wasn't always important enough to keep a record of. Of course, it could have been lost as well. New owners get rid of the old junk from last decade. The newspapers, on the other hand, always kept a copy, maybe just the one copy, in their archives. Lately, all of that stuff has been digitized." Brad answered the query. He mumbled to himself, and then spoke out. "But how different would it be, from print to on air? What more, or less, would we know or could deduce if we had TV coverage? I think we need to let that angle go, unless something tells us we need that perspective." Brad looked around to those present for consent.

"What else do we have?" Very asked.

"Lots of reports, for example. We have the weather report for the day. The day was a mild spring day, high of 70 degrees, sunrise six-thirty, sunset seven-thirty. It was a Wednesday, no holidays that week. School was in session, work all over the valley was going on with no interruptions." Darrell reported.

"So, that means during the time of the 'going missing,' the streets were quiet. Everyone was at home, work or school. Too cool to be out much, everyone, like housewives and little kids, would be inside, where it was warmer. People wouldn't have been at the park, for example." Very spoke, more to herself than to the group.

Darrell continued, "For example, here are the neighbors' statements." Olivia reached up to write on the time line.

"Next door, here, along the street to the east, was a housewife who didn't go outside all day. She was cleaning house and baking. Her husband was at work. She said she watched some TV, but quit after a while as the picture was fuzzy and the sound wasn't coming in well. Her house had no window in the front, so she couldn't see the street while she was in the kitchen or the living room."

Very snorted at the TV comment. "I can't imagine anyone watching TV in Cuyama. I remember trying to watch the Mickey Mouse Club and being frustrated as all get out. I had to go to Bakersfield and visit my grandparents to get any kind of decent reception. I don't know whether to say she is lying by saying she was watching soap operas, or sympathize with her for even trying."

Darrell continued. "Here is the neighbor on the other side. She was also a housewife with two little kids. She and the kids were inside all day. Her husband was at work and he took the car. She talked on the phone to her girlfriend who lived on the next street over and also her Mom in Bakersfield. She said she heard nothing, saw nothing, until Betty Jean raised the alarm late in the afternoon."

"Nothing was stirring, not even a mouse," Very mumbled. "I can believe all of this. It sounds so familiar."

"There are lots of these kinds of statements, from neighbors up and down the street. Across the street was a teacher, and she was at the school that day, until late in the afternoon. There were three women playing bridge at the community center who lived on the street. They started just after lunch, at one, and finished about four. There were ten or so other women with them. There was a general call for information from anyone who saw or heard, or who knew anything. No one answered this call on the public."

"There is one family of interest." Olivia raised her head from the board and looked around.

"The Kentons," said Glen, "they lived there." He pointed to the map, to a small square that designated a building just four houses down the street to the west. "Suspects, both of them, oh yeah, they are suspects."

Very felt jolted out of her seat. She stood and looked around. "Why, when? Who are they and why are they suspects?" She looked at Brad. "I had no idea about this. When did this come up? I thought in this whole thing there was nobody that could have done this? What do you mean, suspects? How so? And when were they identified as suspects?"

"As far as we can tell, at the time. You see, they were referred to as the stepfather and the son, stepbrother to AnnaRose." Darrell explained to Very.

"So when was this? When did this come to light?" Very was still on her feet, confused and just a wee bit angry.

Glen answered. "Then, at the time, they knew it, the cops knew it. Betty Jean and Raymond were together. I mean, I don't think they actually lived together, but there was a lot of spending nights together. It was one of the factors that made him a suspect."

"But I thought that Betty Jean was still married to your dad, to Eugene, at the time of the, the, the incident. How could this Raymond character be AnnaRose's stepdad? And alibis, two of them you say, father and son, do they have alibis?"

Brad stepped in. "Sit, Very. And before you get excited, Raymond Kenton was not married to Betty Jean, then or at any time. And yes, Raymond has an alibi. He was at work, all day with others to corroborate this. Pretty solid alibi. And the son, Mickey, was at school. He was only fourteen at the time, in any case.

"And the relationship, well, that was complicated. There is no doubt that Raymond and Betty Jean were in a relationship, as they say. There were many nights when Raymond came for dinner and didn't go home. Mickey, being a kid, also came to dinner and presumably he went home in the evening. They, Raymond and Betty Jean, never married, never held themselves out to be married, but Betty Jean was disingenuous when telling her neighbors and her daughter. And then, after AnnaRose died, that relationship died with it. But consider this, the neighbors all talked about the connection. They mentioned it in their statements, things like, 'You should consider that Raymond Kenton guy. He was AnnaRose's 'uncle' and you need to look into that.' That was a general consensus. But, in the original and also in the cold case investigation, he was thoroughly considered. They checked out the alibi with more than one workmate. And the kid, Mickey, was in school. That checked out too.

"The real problem was that they lived in a house just up the street. And there was a lot of comings and goings of an adult male not related. It looked really bad, but it was all checked out. And, yes, they should be listed as suspects. If we are really serious, we need to consider them again."

Darrell spoke again, "The creepiest thing about this was, apparently, Betty Jean told neighbors and such that they had gone to Vegas and were married. I mean, in those days, being a divorcee was not nice. So, it seems she told nosy neighbors what they wanted to hear. But she maintained later that they weren't married."

"Was he Cindy's father?" Very asked.

"Not so that anyone could tell. He moved there and met Betty Jean about the time that Cindy was born, so he didn't even know her when Cindy was conceived. But people talked about them as the 'stepfather' and 'stepbrother.'"

"How come I didn't know them? I was around when Cindy was born." Very broke in. "I mean, we left soon after that, but I do remember the baby Cindy because that was one of the reasons Betty Jean asked me over, to entertain AnnaRose while she took care of the baby. Although, I do remember when I was there, there was a lot of sleeping, mostly on the part of the baby. I never saw or heard of anyone that was stepfather or stepbrother. But then again, I was a kid myself, what did I know? What are kids supposed to know?"

"I am assuming that the relationship started after you left, Very," said Brad.

"So, suspects or not?" Olivia had placed photos of Raymond and Mickey on the board under suspects. "And do we need to interview them again, or do we take what we've got?"

"It might be instructive to interview them again. On the other hand, where are they, are they still alive? If he is still alive, Raymond Kenton would be over 90 and Mickey would be, well not young. And can we find them?" Brad mused. "I didn't do any interviews with them, but we have the interviews. Where were they living?"

Darrell consulted a sheet, "In Taft."

"Not far at all. Eleven years and they were still nearby. And what kind of work did Raymond do?" Very asked.

They all looked at her. Brad shook his head, Darrell snorted in derision at her ignorance, Olivia smiled and Glen answered, "Oil. Roustabout most likely. I think Mickey was in the same field."

"Very," Brad asked, "What was your family doing in Cuyama?'

Very sighed, "My dad worked for the oil company. But he was a surveyor, clean job. My mother said that because of his job, she could have coffee with the engineer's wives. She was considered one of the 'elites.' I guess once you have worked in oil, you don't go changing your profession."

"Good money, no education needed," Brad said.

"Yeah, we stayed in Bakersfield. My dad worked for more than the oil companies, but he still was surrounded with the oil fields and the people who worked there. And my mother, she never left. Where would she go?"

Brad asked softly, "And you, why are you still here?

"And what about Cindy?" Very asked.

"She's still there too." Glen answered. "So am I."

"Where have we gotten with this? A bunch of men with alibis, housewives at home alone. No one saw anything. A cold case for sure."

Darrell said, in a loud and commanding voice, "Lunch everyone. Shall we go out? Together?"

"I have work to do at home. And a needy cat. Tomorrow?"

Glen sighed. "I have to check on my dad. If I don't work, I can't afford the nurse and the helper, so I'm the helper today."

"I'm off to check on paperwork that I filed about accessing the case files. Sorry," Brad said rising from his seat.

Olivia and Darrell looked at each other and smiled. The two, lovebirds, and lunch declined by all the others. They had the afternoon to themselves.

As they left, Brad waited to speak with Very, falling in step with her as they descended the stairs. "Ah, if you have some time this evening, I have a suggestion, if you're, ah, interested."

Very looked up at him. "Oh, yeah, maybe."

"I thought you might like to go with me to square dancing," he smiled.

"They still do that?" Very said quickly.

"Well, it is Bakersfield. Not too surprising."

"Okay, I guess, what time?"

"I'll pick you up at six."

"Oh God," Very said. "I don't have one of those big swirly skirts. My mother had a couple of them, but they are long gone."

"Ah, you don't need that. Just a regular skirt is okay, not too tight. Or you could just wear pants, I don't think anyone would mistake you for one of the guys. And leather soled shoes, if you have them, so that you can slide nicely."

"This sounds fun. I did some square dancing when I was in the Girl Scouts, but not since. Okay, see you then. Oh wait, you need the gate code." Very whipped out a pen and a small note pad, writing her address and the gate code for Five Points, the 55+ retirement community where she lived.

They said goodbye and parted at the bottom of the stairs.

As she walked to her car, Very's mind raced. She had been terrible at line dancing, the one time she tried, years ago. What made her think square dancing would be any better? She had fun at the time she did it when she was young, didn't she? Did she have two left feet then? She was probably no worse than the other girls, so it didn't matter much. But in a roomful of experienced dancers, could she hold her own? And then, she had forgotten to tell Brad that she was directionally dyslexic. Oh well, that was only of concern to her. Over the years, she had had come to terms with her inability to quickly chose right or left. She had failed her first driver's test because she had turned left twice when directed to turn right. Why would the examiner want her to do something easy; left was so much more difficult, surely he meant for her to turn left? Even though he said right. The next time, she thought about it for two beats and managed to pass her test. But it was something that hadn't gotten better with age, or education or concentration. She had once met a very smart college professor who suffered from the same malady. Smart man, right-left dyslexia. So, did that have any relationship to the flying pickle balls that confounded her? Well, no pickle balls at square dancing. Do-si-do, do-sa-do.

A date. She had been asked out on a date. A man asks you to go dancing, that's a date. Why didn't it feel like a real ask? Dinner maybe, Saturday night, not square dancing on a Tuesday. Don't look a gift horse in the mouth.

She pictured Bradley's face. This morning, he hadn't shaved; the chin and cheeks had looked a little grizzled. She heard his gravelly voice. And saw the white Stetson.

Chapter Twelve: Square Dancing

Very went home. She noodled around the house, cleaning up breakfast dishes, petting her cat and playing with a string until Cleopatra got bored.

At three she headed to the pool. She donned a UV shirt that slightly inhibited her clean powerful strokes, but it protected her overexposed back. Don't need skin cancer on top of other problems of aging. She swam laps for half an hour, soaked in the hot tub and tried to forget the dead body she had found in the old iteration of the spa. When she felt sufficiently warmed, she got out and shivered against a slight breeze. She walked home wearing her personal 'refrigeration unit' under her coverup. A wet suit is good for cooling off on the walk home. She tried, and mostly succeeded, to forget the state of their investigation. Nothing she could do now.

At home, she showered and then felt hungry. Now, did he say dinner or just dancing? Like Scarlet O'Hara, she needed not to look foolish and stuff her face if food were offered. She made a sandwich and ate it seated at the table. Be civilized, it was one of the things about living alone that became tempting, to ignore the good manners of food preparation and eating.

She looked in her closet. A loose swirly skirt. She had a number of feminine outfits from her days as a teacher/librarian, but they all seemed too tame, or too frilly. She found a blue skirt, spread with white and pink flowers and topped with an elastic waistband that could roll up a bit if she needed a shorter skirt, a matching pink blouse and a short-sleeved sweater topper. Shoes? She hunted in her shoe rack, finally finding an old pair in the back. Dusty, in need of shoe polish, but not her regular rubber-soled teacher shoes or sports shoes. She took a clean rag and rubbed them clear of the dust. Skip the polish, no one will notice.

She carefully applied a thin layer of make-up. Need to look a little pretty, but not too garish, not her style.

At five-thirty she sat down at her computer. She googled square dancing and as she watched the videos, she began to quake, moderately. This was not the square dancing she had done in her youth. The first video showed properly attired dancers whirling around the floor, never missing a step. A third video showed a community in Washington State, which included a few couples of women dancing together. Not enough men, or a political statement? Very sighed and tried to follow the instructions from the caller and to see what maneuvers were made. Too many steps, done too quickly.

Promptly at six, the doorbell rang. Very slammed her computer closed, grabbed her handbag and answered the door. She fumbled with the lock and flung it open so that it banged against the wall. Cleo appeared and cowered just inside the doorway to the second bedroom.

"Good evening," he said.

The cat's eyes grew large and she scooted backwards. Man, deep-voiced male. Her eyes sparkled at the whiff of the outdoors, but the large masculine thing stood in the doorway. She slunk back and cowered under the bed.

Brad doffed his hat and gave an awkward bow. Very looked at him, smiling and said nothing. She turned and locked the door and they proceeded to Brad's truck. He held open the door and Very climbed in, neatly tucking her skirt under her leg. He slid into the drivers' seat and started the motor. A quiet hum, not a dominant roar. A man who cares about his engine, the smooth running of his vehicle and not one who believed the truck was a symbol of his full-throated masculinity. But it was a pick-up truck.

The radio played a soothing medley of innocuous tunes, but Very sat happily watching the world go by and surreptitiously eyeing the driver.

"Thanks for asking me. I'm looking forward to this. Tell me, how did you get involved?" Very looked at him directly, noting his smoothly shaved cheeks and freshly ironed 'cowboy' shirt.

"Well, my folks were square dancers. Not a lot to do in the old days. They had friends, so it was easy. I went at first to look for girls. You know, there are never enough men dancing. I dropped out for years, but recently decided to get back into it. Retired, more time. Nice bunch of people."

Very waited for more, but then offered. "My parents danced too, when I was little. Out in Cuyama there was NOTHING to do and the oil company helped organize things. I think they had fun."

They drove to the other side of town, to a community center, with no more conversation.

A woman at the door greeted Brad enthusiastically. He whipped out his wallet and slapped a bill on the table. "Two," he said.

Very stepped out from behind Brad and smiled at the woman, who immediately frowned at her. Nice bunch of people as long as you didn't show up with an unattached male.

Very kept smiling, refusing to acknowledge the frosty stare, and eventually received a warmer welcome.

In the hall, people mingled, greeting old friends and exchanging stories. Very noticed a long table against one wall with lemonade, water and plastic cups. Other tables and chairs were pushed back against the wall, clearing a space for the dancers. A raised platform at one end held three musicians and a caller. Very recognized the set up from the videos. Very professional, with live musicians. No one under forty, and most over sixty, including the musicians.

Noting that her flat shoes and floaty skirt were the right things to wear, Very surveyed the other clothes. One couple had matching outfits; he wore a lavender colored shirt and she sported a dress of the same shade, edged with rick-rack and ruffles. A petticoat made the skirt pouf out. She continued to look around, to see if she knew anyone, she usually did. But this was a different crowd.

She turned to find a spot to set her purse down, when her phone rang. She turned to see where Brad had gotten to; she saw him talking to a small group of men, laughing and back-slapping. She looked at the caller ID. Gabby.

She immediately pushed the green spot and spoke. "Hey, Gabby, just a minute. I'll find a quieter place to talk." She glanced up to see Brad looking her way. She pointed to the phone and headed back outside.

When she was outside on the quiet side of the building, she spoke again. "Gabby, what's up?"

"Oh, sorry," Gabby answered. "Am I disturbing you?"

"Ah, no, I'm just…on a date."

Gabby let the air hang and then said, "You go on dates? You?"

Very laughed, "Yes, Gabby, I go on dates, but not very often."

"Oh, I didn't know that. I thought…"

"That I was too old to go on a date? It's more like a group date, don't worry. What did you want?"

"Oh, Very, this is an awful thing. You know, I started working at the Catholic Boys and Girls Club. So I went last weekend and after school for a couple of hours. But there's something wrong."

"What?"

Gabby described her duties, checking out balls and other athletic equipment. The kids checking it out had to leave a small deposit, which they got back when they turned in the equipment in good shape. "Twice there've been big arguments about whether the kid had deposited the money or if the ball was returned on time. One kid got kicked out for arguing and another time, a boy left really unhappy. I don't think he'll come back. The supervisor, Sally, she got nasty with the kids. The one, I remembered checking in and writing his name down. But later, it had been erased and there was no mark to say that he had put a deposit down. It was really fishy. Someone was doing something, and I can't say anything. I'm new at this and I'm just a kid. It's terrible."

"It does sound awful. Do this. Make sure you make a note of anytime something like this happens. Take a photo of the book page, write it down. Make a note of date, times, names, everything. Don't' let anyone see you doing it though. Keep it to yourself. Can you do that?"

"Yeah, yeah I get it. It's the docu…docum…"

"Documentation. You understand. Everything in a notebook. And remember, don't say anything to anybody." Very spoke sternly.

"But what if it's Sally, the boss?"

"That's what I'm afraid of. That's why you need to be quiet. Do it surreptitiously." Very paused, "Sneaky like."

Gabby breathed deeply. "Oh gosh, don't you think I should say something to Father Sullivan?"

"Not now, when it's finished, all wrapped up."

Gabby was silent, then she said, "Okay Very. I trust you. I'll do it like you said."

"Bye, talk to you soon," Very said and hung up.

She stood outside and tried to think. She heard the music inside, but she needed time to consider. Wound up from the Cuyama cold case, a date with Brad which she had interrupted, and now a problem with Gabby and her new job.

She heard the music die down and knew she needed to get inside. The table at the door had been abandoned, but Very found Brad and waved. He strode to her and hooked her arm in his as he walked back to a group in one corner. "You missed the introduction to square dancing, just a short refresher for new folks. I thought that since you hadn't done any square dancing in a while that you might appreciate it. But never mind, you don't need it. Just follow the caller. And the others."

They made a square with three other couples and Brad said quietly, "She hasn't done this in a while, so we hope things go smoothly." He smiled at everyone and firmly led Very to her starting position. She stood nervously, looking over her shoulder at the other squares, now all shaping up.

The music started and the caller said something about partners, his 'call' was not as clear as Very could have wished. She felt herself grabbed around the waist and propelled forward in a brisk shuffle. She breathed out in an attempt to relax. She watched the other couples whirl around and was glad of her strong support. Soon, however, after another call which only contained one word of clarity, 'partners,' she felt herself thrown off, spinning in a completely different direction. Then, she was clutched by another man, who also guided her firmly into the next move. She shuffled along, trying to keep her feet in rhythm. Suddenly, she was alone, no firm hand on her wrist or waist and she glanced into the circle. Three women stood in the center, wrists linked and expectant faces turned towards her. She tried to remember what this was called; she had seen it in the video. But the caller's voice was brisk, loud, but not distinct, and she had obviously missed the cue. She leapt into the center and stuck her closest wrist out. It was gripped firmly by the lady to her left, or was it the right?

The women took off quickly in the opposite direction from the men and soon she found herself opposite her original partner. Brad grabbed her swiftly and they hastily shuffled forward, so as not to delay the couple bringing themselves up directly behind them. The caller rapidly uttered another series of directions and Very gave in, letting herself be guided by her experienced series of partners. Left, he said left. Very hesitated. "Left, left left," she muttered to herself, hesitating too long and then she found herself facing the wrong direction.

Her new partner laughed and swung her around, pushing her in the right direction. The rest of the dance was simply a repeat of all the steps so far and Very watched carefully. When the music died down, she found herself once more in her original partner's arms. She turned to him and laughed, "I made it. Just barely, but I made it." She breathed heavily and chuckled again.

"Would you like a drink? We have a few minutes." Brad linked her arm to his and they drifted over to the drinks table.

Very kept a smile on her face. She felt foolish for all the mishaps, but exhilarated with the music, the shuffling, the happy faces of her fellow dancers. Everyone came to say hello to Brad, and few asked who Very was. "My new partner, in dance," he answered.

After a break, the dancers mixed and many formed new groups. Very found herself in a group with the dressed alike duo, as well as another couple who were obviously long-term partners. Most likely married. They, too, were dressed in proper clothes for square dancing. Very glanced at Brad and with a start, realized that he, too, was appropriately attired. His cowboy boots were well-worn and looked comfortable on his feet, as agreeable as could be given that cowboy boots have pointy toes and heels. His jeans were new-ish. Not just from the store new, washed a few times, but still had the dark indigo color of proper jeans. His shirt was delicately striped, with mother-of-pearl buttons, snapped, down the front and on the sleeves. His bolo tie was small, but had a turquoise stone set in silver as a slide. The turquoise matched the faint color of his shirt. Like a professional.

The music started again and the opening moves were similar to the last dance and Very began to relax. Suddenly, a new move was called and Very stumbled, stepping on her new partner's toes. As she tried to apologize, he grabbed her tightly and pulled her along. Then she was spun off and she found herself alone, on the edge of the circle. She watched as two couples went by and then she saw a man, alone, shuffling along without a partner. Her partner. She pushed her way into the circle and joined him.

They moved forward easily for a few steps, and then the caller said something else, but definitely a 'right'. Very hesitated and then turned…left.

She saw the arm in front of her face, too late to do anything as she moved swiftly towards it.

'Wham,' the arm hit her in the face, squarely between the eyes. She felt herself falling backwards and wildly twisted, reaching out for something to break her fall. She found a handful of clothing, but it slipped out of her grasp and she heard herself hit the floor.

There was a loud 'whoosh' just as she fell and she intuited that it was not she who made the sound, but the body that fell on her, full length. She found herself face to face with the handsome man who usually wore the Stetson.

She should have told him about the directional dyslexia.

Chapter Thirteen: The Kentons

Very walked in the door of the Pitts and Blew Agency early on Wednesday morning. Olivia and Darrell were already there.

"Good," said Very to Olivia, "you can help me with this makeup."

Olivia gasped as she looked at Very's face and especially at the two blackened eyes. Very's forehead was still red and a bit puffy. But it was the eyes that sent shivers up the spine.

"What happened? Have you been to the Emergency Care?" Olivia asked.

"No blood, no lasting effects, just a simple accident. I turned left when I should have turned right."

"So, how is your car?" asked Darrell.

"Oh, I wasn't in my car, thank goodness. Just square dancing. I have a small case of directional dyslexia and I sometimes confuse right and left."

"Oh, I do that too," volunteered Olivia. "I thought I was just stupid, but if you have that same problem, and you are one of the smartest people I know, then it must be something else."

"I was up half the night with ice on it, otherwise it would have been much worse. Suffice it to say that I am VERY embarrassed. I think the red is just from the ice. It's the eye stuff that may take a while to fade."

"Here," said Olivia. "Give me that stuff and I'll have you looking great, well, normalish, really soon." Olivia took Very's small makeup kit and riffled through it, looking for the right cream to cover the rapidly expanding area that had been hit. Olivia gently smoothed the base and then put some blusher on. She found an eyebrow pencil and made Very's eyebrows darker, hoping to make the skin look lighter and healthier.

After ten minutes, Very was invited to look. "Wow, it hardly shows. Now, if I just wear sunglasses for the next week… It looks soooo much better. Thanks a million."

"So, how did this accident happen?" Darrell asked.

"I went on a date last night to go square dancing. Well, I thought it was a date. Anyway, they were all experts and I'm a rank beginner. I guess I was having trouble following the calls, and besides, I have this little teeny challenge. You show me this way or that way, I've got no problem, but if you say left, then I have to stop and think. Left, left," she said, putting her left hand out to the side. "But this time, I heard right and I just went with it. I didn't stop to do my 'right-left' thing. And so, I ran into my partner."

"Oh," Olivia said, "Not the guy who took you? Our esteemed colleague?"

"Yes."

"You mean that you deliberately ran into Bradley Parker? Or he ran into you?" Darrell asked.

"None of it was deliberate, it was an accident."

Olivia gave a smirk of dissatisfaction. "Remind me to never go dancing with that guy."

"It wasn't his fault, it was mine." Very sighed.

"Did he suffer?" asked Olivia.

"I think there was a mix-up with legs and the floor and a rather unfortunate foot that kicked. I didn't mean to, but I think it was painful."

"Oh, not in the delicate male place?" Darrell asked softly.

Very hung her head as she answered even more softly, "Yeah."

"Not the best first date, huh?" Olivia declared.

"I can't imagine repeating that. It was a disaster." Very sat quietly, hoping the discussion had ended.

They all looked around for coffee, but the big coffee thermos had gone home with Brad, who had become the go-to coffee man. Regret for the accident of the night before became profound as it meant the absence of coffee.

"Okay, no coffee. What are we doing today?" asked Very.

Darrell started, "I think we need to re-interview the Kentons, father and son. Raymond and Michel, known as Mickey. In the original case notes, they both had alibis for the time period. The whole thing about being referred to as stepfather and stepbrother is just weird, it's the only way of putting it. Then, in the cold case investigation, they were not even contacted. No explanation. I would like to hear what Bradley Parker has to say about this. An oversight, a bad…"

The door opening interrupted Darrell. He looked at the man entering and whispered, "Speak of the devil."

Bradley Parker stood in the doorway. He did not stand as tall as usual, but he did carry the large thermos in one hand. He said slowly, "You were talking about me?" He looked directly and deliberately at Very's face.

She smiled back. "We were wondering why you neglected to interview the Kentons, father and son, in the cold case investigation."

Brad took off his hat and lowered himself gently into the only remaining chair, an old wooden, hard seated one. He winced as he settled himself. "Is that all?"

Very gritted her teeth in an attempt to suppress a smile. "Olivia helped me with my makeup, in a vain attempt to cover up the black eyes, so I had to tell them."

Brad looked blankly at Very. "Well, there's a good simple answer to the Kenton non-questioning. I wasn't allowed. Remember back then, I was very junior and was not calling any shots. I think they were questioned again, it was my impression that it was done. But I don't know who did it, nor where the documentation got to. It's not in the cold case file. Maybe it was lost, maybe the questioning wasn't done, maybe it was deliberately suppressed. Your guess is as good as mine. Although I might have some opinions."

Darrell smiled and plunged in. "Well, I have some good news then. I've found them, both of them."

"Where are they?" Very leaned forward eagerly.

"In Taft. In a house that has been occupied by one or the other since shortly after the occurrence. They left Cuyama almost immediately after this happened. Not surprising, really. Raymond was separated from his wife and he was just renting in Cuyama. Mickey was living with him at the time. He got another job, in the Taft area, so he left. Makes sense, doesn't it."

"Are you saying that they are living together, now, in Taft?"

"Yeah, apparently the old man needs help and Mickey moved in with him, or maybe it was the other way around. Anyway, they are there."

"So, what did they say then and what might they say now?" Very leaned forward. Then she spied the coffee thermos and interrupted herself. "Coffee first. Thank you

Brad for making it. We have come to rely on you. Maybe too much."

Olivia got the cups and they all fixed coffee for themselves. Both Olivia and Darrell made a point to thank Brad for not forgetting the coffee.

Darrell sipped his coffee and pulled out a folder from a stack on his desk. "Here is the original statement. There is nothing from the cold case. Let's see what they say." He began to read the document, both questions and answers. Olivia wrote down the major points on a paper that she had taken down from the wall. Most of the first part was routine. Name, address, age, place of work. Ray gave details where he had been that day. He mentioned names of his fellow workers and exactly when and where they were. When asked about his relationship to Betty Jean, he hesitated."

Darrell read verbatim from the report. "Here's what he says. 'I liked Betty Jean, I thought she was a fine woman. She had a hard life, with those two little girls. I spent some time there; I helped around the house, her husband not being around in town very often. And you know, little things need to be done. Changing light bulbs and fixing the shelf that falls down, you know, things like that. And what if I stayed the night? Those old biddies want to gossip, they can, but I helped pay for the groceries and my boy used to babysit for Betty Jean. And her old man knew. He probably had a bit on the side himself, 'cause he wasn't getting none from Betty Jean. Now, I know that some used to say that the little one, Cindy, wasn't her daddy's daughter. I don't know about that. But she wasn't mine, that I know. And there is no way someone is going to pin that on me. I thought they were nice little girls, well Cindy was a baby. And AnnaRose, well, everyone'll tell you, she was a live wire. She had spunk, courage. Sass you back, could give as quick as you could give it. She was pretty and she knew it. Only six, she was, but I swear, going on sixteen. So sad. It's so sad.'"

"When asked when he got home from work that day and what happened, he said, 'I got back about five-thirty or so. Maybe a little sooner, I don't remember. But the whole town, everybody, was out in the middle of the street yelling their heads off, like AnnaRose had just walked away, or was playing 'Hide and Go Seek' or something. I helped, yelling. I also went in the house and found Betty Jean, crying her heart out, screaming about her baby AnnaRose being kidnapped. I tried to talk with her, but you know women, they get something in their head and nothing can squeeze it out. I looked all over the house again, even peeking into the closets and the laundry basket and the cedar chest. I even went outside and tried the crawl space under the house. No way she could have gotten in, though, so I gave it up. I tried talking to the neighbors, and they went home and did the same thing. She'd been in everybody else's house, so she knew where the good hiding places were. Boy, everybody was looking, hollering and looking. It was getting dark when the sheriff finally arrived.' He was asked about Mickey and he said that Mickey had gone to school that day, but he had come home and gone to bed, said he wasn't feeling well. That is pretty much that interview. Not much help, is it?"

"What did Mickey have to say?" Very asked, trying to peek at the documents in Darrell's hands. They were photocopies of old typed pages, before the age of white out, and long before auto-correction techniques. Corrections were made in the text, but very few. In her typing class, the only one she took, she had the feeling that accuracy was almost as important as speed. Never particularly good at either. She marveled at the accuracy of the document.

"Here it is. He has even less to say. Like his dad said, he went to school and came home right after, and went to bed. He wasn't feeling well. He seemed not to have heard the chaos outside, as his dad woke him up. He then helped look for AnnaRose. That's all for that day. He described his relationship to AnnaRose as a kind of big brother. He babysat for her on occasion, when their parents went out. They never went far, to the community center to go to a dance or function or to the Buckhorn for a drink. He said he hadn't seen AnnaRose for a couple of days. That was the end of the interview. It appeared that for both the Kentons, there were some follow ups on the alibis. Ray Kenton has a note attached to his file that they spoke to two of the guys who were listed as being able to verify he was at work. And there's another note that they had called the school and checked that Mickey had attended. No problems there. And as I said, eleven years later, no other interviews held."

Brad sighed. "Is it worth reopening? Alibis all accounted for, what is there to say? Any more, any other things? I mean, I would have done another round of interviews, delved a little deeper into the Kenton's relationship. Oftentimes, it's family, or near relatives. But, now???"

"Ray Kenton said he was at work. The other guys said he was there," Very dove in with more questions, "but what about lunch? Did he bring his lunch? Go to get it? Did anyone think of that? Did he work with the same fellows all day? Did anyone take any breaks? How far from the township were they?"

"I can check further on some of that," said Darrell.

"He could have gone 'home' for lunch, snatched AnnaRose from her house, took her off to the bushes, did her in… And then gone back to work. Who would have noticed? It's not like he's working in an office standing around the water cooler all day, where, if someone takes off for a long lunch, everyone notices. Countryside, up the little valleys, where were they all, all the time?" Very stopped and breathed. "I think we need to delve into this again. What if he was trying to get back at Betty Jean for some reason? Picking on her little girl? AnnaRose would have known him, wouldn't have fought back, wouldn't have said anything."

Brad added, "And what about the son, Mickey? I know he was only fourteen at the time, but what if there was an accomplice? What if they were in it together?"

Olivia protested. "That sounds awful. That sounds really, really gruesome and terrible and unthinkable. She was a six-year-old. A little girl." Her face crumpled as she said it.

Brad went on relentlessly, "Remember, we always thought it was a man, but we have always thought it was just one. Could Mickey drive? Did he have access to a car? A friend's car?"

"Olivia's right. This is beginning to sound really morbid and awful," Very said.

"Are you ready for a trip to Taft?" Brad turned to Very.

"As ready as you are." Very turned and gave Brad a half-smile.

He stood gingerly and winced as he dug into his pants pocket for his keys. Better not apologize, not say anything, just let him deal with it. He won't say anything about Very's face. We will both pretend that we are fine, not aching, or ugly-looking or walking very slowly. Neither one was upset or to blame or has any grievance. Pretend the evening never happened. Maybe later we can laugh? Or maybe not.

On the way to Taft, Very explained about Gabby, who she was, what she meant to Very, and her current predicament. How did you clarify or justify a tenuous relationship? Very knew that Gabby was tied to her in ways that were unusual and yet deep and inviolable. She had been asked by Darrell to help with a case of a possible suicide. Investigations brought her to the Hernandez family home and there she became enmeshed in the family's tragedy of the drowning of Gabby's older sister and of a cousin. She had listened to Gabby's brother's confession of a crime, and knew that he would die because of it. She had been saved from the fireball that had engulfed him and his motorcycle by Gabby herself. And she carried a memento of that horrific episode in her purse, holding her keys. It was a keychain made from the only thing left of Javier or his possessions, a tiny set of wings that was the logo of the motorcycle. It bound her to Gabby and her family. She owed them. Brad said nothing as he listened to Very's tale.

At the house in Taft, they sat for a minute looking at the small dwelling. The front yard was dusty and contained a big tree that shaded most of the ground. Just out of full sight was a garage and as Brad surmised, more outbuildings.

"More garage than house," Very said.

"Priorities," Brad pointed out.

As they walked up to the front door, Very bit her lip and said, "Will they be at home?"

Brad gave a low chuckle. "Where would they go? He's almost 90 and the son is 70ish and retired. There isn't anyone else."

Brad knocked and waited.

Soon, they heard the shuffle of feet coming to the door. A crack appeared. "Yeah?" Mickey Kenton's face could be seen through the chink.

In a deep melodious voice, Brad explained who they were and what they wanted, to talk with both father and son. "Is that possible?"

Very thought they were after an interview, or rather, an interrogation. 'Talk' was a sad euphemism for what they really wanted.

"If that's okay with you," Brad continued. "Is your dad up and around these days?"

Very heard shouting from inside. Most of it was muffled, but she heard quite clearly, "Who is it, dammit?

Mickey turned, leaving the door momentarily unattended. Brad and Very slowly and unobtrusively stepped inside.

They found him standing over an elderly man ensconced in a sleep chair, adjusting the pillows and pulling up a sheet to cover the old man's skinny legs.

Very smelled the odor of an unchanged diaper. Brad found a hard chair next to the old man and settled in.

He leaned in and spoke softly, but clearly. "We wondered if we could talk with you. I know it's an unhappy past, but do you remember AnnaRose?"

Raymond Kenton's eyes flew open and a knowing look came into them. "Poor little thing, she didn't deserve that." He looked at Brad and wet his lips with his tongue.

Mickey leaned over and placed a straw between the lips of his father. "What do you want, dragging that up again?"

"Glen Bullitt wants to clear his father's name and reputation." Brad answered.

"Nobody accused him, did they? Her own father?"

"Wouldn't be the first time," Brad mumbled.

Mickey sighed. "Eugene Bullitt was a good guy. Getting tangled up with Betty Jean was the worst thing he could have done with his life. She was something else!"

Raymond spoke slowly and carefully, "Don't you say nothing against Betty Jean. She raised those kids alone. She was a good mother. Unlike some."

Silence hung in the air. Mickey fidgeted. Finally, he turned to his guests, or rather, intruders. "I don't know what else I have to say. I said it all the first time. So did he. We don't know anything about how she went missing or what happened to her. We don't know who did it."

Raymond tried to raise himself from his awkward bed-chair. "The car, the car. Tell them about the car."

"There's nothing to tell about the car. Is it about time to get rid of it yet?" Mickey said angrily.

"Over my dead body!" The old man shouted, throwing off his lightweight sheet, exposing thin spindly legs and a pink adult diaper.

Mickey shouted back at him, "Won't be long now, will it?"

He turned to Brad and Very. "You'd better go. He's got dementia, on his way out. We can't tell you anything anyway."

Chapter Fourteen: Who is Related to Whom?

Brad and Very stopped at a local coffee shop in Taft. At the end of forty-five minutes, Very got up, used the restroom and came back.

Brad remarked, "You didn't finish your sandwich, nor your coleslaw. Something the matter?"

"Just because a place is an old-fashioned diner, does not mean the food is good. The coleslaw had way too much mayonnaise and the sandwich, American cheese, commonly called cheese food because it contains almost no cheese. The lettuce and tomato were both soggy. The bread is at least a day old, maybe more, and being toasted does not absolve the owners if they advertise it as fresh. And you noticed that I asked for whole wheat and they gave me white bread. But I see that you finished yours?"

"Put food in front of me and I eat it. It's as simple as that," Brad said, getting up to pay the tab.

"At least it was cheap. Thanks for paying."

"It was the least I could do after the fiasco of last night," he said while opening the door of the pick-up for her.

"The fiasco was of my making, not yours. I was the dumb one who went in the wrong direction. I guess I should have mentioned my little dyslexic problem. And asked you to watch out for me. Although I don't think it would have made much difference. Right and left will always be what they are, whether I get it correct or not. Well, that's another thing I'll never do again. Like pickleball."

"Oh, I'm not so sure about that," Brad answered.

"The pickleball I'm sure about, very, very sure. When you catch the ball with your forehead instead of the paddle, it's time to hang it up. It's not my thing. But I actually enjoyed the square dancing until…"

"Well, maybe try another time?" he asked.

"I'm not so sure you want that." Very looked pointedly at Brad's lap.

"Aw shucks. It wasn't nothing ma'm." Brad replied with a movie cowboy accent.

"Oh, maybe I'll try those moves again," retorted Very.

Before they entered the office, Brad stopped and looked at his phone. "Darrell has texted. It appears as though we may be able to access all, and I mean all, the cold case files. Including the original evidence."

"So fast, when did you request this?"

As they climbed the stairs, Brad pointed out that it may have been the age of the person requesting the reopening. "The fact that Eugene Bullitt is aging, already very aged, and that he is the biological father, may have persuaded them. It makes things more pressing, in a way."

"You being a lawyer, or you knowing someone, didn't have anything to do with it?"

"That could be the case, as well. It's not clear why they have expedited it."

"So, tell me the story of you being a lawyer? I thought you were in law enforcement, a cop to be precise." Very said as they entered the office.

They found it empty.

"That's why Darrell texted. They aren't here. Well, that gives me ten minutes to tell you my life's story."

Panicked, Very sat down gently in 'her' chair. She had asked for his story, and now that he was about to give it to her, she had a minor sense of trepidation. What kind of story would it be? Sob story? Too feminine. Spill the guts out? Confess to the vilest deeds? The truth or many shades of it? More masculine. Heart wrenching or maybe boring? No, at least make it interesting.

"The long version, then? Childhood, normal. One sister, one brother, I was the middle child. No traumas. No bullying or things like that. College, I dropped out for a semester, got a job as a back-country fire fighter. Majored in pre-law, with an idea of being a lawyer, but then switched to law enforcement. I was hired by the Kern County Sheriff's Department and one of the first things I did was work on the AnnaRose Bullitt cold case. There were major difficulties for me with the case; I've told you that before. I think I was being used. I suspected a lot at the time, but the longer I stayed with the department, the more I was sure there were extensive issues waiting, sitting under the radar. I felt uncomfortable. Later events have proven me right, but I had to get out of there. I left, went to law school, got married, had a son, got divorced, drank too much, alienated my family. My son was involved in an accident, sobered me up quickly. Remarried my wife, tried to build up that relationship. Then she got cancer, eight years later she died. I worked too much. Was it too much stress? Did I cause any of that? I never thought of myself as being fragile, that is what women are, but I did suffer. Then, I patched up my relationship with my son. We're not close, but respectful of the obligations and rewards of the link. We have rapport, and each other's back.

"When I became single again, I rethought my life. I knew that connections with people were important. That's when I met Bobby Sanchez. It was a professional relationship at first, then we got closer. I avoided any public contact until I retired. It wouldn't look good if I worked in the public defender's office and he was a cop. I didn't always live in Bakersfield, I actually grew up in Fresno, got my law degree in LA. Been around a little bit. There you have it. And you?"

"Let's start with Joey Sanchez. I met her when we were student teachers together. And I was around when she met Bobby. Urged her to snap him up, having failed in that department myself. Grew up in Bakersfield, went away to college and then came home and met Frankie Monroe. Got pregnant, got stood up at the altar, he disappeared, I lost the baby, went away and got an MA degree in Library Sciences, and a teacher's certificate. Got a job and came back. I lived at home, helped my dad and then my mom negotiate their last years, and recently moved out of the old family cottage. I was an English teacher and librarian at local high schools and retired a few years ago. And of course, you know about the body in the orchard?"

"A little, but you can clarify some things. It wasn't Frankie Monroe who had been buried in the orchard for 37 years?"

"No, but it was his friend, or rather, associate in criminal activities. I found out who had killed Frankie's friend, but never could figure out where Frankie went. There was a body, an historical body, found in the riverbank about a year ago. When I was helping to find out if a woman had committed suicide in the Kern River, the mean old Killer Kern, I got mixed up with the Hernandez family. Gabby saved my life, so I owe her."

"But because she saved your life, you are now a millstone around her neck, you are forever in her life; so an old Chinese saying goes. She is responsible for you."

"It's more like I'm responsible for her. I have a deep need to make sure her life goes more smoothly from here on out. If I can."

"And I've also heard that you are good at finding dead bodies? Especially ones floating in hot tubs?"

"Oh, please don't remind me," Very said sarcastically. "I hear they are seriously talking about having another pool party, maybe to erase the memory of the last fiasco. I had to open the new hot tub. I tried to get out of it, but they said that if I wasn't afraid to go in, others would go too. So, I did. Inaugurated the new, revitalized, restored spa. And then I was going off to Canada."

"To find Frankie. What made you think it was him?"

"A few things. The name, Marvin Franks. And the photograph, it did look like him. It's hard to tell when someone has gotten older. And the photo wasn't very good; it looked like a mug shot or a driver's license ID photo."

"How do you feel about it? What do you think will happen?"

"Conflicted. I don't expect much to happen. I do think he owes me an explanation, though. An apology would be appropriate. And then, maybe it's not him."

The door burst open and Darrell and Olivia spilled into the room, clutching a new poster board. Olivia tore off the paper wrapper from the office supply store and pulled it out. She took a marking pen and wrote at the top, in school teacher printing, 'Who is related to Whom?' She found the photo of AnnaRose and stuck it in the very center. Then she had a photo of Betty Jean as a teenager and put it directly above, close to the first. She drew a line and labeled it 'mother.' She proceeded to attach photos with names, placing them in context to the central photo. Eugene Bullitt was next to Betty Jean; labeled 'father' and 'husband'. She had a photo of Cindy and placed it between AnnaRose and Betty Jean, but not close to Eugene.

Darrell spoke up, "We need to say 'paternity in doubt' for that one. We know that Eugene has always treated Cindy as his, but not his biological daughter."

"Does that matter at this point?" Very asked.

"If we are looking at who is related to whom, I think it might be relevant. But I can't say how." Brad said. "When did Cindy find out Eugene Bullitt wasn't her father? It's on her birth certificate and her name is the same."

"Does it matter when she knew? I mean, if someone came along, said, 'I'm your dad' and he has the same name, what would you do? He treated her like a daughter." Darrell said.

"Compensation for losing his own daughter?" Very said. "Guilt? I know that we are supposed to be trying to clear his name, not muddy it, but…"

"A question for Cindy?" Olivia said. "And by the way, do we know who her dad is? Can we find out?"

"Is it relevant?" Darrell sighed. "Leave it. This is leading us off and down the garden path."

Brad had been silent, but now stirred in his chair. "In the animal kingdom, males will sometimes attack and murder the children of their 'spouses' who are not theirs, to clear the way for their own blood. It may be relevant. But at the moment, it's not crucial…I don't think."

Olivia stared at Brad, "Are you suggesting that Cindy's biological father murdered AnnaRose to 'claim'

Cindy as his own and to send a message to Betty Jean? That's just sick, really sick."

"It is sick, the whole thing is monstrous. It's a tragedy." Darrell said.

"Who is Cindy's father? Can we find out?" Very asked.

"DNA." Brad said.

A moment of silence let them all contemplate the possibility, but expense, of the DNA analysis.

Darrell turned again to the board. "Okay, here is what else we have." Darrell started naming the neighbors, pinpointing the men who lived nearby. He rattled off names, wives, kids and where they had lived. He was also able to indicate which of the potential suspects had died, which then narrowed the field considerably.

"Are you saying that these men are all suspects? What about innocent until proven guilty? You're a lawyer, you know that?" Very said to Brad.

"They can't tell us anything more than we already know if they have gone to their reward. I'm a detective here and I say all of these neighbors are suspects. Which, it turns out, makes for very good suspects. Being a neighbor."

"Don't we need to concentrate on building a profile of these neighbors. Dead or not, they could be our man. We need to ferret out what we know, what they said, what their motives, means and opportunities are." Darrell turned again to the board.

"Motive?" Olivia asked, "Who could have a motive for doing this to a six-year-old? Who would want to?"

"A sick mind. We need to look for someone who is 'off', has some mental or psychological problem."

"With so many of the neighbors gone, how do we do that?"

"Profiles," Darrell said. "We are looking for a man, 70 or older at this time."

"Who raped and murdered a child and then went about his life as if nothing was wrong?" Very muttered her frustration.

"Do we have profiles of all the neighbors to see if they have had further law enforcement problems?" Brad asked. "Once a criminal, always a criminal. Do we have records of someone who left Cuyama soon after, someone who was avoiding being questioned? Easier to leave, run away, rather than sit and watch your life implode."

"That's a lot of work. I can start with the next-door neighbors." Darrell moved over to the map of New Cuyama, laid out street by street. "Next door, here, was the Smith family, father John."

"You have got to be kidding, John Smith? Oh wait, I knew that family, Paul was in my class, the son, Paul." Very said.

Darrell looked at her. "So, what do you think?"

"Well, not Paul, he was just a kid. But there were older brothers, and of course, their dad. And there was the mother, Joan. She and my mom were friends, used to have coffee together. Really nice family, all of them, really nice, nice boys. That's what my mother would have said."

"Okay, kids too young, dad too nice. Does that let them off the hook?"

"They live in Texas now, the oldest son, John Smith, is still alive. But…"

"Next," Very said. "Is there any reason, at all, to pursue this family?"

Darrell ignored this remark and went on. "The next house, in this direction, was a woman alone, husband out of town. Then next were the Kentons."

"No go on that one, dad at work, son too young to drive, only fourteen and…"

Brad interrupted, "Too young to have a license, not too young to drive. Hmm."

Very said, "We need to go back. Remember what the father said about the car?"

Darrell looked puzzled. "What did the father say about the car and what does it matter?"

Brad mumbled, "More and better questions."

"Next house empty," Darrell continued. "House on the corner was empty while the family had gone to a funeral. Now, the house on the corner behind is interesting. I mean on the next street. Wife gone to Taft to do shopping, had dropped sixteen-year-old son off at high school, dad was at work. But on the list, they are crossed off as well. Interviewed, but, they said they didn't know anything, didn't hear anything. Most people who were interviewed said the same thing."

"Can we re-interview these people?" Very asked.

"Hard to find them, but we can try to find out where they are."

"Okay, skip that for now. What about directly across the street?"

"Directly opposite the Bullitt house was a young mother with three small children. They were at home all day, she was watching them in the backyard or in the kitchen. Husband at work. Nobody saw or heard anything."

"Farther down the street?"

"Another mother at home with two sick kids. Never went out. Husband at work. They are all this way. Three doors down on the same side of the street, here," Darrell pointed.

"That's where I lived. Well, before this happened. And…?"

"Same thing. Alibis. Anyone at home saw nothing. Shopping out of town, looking after little kids."

"And were any of these re-interviewed at the time of the cold case? Were all their alibis checked?"

"No wonder the eyes of the law fell on Gene Bullitt. Alibi flimsy. Raping his own child is flimsy too, but…" Brad said.

"Means, what does that really mean? We are all thinking it is a man, but couldn't he have had someone help him? A woman?" Olivia said. "Just because she was sexually interfered with, doesn't rule out a woman, at least as an accomplice."

"Motive, what possible motive could anyone have for this?" Darrell stopped them all with this comment. "Opportunity seems slim, for almost everyone, but why, why would a person…"

"Other than the neighbors and the father, who else was questioned or suspected?" Very interrupted.

"That's about it," Brad said. "The web of connections seemingly dies. They are neighbors, they live in a very small town, everyone knows everyone else's business, but the trail runs cold."

"Cindy isn't telling all she knows. Still, she was too young to remember anything. But there are other memories, passed down. Sort of inherited memory. There's more there. And then again, what do we know about the movements of the child, from sickbed in her bedroom, to a bush miles out of town?"

Darrell found another piece of paper. "Here's a layout of the house. As you can see, there are two ways out of the house from the front. The front door and the garage. The garage door was closed. The car was in the garage, not currently running. And that garage door was far too heavy and difficult for a child to open. The front door opened directly onto the front yard, a very open space. If she had come out here, by herself or with someone else, she should have been seen by someone."

"What about the back door? And the fence, there, was it too high to climb over? I don't remember it being a big barrier," Very said. "I climbed over it."

"The back door from the garage out to the backyard was locked, according to the report."

"What about the back door from AnnaRose's bedroom to the backyard?"

"What door, what are you talking about?" Darrell studied the floor plan again.

"There was a door built into the bedroom that led directly to the outside, to the back yard. I know that, I spent hours in that room. We used it to go outside to play. I remember asking my mother why we didn't have a door like that. She said it was weird, silly. Who would want a door from their bedroom to the outside that way? I told her that it would be good for when I wanted to go outside and play. I could do it whenever I wanted, my secret."

Darrell watched as Very drew a tiny line in the middle of the back bedroom to indicate a door.

"Maybe AnnaRose went out that back door, climbed over the fence, and walked down the sidewalk, here. The same sidewalk her mother took to walk to the store." Very pointed to the bigger map of New Cuyama with a small pedestrian walkway midway down the block of the east-west streets. "If she did that, then she would be here," Very pointed to the open lot on the edge of town, only one hundred yards from the highway.

"She could have walked out to the highway, and anyone could have picked her up. Anyone."

Chapter Fifteen: Visit to Cuyama II

For the rest of the afternoon, the four went back and forth, arguing one scenario after another. They ordered pizza, but then declared it not very good. "We could have ordered from Woolgrowers," Darrell complained.

"We already had some lunch, this was just an afternoon snack." Brad said.

Very declared a stop to everything. "I have a headache coming on, I need to go home."

At home, she made a cold compress out of an old washcloth and some ice. She lay on her mother's couch with a cool cloth over her eyes. Cleopatra jumped up and wanted to share the space. Very opened the back door to let the outside cool air come in. From next door, she noticed the preparations for barbecuing, the putrid smell of gas, the noise of cleaning the grill, the clatter of plates of food, the banging of extra-long utensils. The noises of her childhood, except for the gas for the fire; her dad always used charcoal.

Her childhood in Cuyama had been much on her mind of late. How had those years in the picayune town, the safe environs, the small classes at school, and the wide-open spaces affected her later life? When they had moved, she liked living in Bakersfield, with the big stores, the big school with lots of classmates, the library with its shelves full of books. But her teen years, how had she coped with that time of her life? By eighteen, she had tired of what now seemed the insular, small-town atmosphere of Bakersfield. What had been her hopes, dreams and plans at that time? If she could time-travel back to her eighteen-year old self, what would she have thought of how her life had turned out? What would that 18-year-old say?

For starters, she would have scoffed at the Frankie Monroe chapter. 'What were you thinking?' She would have been ecstatic at the summer travel around the world, dismayed at the life as 'mother's helper,' or maybe it was more like 'mother's slave.' Satisfied at the jobs she had held. Not bad.

As Very prepared for bed, she carefully wiped off the makeup and found her eyes much improved. Must find ways to avoid this whacking in the eyes.

Early the next morning, Brad greeted her at the office with a hearty welcome and no outward signs of lasting damage, either to his ego or his body. Very had carefully hidden the residual signs of the square dance debacle, again a sign of feeling more upbeat.

"Ready to go back to Cuyama?" he asked.

"Sure, whenever you are." She had a look at the crime wall. There was nothing new from yesterday, so they headed outside.

Very looked at Brad's truck. She hoisted herself up and clambered in, there was no other way to describe the contortions she needed to get into her seat. "What is it about men and trucks, especially in Bakersfield?"

Brad smiled his tight sardonic smile. "It's manly."

Very muttered a riff on the 'manliness' or supposed male embrace of certain cultural icons, flaunted at every turn. The speeding on the highway, the loud laughter in restaurants, the back-slapping, the wolf whistles at inappropriate times. She turned to Brad, "You are a well-educated person, at least somewhat sophisticated and traveled. Why the truck, the jeans, the boots, the hat?"

"Convenient, they're convenient. I want to fit in. I want to be part of Bakersfield."

"The hat, really, the white Stetson?"

Brad hesitated and looked sideways at Very. "It was my grandfather's, the last one he bought before he died. My father gave it to me. Family heirloom. And it fits."

Very mumbled an apology and turned on the radio. Brad punched some buttons and country and western music burbled from the speakers. Very turned it down to background music.

As they dipped into the Cuyama Valley, Very asked Brad, "What are we going to ask Cindy?"

"First of all, look at the house, see about this back door from the bedroom. Sounds weird to me. And we need to walk the streets in the area."

"And we need to ask her about the accident, the car accident. That's just so strange, that one. I don't know if that's a red herring, but it's worth pursuing. Remember, Eugene Kenton said something about a car."

"Are cars on your mind today?"

"That's it, the next time, you ride in my little red Prius. I can move the seat back and you only have to crunch up a little."

Silence ensued until they entered the township. "Coffee?" Brad asked.

"Sure." They headed to the Buckhorn.

They sat in a booth with a view of the hills to the south. "I always think of this view as the quintessential view of Cuyama. Not the old oaks, or the green fields, but the white-hot sun and the naked hills. My mother had a view out of her kitchen window, just over the sink, with this exact perspective. Those hills. My dad planted some trees, but she had one moved because she knew that it would grow up and block the vision of those bare folds. She once called them 'giant's knuckles.' Like a great lion, or the Sphinx, with toes thrusting forward, catching the slightest bit of shadow. Late in the afternoon, it's a magical composition. Mere man couldn't do better than nature. It's my definition of the Cuyama Valley."

Brad called Cindy and announced they were in town. "Is now convenient?"

Very heard a squeak of alarm. "My house..."

"Tell her we are not here to visit her house, but to see her," whispered Very.

Brad relayed the message. "Yeah, about five minutes."

As they drove to the house, only two minutes away, Very became overly agitated. "Do you know how this interview is going to go down? I mean, what exactly are we going to ask her? What do we expect her to answer?"

"Start with the door, just like we talked about. Then mementos of AnnaRose and maybe photos. Also, her mother. Okay? Try to worm out of her more about this accident. Remember, she brought it up."

As they walked up to the door, Very turned and stared down the street. It had changed so little since she had lived here. Her brain did some flip-flops and she could see the street, the houses, the old cars in driveways, and the sound of children playing carried on the wind. The air felt soft and slightly humid, the smell of just-mown grass reached her nose. The laughter burbled up and she heard childish voices, 'Red Rover, Red Rover, send Very on over.' A pinch at her heart drew her back to the present day. Running full tilt at a line of bigger boys who linked their arms to keep her out, was never a good thing in Very's book.

"Oh," she breathed, shaking her head to drive the scenes of her childhood away.

Then she noticed that Brad was carrying a bag, a white bag like you got at the bakery.

He knocked. Cindy answered immediately, invited them in, "Coffee?"

"Sure, why not," Very said smiling. Her stomach groaned at the vision of more of the black stuff.

"And here," Brad said, holding out the little white bag.

Cindy accepted the bag and looked inside. A huge grin spread over her face, "Oh, Smith's smiley cookies."

Brad grinned, "Never too old for those guys."

Cindy disappeared into the kitchen at the back of the house. Very peeked in behind her. Yeah, Cindy had the same view that Very's mother had out the window. Blue sky and brown hills. Very watched as Cindy placed the cookies on a flowered plate and brought them into the dining room.

Very noticed that the plate had a few miniature chips in the scalloped edge. "What a pretty plate, is it old?"

"Yeah, my mother's, and she probably got it from her mom. It was the one always used for cookies."

Very asked, "Do you have other things from your mom?"

While the two women talked, Brad moved into the kitchen.

Cindy pointed to a small china cabinet backed into a corner in the dining room. "A silver candy dish, maybe a wedding present? And some glasses I'm too afraid to use."

Very said, "Yeah, me too. And tablecloths."

"Oh, yeah, I know that kind of stuff. Packed away somewhere."

"What about photos? I've got way too many."

Cindy looked at Very, "Yes, of course. Doesn't everyone have old family photos? She made a little collection, old ones of grandparents and so forth."

"Do you have them in an album, like?"

Cindy's eyes narrowed. "You want to know if there are any of AnnaRose." It was a statement, not a question.

Brad appeared from the kitchen. "Yes, we need more information, if we can get it. Anything at all that you have."

Cindy sat down hard on a chair. There was a 'ding' from the kitchen and Brad returned there, reemerging moments later with a tray. On it were three cups and saucers, ones that matched the cookie plate in style, if not in color. A small jug and covered bowl held milk and sugar. The modern glass carafe of coffee looked out-of-place with the antique settings.

Brad poured three cups of coffee and let the women add their own milk and sugar.

Very said softly, "You know, it's not just Eugene and Glen that want to know more. You can know more too. And don't you want to clear Eugene's name?"

Cindy sighed, "He's been good to me, always. Not knowing who your father is, is hard, but he never acted as anything other than a real father to me. Even though I didn't know my real father, my biological father, Gene is my father. To try to find out who that other man is, or was, seemed like betrayal to me. I had a father, just not...]

\\\\`1"

"So, do this for him, even if not for yourself. Help us find out who killed your sister." Very leaned forward and spoke softly.

"Okay," said Cindy. "They're in a box in the closet. It may take a few minutes to dig it out."

"If you trust us, we can take the box and return it."

They ate their cookies, Very feeling a bit sick at all the sugar. She had changed her diet after her mother died and normally shunned the overly sugary treats her mother loved so well. This was her third cup of coffee for the day and she felt her fingertips beginning to shake. She put down her cup and concentrated on nibbling the cookie. Did imbibing sugar negate the ingestion of caffeine?

"You lived here as a kid, and now as an adult, can you see changes in Cuyama?" Brad asked.

"Well, the population went down when the oil company pulled out. They stopped doing exploration and new wells, although they kept some old ones going. They needed a smaller workforce. I was a young teenager, but I could see that. You needed a job to stay here. Then, the houses became really cheap, just about the time I left. Every other house was empty, and the school didn't have many kids in it. Later, I remember coming back to have a look at my house and saw that the houses were occupied again. They had mostly gone downhill, but they were cheap, in all senses of that word. Yards with no grass, broken windows that got boarded up. Maybe people on welfare. Eugene Bullitt, dad, always made sure that we had tenants. And one time, someone lived here for fifteen years, an older couple that had retired and lived on and on. Even though I own this house, I hadn't lived here until about six years ago. I was just working from home, doing books for small businesses, doing handiwork to sell at boutiques, crocheting afghans. I didn't need much of an income. And I liked living here."

"Is that where those throws on the couch came from? You did all of them?" Very got up and went to the couch in the living room. She ran her hand over the one on top and then sat down. A strange sinking, sliding, slithering movement startled Very. She understood where they were all stored, one on top of another. The feeling of sitting on something that was not stable was disconcerting.

"I needed to keep my hands busy." Cindy shrugged.

"But why so many?" Very shook her head in wonder.

"Oh, those are the ones that didn't sell. I just put them there. Maybe the ones on the bottom might sell now. Sort of, if I discounted them, maybe…"

"Would you give them away? I know a place that has things like this to give to young mothers with children who need them."

"Hmm, mothers and children. That would be nice. Better than sitting on my couch forever." Cindy looked over at the afghan-filled couch. She squinted.

Very said, "We came today to see if you'd talk to us some more about your mother and AnnaRose. Can you tell us anything more?"

Brad said, "You said it wasn't an accident. What did you mean?"

Cindy turned to Brad with a look of dismay on her face. "You might know. I remember you now. You talked to her and then she died."

Very looked from one to the other. "When? When did this happen?"

"It was you, wasn't it? I couldn't remember at first, I wasn't sure. There were two of you. The older guy, he really scared Mom. But you were there too. I remember." Cindy crossed her arms over her chest.

Very looked at Brad with a question mark in her eyes.

He shrugged and said quietly, "You knew that; I worked on the cold case."

Cindy breathed deeply. 'You came and then she died."

"It was an accident," Brad said.

Cindy stood and shouted back, "No, it just looked like one. She couldn't take it. YOU made it happen. You killed her!"

Brad stepped back, into the doorway of the kitchen.

Suddenly, Cindy picked up her cup and saucer and threw it in Brad's direction.

His reflexes kicked in and he sidestepped.

Very watched as the cup and saucer separated. The dregs of the coffee made a delicate arc in the air, flinging themselves across the whole of the doorway. The delicate pattern of flowers and vines flashed in Very's eyes as they flew inexorably towards the kitchen floor.

The crashing sounded as if a bomb had gone off. Sobriety fell on the three. Cindy cried out in anguish, "My mother's china!"

Chapter Sixteen: More Answers and More Questions

When the dust had cleared, the cup and saucer swept up and disposed of, they sat again. Brad sighed, and said, "The brakes on her car were worn. That hill, you know that hill, you need your brakes and she basically didn't have any."

Very look puzzled. "You mean the hill, the long one, down to Maricopa?"

"Yes, that one. The brakes were checked. They were worn, they didn't hold."

Cindy looked out the front window, and spoke in a flat voice, as if retelling the story for the hundredth time. "She left me alone that afternoon. She was angry, she wasn't herself. She didn't say where she was going, but she was upset. Maybe she was going shopping in Taft. I don't know. When she didn't come back, I didn't know what to think. I went to the next-door neighbor's, where the Highway Patrol found me. That neighbor kept me for two days, then my aunt came and took me with her. Dad came too, and he apologized for not being able to take me in. Wife, a new kid, not a big enough house. But my aunt had room. I went to high school in Santa Maria. She was good to me. It was better than high school here, that's the truth. At Cuyama High School, very few of the kids reached their senior year, and then half of them were pregnant by the other half and nobody got anywhere. No, no, that's unkind. It's just in Santa Maria, kids really aspired to go to college. And dad kept in touch. I got to know Glen, he's my little brother, my baby bro."

Cindy sat on the couch, lost in her thoughts of the past.

"Thanks for sharing these things with us. Sounds like you had a hard time as a child and teenager," Very said.

"What doesn't kill you makes you stronger."

"I'm not so sure about that, but it is a philosophy that can take you into the future." Very hesitated slightly. "So, you said it wasn't an accident, you mom's accident wasn't. What do you think happened?"

"She was tired of it all, angry and tired. She just let the car go off the road. If you jump off a ten-story building, you'll die when you hit the pavement. She knew she'd die. It was suicide."

"Did she leave a note or any indication? Did she say anything to anyone? Did she phone anyone?" Very tried to keep her voice low and with overtones of deep concern. She had known Betty Jean, but only as a child knowing an adult. Adults were all the same, weren't they? Capable, logical, always had it together?

"Adults always think they know better. The adults told me what happened. But I know it wasn't an accident. Ask him," she said pointing a finger at Brad. "Ask him what he said to my mom. What did my mom say to you?" She stared at Brad.

Brad sat, his lips closed, teeth grinding. "I said nothing, nothing at all. The officer in charge asked the questions. Maybe," he hesitated. "Maybe it wasn't so much what he asked as how he asked it. Lots of people thought Betty Jean was careless. I think his questions and techniques reflected that. She was upset. I remember that. But nobody threatened her. I know that it's a horrible thing, and so difficult for some, to bring things like this up, years after." Brad sat forward. "I apologize for the way my superiors handled the situation. I'm sorry it was so harsh and…"

Cindy murmured, "I guess so, I guess I need to accept your apology. It's just that it was unfair. I thought a lot about it afterwards. Everyone kept saying it was an accident. But I thought I knew better. My aunt told me to keep quiet. She said my mom was gone, nothing was going to bring her back. We should remember her as she was, a good woman, that unfortunate things happened to. And I had my dad, and Glen."

Brad hung his head, then asked, "Do you still have the back door? The one from the bedroom to the back yard?"

Cindy's head jerked up. "How do you know that?"

"Very told us."

"Not many people know about that door. One tenant didn't like it and wanted me to close it up, cover it over. I just locked it and put a big bookcase in front of it. Told them to just forget it. Tenants, really!"

Very looked at her, "You had that much contact with the tenants? I thought you were so young…"

"Yeah, I did. At one point, Gene had an accident and he couldn't get out and about very well, so I just did it. I told him I could do it all and I did. I was living in Bakersfield with Number Two and it gave me something to do. After all, it was my house. So, I started doing all the rental stuff, even doing yard work and cleaning it up between tenants. It's always been my house, in my name, ever since Mom died."

Cindy paused and they all took a moment to honor Betty Jean.

"I'll show you the door," Cindy said, rising and leading the way. Very needed no directions.

The room was obviously used, the bed made, but the night table strewn with books, cough drops and boxes of tissues. The door was set in the middle of the back wall, with windows on either side. The door sported an old-fashioned handle of brass. Cindy opened it and then pushed on the screen door. She stepped out and down two cement steps to the lawn.

Very and Brad followed. Very smiled at the well-kept patch of lawn, but it was the garden that elicited her admiration. A well-tended vegetable patch sat between rows and rows of fruit trees. They were in flower, or had set their fruit. The vegetables were thriving; their green leaves spreading out; their flowers just beginning to open. "It's beautiful, your back yard is amazing. You've done such a great job."

"It's my baby. New life, fruit."

Very walked over to the fence. "Has it always been like this? I don't remember it being so high. But then again, I was a kid, so it should have seemed tall to me."

"No, it was shorter, you could see the back yard there. I could always climb over the fence, over to the sidewalk, just there. See, behind the fence. One tenant put up this higher fence. He also put up sheds and worked on cars and motorcycles back here. He ruined the soil over there." Cindy pointed to a place in the far back of the lot where nothing was growing but some sad looking weeds.

"Oh yuck," said Very.

"Yeah, yuck is right. That's when I decided to move back in. My house, have it the way I wanted. I was single, again, so I just did it."

Very walked over to the fence near the sidewalk. "Could someone have gotten into and out of the house that day this way? Over the fence?" Very looked at Cindy, judging her reactions to the mention of the day AnnaRose went missing. "Could she have done it herself?"

Cindy looked back at the door. "She could have gotten out the door, I guess, if it wasn't locked, or even if it was, she could have unlocked it. We used it, I remember as a kid using it. But the fence? Maybe. I used to leave a box out here and shove it up to climb over the fence. I don't know if mom knew or not. She must have known. But, mom wasn't always 'here.' She drank and went on benders. I don't know if she ever used drugs, sleeping pills maybe. Don't get me wrong, she was a loving mother. Always a kiss, a hug, a special treat. I felt loved, and I loved her back. But she was so sad. That's why I told her a lot of funny stories. I had dozens of them and I would retell my friends' whacky stories too. My mother liked it, I don't believe any of my husbands appreciated my talents for storytelling."

"Oh, husbands, how many did you have?" Very asked innocently.

"Three. Three really handsome, friendly, party-loving deadbeats. God, could I pick 'em. I finally quit, and quit looking."

"Me too. Only one, but not really. I got pregnant, he left me at the altar, disappeared. Never heard from him again. Lost the baby. Never managed to find anyone else. Leery of getting involved again."

"So, only one that got away?"

Very laughed. "I guess it is never again. And you?"

"Bad taste in men. Join the club. So, no kids?" Cindy asked.

Very shook her head and said, "And you?"

Cindy walked towards one of the fruit trees. The flowers had faded and now tiny green orbs dotted the branches, dragging the tree downwards. Cindy reached out to the trunk to steady herself. She stood there, among the ripening fruit. Gaining strength from the fecund tree?

"No children," Cindy answered. "I had five miscarriages. All of them, not even born, or close to it. And it wasn't the man, all of them, different husbands. And then, I had one, a tiny little girl. Born too soon, so small. I named her AnnaRose. I named all of them AnnaRose. But that last one had a birth certificate. She was real, she was my real AnnaRose. But she died. My little special AnnaRose died too. All of them."

Now, Cindy was sobbing, holding onto the tree, the one carrying myriad babies. Very took a step closer. She turned around to find Brad.

He stood on the tiny step of the doorway, watching the two women in the back yard.

Very leaned towards the distraught woman, "Cynthia, Cindy, I understand." It was a whisper. A communication between women.

"But my mother kept AnnaRose. She kept everything. Especially pictures. She had a little Brownie camera and took photos. They're here, I can find them. Next time, next time you come back, I'll have them for you." She sobbed again. "AnnaRose only lives in photographs."

Very opened her mouth, intending to ask about the other things that mothers sometimes keep, like clothes, hair. But she shut her mouth.

She put her hand on Cindy's shoulder as the sobs went on and on. The anguish of the lost AnnaRose. AnnaRoses.

Chapter Seventeen: The Cold Case Files

Very had demanded to be taken home. She said she didn't want to talk to anyone. Nothing to say. Brad complied with her request. He took her back downtown to pick up her car, but followed her all the way out Hwy 178 until she reached the gate of Five Points. He let her drive in by herself.

The stuff kept creeping, shoving, bursting into her mind. She tried to push it out by busying herself doing some housework; cleaning the toilet; vacuuming the hallway and living room carpet. The cat left hair everywhere, even vacuuming everyday wasn't enough. Was it?

She sat with Cleopatra on her lap and watched dumb shows on the 'idiot box'. She petted Cleopatra so hard that the cat rebelled. At first, she stalked off, but came back when Very settled down. It was not good to let your feelings affect your cat. Finally, after one rather heavy pet, Cleopatra turned on her, hissing and lunging to bite Very's arm. Very shouted, the frustration of the day flying towards the cat. Cleo went and crawled under a bed.

At ten, Very took a sleeping pill, determined to get a whole night's sleep.

The next morning, she sat with her coffee, reading the day's obituaries. "Sheesh, what am I doing, reading about dead people!" she said, throwing the paper on the table. Why had she taken this so personally? Why was this case driving her crazy? Even looking for Frankie was never this nerve-wracking.

When she arrived at the office, Brad was there with his big thermos full of aromatic coffee. Darrell and Olivia were busy filling in notes on all the persons involved. Brad had already filled them in about what Cindy had told them regarding Betty Jean.

"I've already checked the newspaper archives about the accident. I can confirm that the official report was that the brakes were worn and didn't hold, causing Betty Jean Bullitt to swerve and leave the road, plunging over the side. I was wondering, given that name, Bullitt, if the newspaper reading audience would want to know that she was the mother of the murdered child. There was nothing there about it, but I suspect that many remembered her. It was a very short article. And then no follow-up, except a very short obit. Only mentioned where she was born, when died. Survived by daughter. Didn't even mention husband."

"Were they still married? Surely they would have gotten divorced? Sometime?" Very asked.

"Divorce is not always convenient. We know that Eugene was 'married' to Glen's mother. Or was he? Does it matter? Betty Jean always referred to herself as Bullitt, and let us not forget that Cindy carries the Bullitt name even though everyone seems to agree that he is not her biological father." Brad said. "I'm glad the newspaper never printed that she was the mother of the murdered girl. Let her rest in peace, at least."

'How come we keep NOT going forward? We find out something, but it's nothing. We followed up the wild goose chase of the 'It wasn't an accident', but it sure does look like an accident. Nothing there." Very said, looking around at the others. "What? Am I being 'Grumpy Very' that no one wants to listen to?"

Darrell looked away, Olivia smiled, but it was really a grimace. Brad whispered, "Yes."

Brad's phone rang, an old fashioned 'brinnnnng'. He whipped it out of his pocket and read the caller ID. "Hello?"

They all tried to eavesdrop, but Brad held the phone tightly to his ear. "Yeah, thanks." He smiled at all of them. "Good to go. We can look at the cold case file, all of it. The judge or whoever, said that it was too old, not likely to affect anyone, privacy wise. Very, are you ready to do some more investigating, helping push this case forward?"

"Are you willing for Grumpy Very to accompany you? Then, yes, I'll go." She reached for her coffee and drained the cup.

Darrell and Olivia had put up a blank face on the board with all the pictures of the players. It was masculine, with '?' in place of features.

"What's that?" Very asked.

"That is our mystery man. If we consider that AnnaRose could exit the house by herself, there is no need for finding a strange man inside the house, or even along the street. If she had walked away, she could have been picked up by some random person on the street or the highway."

"No, oh no," Very said shaking her head. "I don't even want to contemplate that."

"Better or worse than her father or the friend of her mother?" Brad said.

"Okay, you're right. Faceless man it is." Very shivered. "Let's go."

On the way to the county storeroom for cold case files, along with numerous other old or outdated files,

Brad and Very did not communicate. The basement room they were directed to was a dumping ground. Brad presented his papers from the court and their ID. The clerk in charge seemed stumped. Had he never encountered someone looking for files? Was he new? Was he deliberately trying to obstruct them? Was he stupid? Was he trying to make an impression on someone by taking his time?

Very whispered to Brad, "Does it always take this long, with this much fuss?"

Brad shrugged and smiled at the clerk. Out of the side of his mouth, he said, "Let the poor man do his job. Perhaps it's because we're essentially civilians getting into his files. He's got to keep an eye on us, make sure we only look at what we're supposed to."

Very assented, "Yeah, I guess you're right. He needs to keep an eagle eye on the criminals, of which we may be two."

"If necessary, I'll remind him of my status."

The clerk eventually led them deep into the archives and waved his hand at a row. "What you're looking for must be here. I'm not sure how everything is stored. Some in boxes, other things in files. You'll have to check with me if you want to look at something else or take something with you. I notice you have authorization. Good luck." He walked back to his position at the front of the vast room.

The place was a warehouse, cool and dry, but musty and dusty. As indicated, the industrial metal shelving contained a mixture of files and boxes. They slowly walked down a row, Very checking the contents of the boxes. They were loosely filed by date. But of course, some were related to trials that had taken years. Others were just reports of crimes and then, they were forgotten.

Brad started mumbling as they passed down the row. "You know, there was a jurisdictional dispute with this case. Santa Barbara County was quite happy to get rid of it, but of course, most of the interviewing, all of the main persons involved lived in their county. The body was found in Kern County, by a Kern County deputy. But everyone knew that it was a Santa Barbara case, really. I mean, Kern County sheriffs, in Bakersfield, were no closer than the guys from Santa Barbara. It's an angle that still puzzles me, except if we were looking at who hoped to benefit, like get kudos for hauling in a murderer. Kern County has had too many, they could have let the guys from another county take the credit. As it was, no one caught anyone. It appears that no one got to take the accolades, either. I wonder if Santa Barbara County has anything in their archives, something they collected that we hadn't known about?"

"Is there some kind of number of the case? A lot of these boxes have case numbers as well as a year. Or rather a number that incorporates the year." Very shuffled down the aisles looking for boxes and files with numbers.

Very bent down low, checking boxes on the bottom shelf. "Oh no, these aren't in order." She pulled out a box and began looking more carefully. "This belongs up here, higher on the shelf, or maybe in the one to the left." She looked and checked the numbers above and below, rearranging and inserting the small box in another place.

"Very, we don't have time to reshuffle anything. Leave it. It's not our job."

"I'm a librarian. A mis-shelved book is a lost book."

"Our case isn't lost. That isn't where it's supposed to be. It's down here," Brad said, bending to look at items on the bottom shelf. "Got it, here's our stuff."

Very hastily repositioned two more files and then scurried to Brad's side.

Brad put the box on the floor and opened it. They peered inside. They could see old file folders, and something underneath.

"Too dark to see anything. Is there somewhere we can take it where the light is better?" Very asked.

"At the front?"

They returned towards the front and found a table set up in the middle of the files. Decent light over their heads.

Brad set the box down on the table and immediately pulled it wide open. He grabbed the two files on top, opening them eagerly. He glanced through and then 'umphed'. "These are just copies of the cold case files. Just papers. Nothing new here." He put them aside.

He stuck his hand back into the box and grabbed. As he drew out the bag, Very looked carefully. It was plastic, but very old. The plastic had yellowed and gone opaque with age. Tape was coming off of one side. Very turned her head to read it. 'Clothes.'

Brad gingerly held the bag up, trying to see through the decayed plastic to its contents.

Very peered as well. "What is that? Clothes, her clothes?"

Brad's grip grew tight. "Damn them." Very turned to look at Brad's face, trying to read it.

"You haven't seen these before, have you?" she asked.

Brad gritted his teeth in an attempt to quiet the storm raging across his face. "No, I wasn't allowed to look this far. I told you, the guys in charge wanted to get it over with. The re-interviews were cursory, at the very best. And this… I never saw. Never knew it was here."

"So, we have it, now. But what are we looking for?"

"Something with DNA on it? Clothes might do, but so many people handled them. Blood, hair?"

"I'd forgotten. They didn't know about DNA in those days. Blood type, maybe, but not what we have now. So many more tools to do investigations with." Very looked at the bag that Brad held in his hand. Her hands began to reach, but pulled back.

"Whose DNA?" she asked.

Brad said, "AnnaRose's DNA to start with. But then, the killer's too."

Brad put aside the plastic bag and dug deeper. He pulled out another bag, this one much smaller. He read the description. "Vials of bodily fluids. Blood and possible semen."

Brad held it up and both squinted at the two glass vials. Brad opened the bag, whose seal had disintegrated, and took the first vial out. It was sealed on the end, but the liquid that had been inside was no longer liquid. The blood had dried up and now only flecks of brown clung to the insides of the small tube. Brad held up the second vial. There had been something inside, but the seal had obviously failed during the last fifty plus years.

"It's hard to tell if there is anything left in this one," Brad said. "But the blood, could get something there." He took out a new plastic bag from his pocket and bagged the two vials and the original plastic bag.

He took out the cold case file and opened the manila folder. "Cold case files. Here's my name." He flipped through it quickly and snorted. "We have all of this from the public record. Did you see all of this?" He leaned back and let Very look.

"It looks like I have. Where are the original files?" Very asked.

Brad dug deeper into the box. He lifted out a stack of envelopes and folders. "Original case files." He opened the top one and flipped through. "No, I've never seen this!" He looked through more and then at Very. "These are original files that I knew nothing about. Not the blood, not the semen, not the bag. And some of these interviews, I've missed seeing them." He slammed them shut and cursed. "Or maybe they were kept from me. These interviews, original. No, I guess I knew that they were here, or somewhere, but we should have had all this to do our re-interviews. I need to take this whole box."

"The clothes?" Very picked up the opaque bag. "Can I touch them? Oh, do I need gloves?"

Brad laughed. "You don't need gloves. Back then, they didn't use gloves, so you won't contaminate them any more than they were originally contaminated. Nowadays, we would go over it all for minute fibers, or sweat, or traces of blood. Anything might be there. But in those days, the police weren't as careful."

"Locard's principle. The criminal leaves and takes away from the crime scene. Is that why they kept these?"

"Don't know why they kept them. You can look at them if you want. I don't see that they will do us much good. They should have given them back to the mother."

"Maybe Betty Jean didn't want these clothes. She would have had other clothes that weren't…tainted," Very said, reaching into the bag.

"There might be more blood or other things on the clothes. Are you thinking of DNA? Yeah, that. If we could get it from the clothes, we could then say that it was relevant. We could tell if it were AnnaRose's."

Very carefully pulled out a small dress, shoes, but no socks, no underwear. There was also a small blue jacket. It was made of nubby material. It would be warm on a cool day. Or if you were planning on running away. "This looks new. There are no buttons missing, or repaired. There's no dirt or wear. It doesn't look like it was worn during a brutal murder."

"Check to see if there is any hair on these pieces. Although I'm fairly certain someone did check for that."

Very checked the jacket, then the dress. She noticed a brown smudge on the back of the dress, as if it had been worn while falling, or being pushed, into the dirt. "Here," she said. "Need to check this out." She shoved the dress in Brad's direction.

She took the jacket, checking the neck carefully for hairs. She stuck her hand into the jacket pocket. Maybe there was a tissue in a pocket? Her mother had always stuck a clean one into her pocket whenever Very went out. No, a tissue would have been found before now. She stuck her hand into the other pocket and felt a small ball of something stuck far into the corner. She used her fingernail to dig at the small rock or clod of dirt.

When she had retrieved it, she held it up to Brad. "You want AnnaRose's DNA? This is it for sure. Nothing better." She held up a tiny tooth, the end was still brown with dried blood. "And this might explain why she wasn't feeling well. Tooth getting loose, so she doesn't feel good. Maybe it was her first? Maybe she was feeling frightened and unsure. And when she lost it, she put it in her pocket so she wouldn't lose it. If you lose the tooth, the Tooth Fairy doesn't come. This was worth a dime, maybe even a quarter. Valuable."

Chapter Eighteen: DNA, the Tooth and the Cigarette Butt

Brad smiled broadly. "Now, we've got a good source of DNA for AnnaRose. We can tell easily if the blood is hers, and if it isn't, we have a place from which to start looking seriously."

Very said, "And the other liquid, that's no longer liquid?"

"If it isn't hers, remember, it could be other bodily fluid. If it isn't hers, then we have something." He held up the vial. "If there is anything left."

Very felt a certain excitement. "What else do we have in that box?"

Brad dug deeper and found a few more files. He glanced at them. "A list of those who were out looking for AnnaRose, officially, that is. There were lots of others. And I mean it, I need to contact Santa Barbara County. They were in charge of the whole thing until her body was found on the Kern County side of the county line. They had more than a day to interview witnesses, gather evidence. They should have turned it all over, but sometimes things get lost."

Brad stuck his hand in and scrabbled around the bottom of the box. "Whoa, look what's here?"

Very looked at the small plastic bag he held up. The age made the bag opaque but there was one small item at the bottom. "A cigarette butt?" Very said. "Not AnnaRose's."

"Could be the killer's. But knowing how the scene was such a mess, it could be anyone's. No note with it, maybe there is something in this mess," he held up a stack of folders. "Somewhere in here, someone must have noted picking this up. But, most likely, someone on the crew looking for her or a person who gathered around when the body was found and removed."

"But if we do find DNA on it, it might lead us to the killer," Very said. "Or it might eliminate someone?"

"Or it could be a dead end."

Very sighed. "Let's say that Old Man Bullitt was there, smoking, then it could be his. But that doesn't rule him in or out."

Brad said, "In the end, it's not going to tell us much."

"What if that cigarette has DNA on it from someone who supposedly wasn't there? If we can eliminate the people who were there, then if it belongs to someone else, then it could lead us to a killer."

"DNA from a bunch of dead, or dying, sheriff's deputies? Cost, Very, it would cost too much to eliminate all of them. Maybe we can find something else that will tell us when this was picked up."

They looked at the stack of folders, all of them old and yellowed. The dates were mixed up between the original and the cold case. Repetitions, copies, piles of paper.

"Look," Brad said. He held up the cigarette butt in its old yellowed bag, the two vials in their ancient plastic and pointed at Very's tooth. "There may be a thread here."

"Or maybe not, but it's the best we have."

"And more than we had an hour ago. We have work to do on this. We have papers to file, DNA to get. Let's go." Brad smiled at Very, picked up the box and they made their way out of the musty storage facility.

Back at the office, the new artifacts generated excitement, a stimulus to push everyone forward. Olivia pounced on the box and started taking things out, laying them carefully on the small table. She took a new pad of paper and, with her multicolored markers, started making a series of labels. Original case files, cold case files, artifacts. Then she pulled out a small laptop and started a new document. She consulted with Darrell as to how they would organize the mess from the box. It would need someone, or more than one, to sift through, looking for something that so far hadn't been recorded, or something that may have a meaning. Or maybe just a clue that needed to be examined from an alternative prospective. Creativity was needed. Generative innovation. Thinking way outside the box.

Darrell made a phone call and they all settled in to work. Very helped Olivia organize the files. Brad got on the phone and started making calls to Santa Barbara County, trying to find someone who could help him locate any cold case files. The small office seemed much too small for all of them.

Then Glen arrived. He flung open the door and surveyed the scene, "I hope this is okay, to just barge in like this. Darrell called me."

Very was closest to him and she smiled a welcome. "We have found some more evidence. We're not sure what it all means, but we have artifacts."

Brad continued, "We need DNA from your dad. He's the closest relative and there should be a good match. We have this," he held up the plastic bag, now a new clear one, that contained the tooth. "We are almost 100% sure it's AnnaRose's. It was jammed down in the pocket of her jacket. If we can get a match with these two DNA samples, then when we look for DNA in some of the other samples, we will know for sure, what belongs to whom."

"Other samples? More teeth?" Glen asked.

"No, blood and other," Brad held them up. "Much the worse for wear. And also this." He showed Glen the cigarette butt. "Did your dad smoke?"

"The men all did, didn't they? I have no idea if it is his. Where was it found?" Glen said.

"Don't know yet," Very answered.

"The jacket, you said. You found a tooth in a jacket? Other than photos, I've never seen anything of hers."

Very took the blue jacket, now re-housed in a larger, cleaner bag and passed it to Glen. He reached out his hand, but then hesitated. "Oh. Was it found with her, on her? Oh no, don't tell me. I'll imagine."

Brad had gotten another phone call and was talking quietly while the rest were taking another look at the jacket.

Brad hung up and turned to Glen. "When can we get the DNA sample? Today?"

"I need to prepare him. He sometimes loses it and doesn't follow what is happening. I'll call him. See if he answers."

Another phone rang and the five sat there staring at one another. Finally, Darrell said, "Very, that's your phone. Are you going to answer it?"

Very quickly checked the caller ID. She answered, "Gabby. How's it going?"

"I'm glad you answered. I'm scared."

"Oh no, what's happened. Are you in danger?"

Gabby hesitated and then said, "No danger, really, I don't think. But let me tell you."

"Okay."

"Are you surrounded by people? I hear noise. Can we talk, privately? I don't want, I don't need…"

"Sure." Very looked at the small office, now crowded with people, desks, computers, maps, crime boards and boxes. Three of the other four were on their phones. Olivia tried to squirm her way in between others to get at the computer on the second desk.

It was a repeat of the scene from the Marx Brothers movie. There was a stateroom on a ship. The four brothers were in the room, then maids came to make up the room, room service arrived with food, plumbers, workmen, guests pushed and shoved around one another, trying to do their business. Finally, the door opened and then all began to fall out the door. Very laughed at the thought and said, again, "The Marx Brother's movie, again. Too many people."

Brad looked up from his phone call and said, "A Night at the Opera, that's the name of it. Do we have to keep doing this?"

Very went out into the hallway. "Now, Gabby, tell me what's been happening?"

"I did as you said, I checked, double checked, made sure no one was watching, took photos even. There were two more disputes. The first time, she argued with the kid, then tried to fob the blame off on me. The second time, she just told the kid it was my fault. She said it with a straight face and I know she was watching to see what I would do. So, I said yeah, it was my mistake. And then she made me get the money out of my purse and pay the boy. He was still really mad about it. When I left, he caught me outside and threatened me. I couldn't tell him it wasn't my fault. How can a kid say that it's an adult that it cheating them, and not a child. Big people aren't supposed to make mistakes, so of course, it is my fault. Oh Very, it's so unfair. What can I do?"

"Don't worry, you are doing the right thing. And adults do make mistakes, and they can be mean and tell lies. You know that! Are you working this weekend?"

"Yeah, all weekend.

"Protect yourself. Be vocal when you take money. Say the amount out loud so everyone can hear, and then make a show of entering it into the book and counting it carefully. Then make a big production of watching the kids sign their names, and repeating the time and amount. Make others hear as well. Then take photos of the book, many times during the day. At the lunch break or rest break, make sure you count the money and enter an amount somewhere. Make sure it's all written in big letters and hopefully, make sure that others see you doing everything as it should be. Is the box ever left unattended?"

"No, never."

"Gabby, you are in the right. It's not you doing this, it's someone else, and I think you know who."

"I do, it's just being able to prove it. And like I said, I'm a kid. It's easy to take advantage."

"You've said it. Don't let anyone treat you badly. Stand up for yourself. And know that I have your back."

"Oh Very, thanks for that. I feel better, more confident. I am learning a lot at this job, so much more than I ever thought I would. I'm a detective. I'm like your assistant. No, I'm a detective, a real one. And you are my mentor. Yeah, that's it."

"You take care and call me if you need to. I'll answer, I promise."

"Oh, Very, what would I do without you?" Gabby rang off.

Brad and Glen burst from the office. Very had to laugh at the force of their exit. "Getting too crowded in there for you?" she asked.

"We're on a mission, you want to come?" Brad asked.

"We're going to visit the old man. This time we will get the truth. He's promised." Glen said.

Brad gave Very a look. Eugene Bullitt had over fifty years to tell the truth, but he had only told the same tired story over and over. A promise? At whose expense? Would he tell them he wasn't AnnaRose's father? Would he tell them about Cindy's birth and heritage? Would he tell them where he had been all that day? It didn't seem likely that he was now going to confess, after having enlisted his son's help to clear his name. But something was up and Brad wasn't going to miss it. Very saw determination in his face, a race for time with an old man who was surely close to the end of his life. Glen said his dad had promised to tell the truth, and Brad was going to hold him to it. Even if he had to physically hold him.

Chapter Nineteen: Old Man Bullitt's Statement

Glen left first. Brad and Very followed and when they got there, stood in the street and waited for Glen to prepare their house and his father.

"First, let's ask for the DNA. I'll just say that it's for identification of AnnaRose's. But, of course, it's for double duty." Brad rocked back and forth on his feet in irritation, or anxiety?

"Is that legal? Can we use it to eliminate him, or convict him? Even if we say it is just to match his daughter's? Oh, I fear we are skating on thin ice here."

"If his DNA comes up on that cigarette butt and there is no evidence that he was at the scene, when the sheriff was looking at it, then it will look very, very bad for him. But if it is not his DNA on the cigarette, then we are still left with questions."

"But," Very protested, "he was the one who wanted this investigation. He can't really be the one who did it and then ask for his name to be cleared, can he? I mean, is he senile, have dementia, or just conveniently forgot?"

"I'm assuming he is within normal range of intelligence and that he knows what he is asking."

"But can we ask him, and surely this is relevant, why now? Why so late in the process?"

"Glen did say that it was a 'before I die' thing. He's pushing ninety and not, I take it, in the best of health. Perhaps he feels his mortality very keenly these days. Perhaps he is thinking more and more of his legacy. Maybe he fears that life will deal him the final blow and he needs closure on this. We do get funny headed when we get old."

"Don't I know it," said Very. "My mother began to do a lot of weird and silly things as she aged. She was always a hoarder, but yogurt buckets? I counted over 100 of them, in two monster stacks in the back of the pantry. And there were other strange things she wanted. She wanted all of her albums of her trips, full of labeled photos, to be put in one easily accessible place. And then she never looked at them again. She collected greeting cards, and never threw them away. There were eight boxes, bags and baskets full of them. Some of them had cash in them that were given to her on her birthday. She never spent it, just saved it, stuck in a card. So, yes, when we get old, we want some things that are just not really feasible. Or even undesirable. Maybe he did do it, Eugene that is, and he conveniently forgot."

"If so, he himself, it appears, has asked for this. I can't see Glen putting ideas into his head, not at this stage." Brad led Very to his truck and they got in.

"So, why do we need to talk with him, again?" Very said. "Didn't he give a formal statement in the first investigation? Did he get another interview at the time of the cold case investigation?"

"Because," Brad said, his teeth clenched firmly. "He lied. He lied the first time, he lied the second time. He doesn't have an alibi. We just need to see what he says this time. Hopefully the truth."

"Do you have his statement?" Very asked, "Here? I mean, if you can show him what he said before, then he can come clean. Some of it must be true. What we need is to separate the truth from the lies."

"It's here," he said, patting a folder on the front seat. "Truth and lies."

Very took it and flipped it open. She shuffled through a few pages and then pulled on one, tearing it where it was stapled to two others. She reconstructed the three pages and looked. There was a time and place typed and note of who interviewed and who responded. It was a series of questions and answers. "I found it."

She read aloud the questions and answers. The first one was about when he left home that morning. He noted that he had called Betty Jean and was going to come to visit AnnaRose. They agreed on the afternoon. But Brad interrupted this flow. "Find out what he says, both times."

"Oh, here is the re-interview. The first one says he left at ten-thirty in the morning. The second one is unclear, he says morning. And then, get this, 'Where did you go?' And the first time he says he went for a drive, but he couldn't remember exactly where. Later on, he says he went to a park. When asked which park, he says he couldn't remember. He just drove around."

"The first interview was only days after the incident, not weeks or months. Why can't someone remember what happened just days before. I can understand the not remembering the exact time, but where? The next time, what does he say?" Brad gripped the steering wheel and scowled.

"The re-interview, hum. Now, he says he went to Aliso Canyon. Isn't that on the other side of town from Taft? I mean he would have to drive through the whole valley until he got to the turn off." Very read further. "He says that when he showed up about four-thirty, when he was expected, all hell had broken loose. They hadn't called the authorities yet, but the whole neighborhood was out looking for AnnaRose. Gosh, no wonder he was a suspect. This stuff is basically useless. He needs to come clean."

"You figure?" Brad said.

"Oh, and was he a smoker?"

"Who wasn't?"

Very sat up straight. "I wasn't. I never smoked."

"Goody Two-Shoes!"

"Actually, I did try. My mother caught me and smacked me alongside the head. That was the end of that. And come to think, it was really out of character for her. To hit me like that. Ooooh, my ears rang."

"Did your mother smoke?" Brad asked.

"Where do you think I got the cigarettes?"

Brad had been carefully checking the addresses and he pulled up to the front of a house in the old neighborhood just north of Brundage.

"Just a thought," Very said as they got out. "Did anyone ever ask what kind of cigarettes anyone smoked? A brand? Suspects, lawmen, what did they smoke?"

"I don't think that a brand was a thing back in the day. I think 'the cheapest' would have been the answer. Or 'the one I could bum off someone else.' Do we even know what brand the butt we have is?"

Very shrugged and got out of the car. "So, we cannot be Sherlock Holmes and investigate varieties of tobacco, can we? No, I don't think we know what brand we have. I haven't even looked through the evidence file to find out when and where they found it. If they kept it, it must have been because they found it at the scene. You would think so, huh?"

"If we don't have more evidence, then it isn't of much value. Most likely, it was some law enforcement personnel who smoked and threw it out. DNA though, maybe."

They stood on the sidewalk and looked at the house. A cement walkway ran from the street directly to the front door. Two huge trees shaded the front lawn. As they approached, Very calculated. Post World War Two; three bedrooms, two baths, 1500-1600 square feet. As they passed under the trees, Very felt the coolness under the canopy. Now, if every house in Bakersfield had shade like this, the whole place would be cooler.

Glen met them at the door. He had obviously been waiting for them to arrive and listening for the car. "He's as ready as he'll ever be," he said.

Brad walked in first, and Very let him go. If he wanted to lead on this, let him. He should have had this conversation years ago. Part of this case was his. His chance for a re-do.

They came directly into the living room. Old Man Bullitt, Eugene, sat in a comfortable chair. The rest of the room was furnished as expected; couch, love-seat, coffee table, TV. Bland artwork on one wall. Nothing on the others.

Brad and Very sat on the couch, opposite Eugene. Glen brought them each a glass of cool lemonade. Very looked around for a coaster, and seeing none, put the glass directly on the glass-topped coffee table. Other rings there meant that she was doing nothing new. She took out a notebook.

Brad cleared his throat. "Mr. Bullitt, do you remember me? I came with an older man, the head investigator, more than forty years ago. You were living in Taft then."

"I don't remember you," Eugene said. His voice was thin and weak, a smoker's hoarseness thrust itself to the fore. "But I remember talking to someone. He asked me where I was the day AnnaRose went missing. I told the same lies I did before. The second time, I had a chance to rehearse. I had been rehearsing for ten or twelve years, trying to convince myself it was the truth."

"And was it?" Very asked.

"No." The old man closed his eyes and leaned back in the chair.

"So?" Brad asked.

A silence filled the air.

Very spoke, "Is it true that you are not Cynthia Bullitt's biological father, but allowed that lie to stand?"

Eugene opened his eyes, red-rimmed and rheumy. "Betty Jean and I had gone our separate ways by the time Cindy was expected. She's not mine. I never asked who it was. I was still married and 'coming around' as it were, because AnnaRose was my daughter and I was still paying for things. But we weren't sleeping together. Poor little thing needed a father, especially after Betty Jean died in the car crash. I'm on the birth certificate, so… She's been grateful, a dutiful daughter. I helped her through life; it's not been easy for her. She couldn't pick a good man. She married three of them for god's sake, and I don't know how many others there were. But I always tried. I didn't do well by Betty Jean's other girl, so I tried really hard to be good to Cindy.

"She didn't know much until she came into her inheritance. But like I said, she couldn't find a good man, so I looked after her. And Glen has been a brother. She's family."

"Did you ever think of trying to find her biological father? Very asked.

"Oh, that died with Betty Jean. I never asked. I guess I was afraid of the answer. Afraid it would be something like, 'Oh, I don't know his name.' So, I decided not to ask. It was too difficult."

Eugene stopped and laid his head back on the chair. "Could I have…water?"

Glen jumped up and ran to the kitchen. He reappeared with a glass and straw. He held the straw to Eugene's lips and watched as the old man tried to suck and take a few sips.

Brad leaned over to Very and whispered. "We need to ask the big question now, before he gets too tired."

Very whispered back, "Do you want me to do it? Feminine softness and all?"

"No, I need to do this. It's mine."

Glen asked then if they'd like a coke or something.

"Yeah, that would be nice, if it's easy, that is." Very said. "Can I help you?"

"No, just cans." He left and returned within a minute with three cold coke cans.

Everyone settled and Eugene had another sip of water.

"Eugene," Brad asked softly. "There's something I need to ask."

Eugene moved his head to look at Brad. "You want to know where I was that day."

"Yes, the truth this time."

Eugene arched his back and looked around to find Glen. "I didn't want to complicate things with your mother. I was seeing her, we were making plans. But I still hadn't gotten the divorce, so she was stalling. In the private part of courting, you understand. She was not accommodating. I didn't want to hurt her, but I had my needs, or so I thought. AnnaRose going missing made me rethink all of that. But you see, once I'd told the lies, it was so much easier to just keep telling them. I made it sure in my mind, the park, the store, the roads I drove on. I fixed it in my mind, in case they came after me, like the cold case guy did. So, if they questioned me again, it was all there, all rehearsed, all ready. I went over it again and again."

"But it wasn't true," Glen said.

Eugene shook his head.

Glen stood over his father and said sharply, "What is the truth? Where were you?"

Brad stood and put a hand on Glen's arm. "Steady, steady. He's going to do it. He's going to be honest, now." Brad pulled Glen away from the old man in the chair.

Eugene screwed up his face and tears welled in his eyes. "I was with another woman. I saw her every week or so. She needed the money, I needed the 'loving.'"

"Name, place? Any proof?" Brad asked.

Eugene snorted, "No, all gone. Her name was Mary, or maybe not. That's what she told me. It was all in cash. The house in Taft has long gone." He closed his eyes and relaxed. "There, the truth. Now are we all happy? Are we satisfied?"

Shoulders drooped, sighs of relief.

"I didn't rape and kill my daughter. Not me." He closed his eyes. "Not me."

Chapter Twenty: Visit to Cuyama III

Very went home tired on Friday afternoon. Darrell had tried to interest Brad and Very in going out to dinner with him and Olivia. A double date? Who wanted more talk of the case? Who hadn't had enough of looking at the same board of photos, of persons of interest, of possible suspects, of people to talk with again. Very made her preference known. She was tired, tired of all of this. Wasn't there anything else in the universe to talk about? This had filled her head for more than a week, and now, she wanted to be left alone, she wanted quiet.

She arrived home to find little to eat in the fridge. Maybe going out with Darrell and Olivia wasn't such a bad plan. At least she would have food to eat rather than leftovers from the week before last. She rooted in the freezer and came up with a plastic tub of something from weeks or months before. She had cleaned out the fridge and the freezer when she left her mother's house and bought this one just a few months before, so she knew it wasn't from last year. But there was no date or indication on it of the contents. Food, that was all Very needed to know. Sustenance.

As she ate, she read an old magazine. Cleopatra begged to be petted, so she tried all three at once. She had had her mail held at the post office and had neglected to restart delivery. Even though she chose another time for her flight to Canada, she could always change it. The airline had pressured her into choosing another date, so she had. But she had no investment in that day. She now thought she needed to bring some closure to the current case. Was it possible? Could she choose a time and date for that, or had they all been immobilized by the AnnaRose case? She put aside the magazine and tried to focus on her food and her cat, but that left her mind to wander.

She turned on the TV. There was an old movie playing, but it seemed out-of-date and boring. The action was slow, the characterizations drawn with broad strokes, the bad guys bad, the good girls good, the movie set unrealistic. She had seen it before. After she had channel surfed for five minutes, she turned it off.

Very sat in her lounge chair, with the cat beside her. She petted and ruminated. She thought of the Cuyama of her childhood. The soft summer nights. Why was it always summer when she thought of the place? Could she recall winter? Snow, surely they had snow? How about the cool autumn nights? What had she worn to go 'trick or treating' in? Sweater underneath her costume? Gloves, hats? Few memories of those, but many of the carefree play of the long warm summer evenings.

Photos, she must have saved some pictures of that time. She wandered into the library and pulled out three boxes of miscellaneous junk from her childhood. She had yet to rid herself of these shoeboxes, probably because they held photos. Her mother had a Brownie camera and took lots of pictures. There must have been dozens of them in these boxes. She had cousins and that was always an opportunity to snap some special poses. They would sometimes come to Cuyama for the day and then there would be a potluck in the backyard. Her dad would haul out the crank ice cream maker. Very's throat constricted at the thought of the taste of home-made ice cream. Especially when she licked the paddle, she had tasted the sharp tang of the tin parts. Strangely enough, she had craved this thrill and the vanilla scent that lingered for hours. This seemed mostly because so much of the ice cream had gotten into her hair and the sticky mess had taken hours to comb or wash out.

Photos were such an easy thing to keep that her mother had neglected to toss out the blurry ones. Very simply shoved them all, willy-nilly, into these handy containers. They had lingered for too long. Might as well use this unexpected time to sort them out and find if her childhood remembrances were correct or not. Photos were flat, easy to store many in a small place. Just store them where the rats or mice can't get them and keep them dry. Arid conditions were easy in Bakersfield; the air was ultra-dry all year. Things like this would keep forever. Photographs and mummies.

Very sat on the floor and pulled out the first box. She started sorting. Soon she was deep into laughter at the memories. She had begun with those before high school graduation, then took the younger photos and sorted them again, pre and post Cuyama. The baby photos could have been taken anywhere, she had never figured out exactly when they had moved to Cuyama, but Bakersfield was still a touchpoint as both sets of grandparents lived there. There were photos with Santa in the front window of Brock's Department Store. She looked and determined her age at about three or four, so they had lived in Cuyama at the time, but there wasn't a place to take Santa photos in the dusty township of New Cuyama. Therefore, to Bakersfield, to grandma's house they went. So, the baby ones were a question mark. The older childhood ones were definitely Bakersfield, and the ones up until age eight, were mostly Cuyama.

Wildflowers in the spring, picking dozens of them and then watching as her mother had carefully pressed them into a book.

On the steps of the house. Even in black and white, it resembled Cindy's house. As it should because they were all made to a cookie cutter plan. And then here was one with Mom and Sissy. But when was that? Sissy wasn't born until they had moved back to Bakersfield. So, this must have been taken the day the family had returned to Cuyama. She turned the picture over. The date on the back was years after they had moved. Yes, taken that day, by her father for a change.

They had been on their way to the coast. It was perhaps longer, but a 'wouldn't it be fun to…' atmosphere had prevailed. At first, Very had protested. She got car sick, they knew that. She would get car sick, she said. But that made no difference to her parents, who seemed intent upon re-visiting their old house, stopping by the Buckhorn and poking their noses into the local grocery store. So, they were forced into the car. Sissy was too young to protest, in fact, she probably slept all the way there, sitting in the front seat in her 'safety car seat'. Very laughed as she remembered it. Plastic and aluminum, with two hooks on the back that held it onto the seat. Did her parents really think it would keep her sister from flying into the front windshield if there was a crash? Did the makers of the seat believe this was better than sitting on someone's lap? Certainly better than crawling around free. But that meant that Very had the whole back seat to herself. She had laid down and covered her head.

She had not fully understood it at the time. She knew that AnnaRose's death had affected her; had caused her to become frightened at all kinds of things. She had never been one to shy away from doing things by herself, but from the day she had first heard about the kidnapping and murder, she had turned inward. She still went outside to play, but a nugget of fear had kept her head up and curtailed her lingering in the twilight. Now, that fear had come back. Roaring in her head, forcing her to plead a stomachache. All the way there, she had been curled into a ball in the back, listening to her parents reminisce.

When they stopped at the Buckhorn, she had refused to get out of the car. Her dad parked the car just opposite the big plate glass windows and they must have watched the car the whole time they had their coffee. She remembered the slow drive down Sisquoc Street and the brief stop at their old house. She mumbled a complaint and stayed hidden in the backseat. She knew that it was because of AnnaRose, but she couldn't say it out loud. They had returned the long way to Bakersfield, through Santa Barbara and over the Grapevine. She had never been back.

She looked at the photo now, trying to figure out what to do with it. Should she save it for Sissy? Sissy had never had any interest in Cuyama; it was just a place where her family had once lived. Very set the photo aside. She glanced at the clock. Late, very late, time to go to bed.

Very avoided the phone on Saturday, leaving it perched on the desk in the library. She enjoyed swimming, chatting with new friends at the pool and later in the hot tub. As she sat in the hot tub, she tried hard to put the sight out of her mind of the floating body she had found here. It was always best during the daytime, as it now appeared so changed from that fateful night, just a few months ago. In the afternoon, she cleaned her house. Running the vacuum over the carpet, sucking up wispy hairs of Cleopatra's, she felt empowered. This was her home, her carpet, her job to do.

In the evening, she turned on the TV again and let it blast in the background. She found a button that needed to be sewn on, and a frayed cuff. The rest of the sweatshirt was perfectly good, just a few stiches to perk it up. She found crochet hooks tucked into the bottom of the sewing box. She remembered her days of crocheting baby blankets for Sissy's two, and shawls for all her friends. Maybe she should take that hobby up again, for real. After all, the Crafter's Club would help her.

She slept in on Sunday again. She sorted through the photos that she had found in the box. Almost none of Cuyama, but memories of high school and college flooded her brain.

At four, Gabby called. Very was in the process of making a pasta salad for the evening and she propped the phone up in the kitchen. Gabby whispered. "I'm doing like you said, keeping track of everything. Should I talk with Father Sullivan?"

"No, I don't think the time is right. How much evidence of taking money out of the box do you have?"

"Not enough yet," Gabby whispered. "You know, I'm just a kid. I need an airtight case, don't I?"

"You are right on that one. I've got your back. You know that?"

"Yeah, thanks Very. Gotta go, just felt the need to touch bases. Life isn't always easy for us little guys. Bye." Gabby hung up before Very could answer or comment on this last statement.

The phone call from Gabby had caused Very to be late for dinner at the Sanchez house. As she pulled up, she noticed Brad's truck. She smiled to herself, realizing that she was looking forward to seeing him again.

She entered the back yard, to the smells of barbecue, the easy laughter of the family and friends. A daughter-in-law of Joey's took her salad. Glancing at the barbecue, she saw the group of men gathered around. There was the white Stetson, pushed back on his head. He was smiling, laughing.

She moved towards him, at what seemed like slow motion. She knew she shouldn't run happily in his direction, but the pull of his presence drew her onwards. Like some sort of movie sequence, he turned towards her. He smiled. His lips parted and white teeth shone in a grin that opened wider and wider. Her own smile matched his, growing broader and broader as she moved ever so slowly forward. When she was near enough, his hand reached out to touch her hand.

"Hi," he said. "Let's get you a drink."

He gripped her hand and pulled her towards the table that held plastic glasses and liquid refreshments. He stood close to her as he poured her the drink she requested. She leaned into the heat of his body as she took it from his hand.

The next thing Very realized was that the back yard was empty. Somehow, dinner had been eaten, drinks drunk, conversation shared. But now, sounds of car doors and cranky kids had reached Very from the street. Laughter floated towards them from the kitchen as cupboards slammed and dishes rattled.

"Oh gosh, we didn't help clean up, we didn't help with anything!" Very said, standing quickly.

"Trash," Brad replied, "we can do the trash at least."

They quickly set to with big garbage bags, bending to pick up soiled napkins and abandoned plastic.

As they rushed about, Very said quietly, "Thanks."

"What for?" Brad answered.

"For not talking about the case. For all the funny stories. For letting me hear about your life."

"As I heard about yours. I can't decide which story was funnier, the horse or the camel."

They laughed together. As they neared the back door, Brad held out his hand. Very took it. He used it to come closer to her. Very stood very quietly, waiting for the next move. What would she do if he tried to kiss her? Is that what he was planning? She held her breath.

Bobby Sanchez's voice rang out, just behind them. "Trash, did anyone get the trash?"

Brad backed away and turned to Bobby. "We have it here."

Very stood still, very still. Had anyone noticed they had only talked to each other all evening? She needed to leave, now. Before her face turned red with embarrassment. "Bye, Bobby. Say goodnight to Joey for me. I need to get home, big day tomorrow. See you Brad." She waved to all as she headed out the side gate towards her car.

He heart was beating and she felt sweaty. Fear? Mortification? She had acted like a teenager all evening. She scurried to her car, hurried to get home. Her precipitous drive took her two minutes less than usual to reach her house.

"Cleopatra," she sang out as she came into the house. As usual, her cat had rushed to the laundry room and waited for her. "Oh, come to bed and snuggle with me. I'm such a foolish woman. And you are a faithful cat."

Monday morning Very arrived before anyone else. She had brought her breakfast and a cup of instant coffee in a travel mug. She stared at the story boards. Timelines, maps of the valley and the township. Photos of people of interest. Even Cindy and Glen were pictured on that board. They were people who knew things. Cindy had a box of photos that her mother had kept. That was the number one project for the day; retrieve that, hopefully, treasure trove of memories that contained a clue. Maybe more than one. Very felt upbeat. That board of photos also had an empty spot for the 'outsider,' representing the theory that some outside, random man, had encountered AnnaRose. Alone, unprotected, vulnerable. Maybe the cigarette butt belonged to him.

A key jiggled in the lock and the door opened. Brad, Darrell and Olivia poured into the office. Brad produced the thermos and coffee was poured all around. Very found herself grateful for the refill.

The schedule for the day was outlined. Darrell and Olivia were tasked with making sure the tooth and the cigarette butt were taken in for DNA samples. But Darrell reminded them that all the photos on the board represented possible lines of inquiry, including Eugene Bullitt.

"I don't care that he has spilled his guts and that you two believe him," Darrell said. "That alibi cannot be confirmed. He's still there and he may have more to tell us. And you might try the Kentons again."

Brad and Very look at each other. "We'd rather not, but if we must, we must," grumbled Brad. "But first, we are off to see Cindy."

"She might have something for us. I know that we will find some more photos, but we might jog her memory about something her mother knew, or…" Very said over her shoulder as she and Brad hurried out the door.

The drive to Cuyama seemed to take less time than usual. Very and Brad continued the conversation from the evening before. The short, awful, version of their lives had been spoken about the week before. Disappointment, loss, life events that might impact their lives, their relationships or their psyches, had already been given the quick version. But now, they spoke of the funny, the good, the beautiful, the accomplishments, the rosy, the positives. They laughed together, they reveled in the heartening parts of their lives.

Just as they entered the valley, Brad slowed down. On the right side of the road was a small sign that read 'San Luis Obispo County.' Then he pressed swiftly on his brakes and swerved onto the narrow road that had once been paved, but the dust, dirt and detritus of the valley had covered it, making it a road, but only because it was still used by traffic. Very stiffened as they neared the tall iron gate that stood open.

Brad hesitated, looking at the farm house that sat not far past the gate.

"We don't need to do this again," Very said softly.

Brad's head hung and then he lifted it to gaze at the landscape. Very looked around too. The dry rolling hills of the valley to the south lay close here. The morning sun raked over the gentle hills, putting them in sharp relief. They were a soft gray-green color. Everything was dry here. In contrast, the gullies to the north were made by the rain water that would plunge and gouge the rocky hills, digging deeper and deeper as each decade passed. The rain water never stayed long enough to nourish anything green there.

Very looked towards the spot which lay just a few hundred yards away.

Brad mumbled, "She lay there all night and all the next day, face down in the dirt."

Chapter Twenty-one: The Doll with the Red Dress

They stopped at the Buckhorn and bought some doughnuts and two coffees to go. They sat in the truck having their mid-morning snack. Very drank the coffee, but wondered if she was having too much caffeine.

Finally, Very let out a sigh. "I guess we had better see what Cindy has for us."

"No more coffee, though," Brad said.

They drove the two short blocks to Cindy's house. Parking the truck out front, they slowly approached the door.

Before they could knock, Cindy pulled it open. She smiled at them, glad to see them, happy to have them as guests in her house. "I found the box. Come in, let me show you."

Cindy disappeared towards the back of the house, and Very and Brad were left to choose seats for themselves. The couch, with a coffee table directly in front of it, seemed like the obvious place to sit. But Very was aware of the stack of afghans. She sat, sinking and sliding around. When she had stopped moving, she bent over to pick up the top crocheted blanket to look underneath. She marveled at the color and variety of afghans as she discovered each one. She attempted to count them, but lost track at fifteen.

Cindy returned with a box and placed it on the coffee table. Brad was looking at the unsteady seat on the couch and stood aside. Cindy sat next to Very.

"Once again, I admire your output of afghans. Any more thoughts as to what you will do with them?" Very asked.

"Oh, I think your idea is good. Maybe I should go through them, select a few for myself and give away the rest. There are at least thirty on the couch, and more in the cupboard. I just do, I don't think. I just crochet and when I'm finished, I do more. It's a hobby. Better than gambling, isn't it? Or drinking?"

"Yes," agreed Very. "The making is obviously the important thing. Don't stop if it gives you pleasure. And, they are very pretty, beautiful colors and a tremendous variety of patterns. There are many things you can do with them. But maybe, stop stacking them on your couch. It's not easy to sit here!"

Cindy wiggled her backside, digging a hole into the stack. "You're right on that one."

They both bent over the box in front of them. Cindy had obviously wiped it as the streaks of dust and years of grime clung to the sides, if not the top. Very's hands reached out to the box, but then she pulled them back. This was Cindy's box to open.

"Now, this box only has a few things. The boxes with other things, clothes, toys and so forth, were thrown out years ago. Or… So, one day, Mom pulls this series of cardboard boxes out of the back of her closet and asks me if I would to go through them and see if I wanted anything. It was all of AnnaRose's clothes and toys, her personal things. What was I supposed to say to my mother? I was at least ten years old and nothing was going to fit. And besides, even if there was a doll or hat or something like that, I wanted my own, not my dead sister's. I didn't say much, but then she started crying. She had to go over each item. Each dress, each sweater, each doll, each book. There was even her hair brush, with hair still in it. I told her to throw it away. Then she got even sadder. So, I suggested giving to charity or the toy collections at Christmastime. But she had been dead for years and no one wanted dusty, out-of-date clothes from a murdered girl. No one."

"But where are those things? If you didn't give them away, what happened to them?"

"We burned them. We waited until dark and then we went out to the back. You know, everyone had an oil drum they used to burn papers. The garbage cans were small and you burned paper rather than throwing it away. I guess no one does that nowadays, do they?"

"It would pollute the air. I'm sure that if you started burning your old clothes and stuff now, you'd be stopped, fined, or at least admonished. So, you burned everything?" Very asked sadly. She hoped that there wasn't something they could have looked at. They might have found out more about AnnaRose.

"Yeah. Mom said we were sending these things to heaven for her. She said AnnaRose was for sure in heaven, and she could at least see her old things, even if she'd never be able to use them. She talked about AnnaRose. She said she would have liked the bonfire. And we had cocoa. AnnaRose liked cocoa. Mom was sure she would be happy. And ice cream. AnnaRose loved ice cream. But I don't think we had any, just the chocolate." Cindy stopped and looked at the box, the remainder of anything of AnnaRose's.

She reached over and pulled on the lid. Even though it had been cleaned, a puff of dust flew into the room.

"Here, photos, and some papers. Yeah, Mom enrolled her in the church rolls for kids. That's why Mom was sure AnnaRose had gone to heaven. She was just a little kid and she wasn't old enough to sin hard. So, she explained to me that the church would make sure all the little kids would go to heaven if they died young. Mom always knew that AnnaRose was in a safe place. Oh, here is what I was looking for." Cindy held up a small brown covered photo album. The plastic was beginning to disintegrate. And when Cindy pulled on the cover, more flecks of cheap brown plastic fell off into her hands. It protested with squeaks and cracks as she opened the book.

"Baby photos, look," she said, handing the book over so Very could see. There was a photo of a cake with a big candle on it and Eugene Bullitt with his arms around a tiny AnnaRose. Another one was labeled 'First day of school.' AnnaRose had on a frilly dress, starched to a stiffness that must have been uncomfortable. Very shivered at the thought of the prickly underarms and back of the legs. Her hair was combed into numerous ringlets, unnaturally curly. It took a whole night sleeping on plastic curlers to get that look, or maybe an afternoon sitting quietly while Betty Jean put smelly chemicals on the poor kid's head in a home permanent.

"Oh, here I am," Cindy said, pointing out a laughing AnnaRose holding an infant, with eyes scrunched closed.

Very peeked over Cindy's shoulder. "That's about the age when I knew her."

"What was she like?" Cindy asked.

Very stared again at the curly haired first grader. "She was happy, and giggled a lot. She wanted to explore something new every day. She loved to sing, mostly off-key, but we sang nursery rhyme songs. We played cards. I remember trying to teach her 'Go Fish.' It wasn't hard, but she just had so many problems with it. I think she always wanted to win, to have the most cards, so she would cheat. Not in a mean way, just a wanting to say that she won, she was good at something. I tried to teach her how to shuffle. It's hard for little kid's hands to hold a grown-up deck of cards and make them flap into place easily. My dad had taught me, and so I thought it would be fun. She loved it, but in the end, she couldn't maneuver her fingers around the deck, so she just threw them in the air. She screamed, 'I shuffled them.' And then she laughed. She loved to laugh. She also wanted to grow up fast. She wanted to wander off by herself. That's one of the reasons I think your mom wanted me there, to rein her in, or at least to accompany her on her meanderings. She was always sneaking off to the store by herself. My mom let me do that, go by myself to the store. She said that everyone in Cuyama knew me and so I couldn't get lost. She'd give me a dime and tell me to take the sidewalk and be careful crossing the street. And so AnnaRose would want that too."

Very sat back and closed her eyes. "We went a lot of places together. Your mom trusted my mom. And maybe I knew that I was trusted because I was older. It gave me a sense of accomplishment, of maturity. My god, no mother would ever let their kids do what we did then. Nowadays, you'd never let a six-year-old, even an eight-year-old, out of your sight. What freedom we had." Very hung her head. Her words hung in the air. What was freedom, and what was danger? Would a mother ever choose self-determination for her young one if it meant putting that child in the way of peril, in the path of a murderer?

Cindy said softly, "So, you think it's possible she got out by herself?"

"That door to the back, that walkway between the houses, sure it's possible. And another thing. I taught her to do it. But you know," she turned to Brad. "The statement that Betty Jean had checked on AnnaRose about eleven or so? Well, it might have been a dummy made up in the bed, and not AnnaRose herself. I did that one day, showed her how you could get a blanket and an extra pillow, and make a fake body in your bed. It was probably dark in the bedroom, with the curtains pulled and if Betty Jean was in a hurry, she might have just glanced in briefly, saw a lump in the bed, and left. Her little girl was tucked up in bed, feeling sick."

"But this is a small town," Cindy said. "And you said it yourself. Everybody knew everybody else, and everybody else's kids."

Cindy bent to the box and pulled out another photo. "This is the one I was looking for. She was holding her doll with the red dress. See, my mom took a colored pencil to it, because it's a black and white photo, and she made it look red."

Very put her hand out and Cindy handed her the photo. It had been taken in a photo studio and AnnaRose was sitting in a small chair. She held a medium-sized doll with a flouncy dress. Very could believe it was red.

"Mom said that she took it everywhere with her; that it was her all-time favorite."

"What happened to the doll?"

"Maybe she was buried with it. I don't ever remember seeing it myself. Maybe we burned it that day, in the bonfire of the past. But I don't recall it at all. I don't ever think I saw it in the flesh or in reality. Just this photo. Or yeah, here is another one."

The second photo that Cindy showed Very was a candid shot, taken with the same Brownie that some of the others were taken with. She could see that the doll was the same, with the same dress. This time, the dress looked more worn and AnnaRose held the much beloved toy by an arm.

"I don't remember that doll at all," Very said. "She must have gotten it after I left. I am sure I would have had a clear memory of such a beloved dolly."

Cindy and Very looked at Brad, the one who had seen, who had investigated, who would have known. "Was it in the files? The cold case files? Was there any mention of it?" Very asked.

Brad leaned over to look at the two photos. "No, I've never seen that, I've never seen these photos and I'm sure I would have recalled seeing a doll like this. We can certainly look at the notes, see if anyone else noted a doll."

"She must have had it that day," Cindy said. "The way Mom talked about it, she wouldn't have gone anywhere without it. Like it was attached to her. Wow, I remember Mom looking at this photo and saying that it got wet one day when AnnaRose refused to take a bath without it. She wouldn't have run off and left her 'baby' at home."

"What happened to it?" Very asked.

Brad looked at Cindy.

Cindy's eyes opened wide. "You mean, it went missing with her?"

"And never found," Brad concluded.

Chapter Twenty-two: A Visit to Cuyama High School

They continued looking at photos, but there were few that were new, or could give them any more information. Cindy offered to make some lunch, but Brad and Very declined.

At the Buckhorn's café, they ate sandwiches and looked at the hills out of the plate glass window. They quietly discussed the morning. Nothing new seemed to have been learned, except for the doll. But as that had been missing for over fifty years, it didn't seem relevant to the ongoing investigation.

Very looked at her sandwich. "It was good seeing the doll. I could imagine her loving that toy to death, she was like that. Loyal and intense. But actually finding the doll would have been nice. Her DNA would have been all over it. I guess we have the tooth for that. What else could the doll have told us?"

"Missing," Brad said. "That's what it would have told us. And it seems as though she had it when she went missing. First of all, she was reputedly attached to it, very attached. And secondly, it didn't show up at the crime scene or, if Cindy remembers rightly, at the house, with the rest of her possessions."

"Can we find it?" Very asked.

Brad shook his head. "It's like a needle in a haystack. After all these years? Most likely got thrown away by someone years ago. Given away by Betty Jean after AnnaRose was gone? Given to charity or some other child?"

"Oh no, I'm sure it wasn't. Remember what Cindy said about the boxes of clothes they burned? I'm sure Betty Jean had saved those things because they were AnnaRose's. It makes sense that she wouldn't have given away a favorite doll. Maybe burned with the rest of the clothes and things, but not given away. Do we know where it came from? Mother, Santa Claus, grandma?"

Brad sat musing. How could that question be answered? They had only a few hints about the doll, and two photos, one staged and one candid. AnnaRose and a doll with a bright red dress.

Very spoke, "What else do we have?"

"The Kentons."

"Really, you are barking up that tree again? I thought that had been settled. Mickey was eliminated because he was too young, and besides, he was at school."

"Not a good alibi," Brad grumbled. "I guess you are right, though. But what about the father, Raymond?"

"I thought that was a watertight alibi?"

"I checked that one out myself. I was able to access the personnel records of the oil company. As far as we could figure out, he was where he said he was. And there was also corroboration from his fellow workers."

"How long does it take to drive to Sisquoc Street, pick her up and take her to the place…"

"Listen Very. He drove to work with friends, he didn't have his own car that day. They could all have been lying. It's hard to tell."

"So, what are we going to do next?"

"See if Mickey Kenton was at school, like he said he was."

"And we can find out, how?"

"Check the school records."

"Really, check attendance records that are over 50 years old?"

Brad stood, "Don't worry, I've got this." He pulled out his wallet and extracted a credit card.

While he paid, Very wandered into the bar. It felt naughty to be in the bar, the grown-ups' place. The wall was covered with heads of bucks, their fabulous racks of horns reaching to the ceiling. There wasn't just one, but a dozen. They were all majestic specimens of the local deer, and had been preserved in magnificent, elegant poses. Representatives of the Buckhorn. Very tried to recall if they had been hanging on this wall all these years. She couldn't picture them in her mind. There had probably been some of them, years ago. She peered closely and noticed thin strands of spider webs and dust accumulation along the horns. A bitch of a place to clean.

She wandered out the door to the patio. It was a lovely space, but now the cement covered the place where the pool had been. It was a tiny place; how could they have had a pool here? How could they teach kids to swim in the tiny pond? But she and all the other kids had taken lessons here and had managed to master the basics. She sat in one of the lounge chairs that had been placed under an olive tree. The thin shade threw fluttery shadows on her legs. She sat, lost in thought. Reflections about the past, about her time in Cuyama, her life as she saw it, as she relived it by being here now.

Brad appeared at her side and slipped into the chair next to hers. "Thinking about your past?"

"How did you know?" Very asked.

"I would too, if I went back to a place I grew up in, but had avoided for years." He sighed. "The sky here is so blue, so clear and clean."

"Usually, but when the wind blows, it can be nasty. My mother always complained about the wind, and the dust. With the agriculture that has come in the last few years, it might not be as dirty, but I doubt it. I think it's the weather patterns here that make the wind. And the soil that is like soft flour. It covers everything with a fine layer of pale tan color. And carries the spores that give you Valley Fever. My neighbor missed out on the last three months of fourth grade because he had to stay in bed. Nasty stuff. And it comes to us on the breeze. But when the wind isn't blowing… Maybe I could retire here."

"I thought you liked your pool, and your clubhouse and…"

"And my newly renovated hot tub. You are right, I like where I am. But it is beautiful here."

They got into Brad's truck and drove a mile to Cuyama High School. They pulled into the school, past the elegant sign that indicated their destination and Brad parked near the office.

"They built this when I lived here. Remember I said I learned how to swim in the Buckhorn pool? But by the time we left, I was swimming here. They built a huge pool, for competition, and a diving pool as well."

They stepped out of the truck. The parking lot was mostly deserted except for five cars parked altogether near the front office. The administration building was obvious. Low, one story buildings spread around, all connected by covered walkways. Picnic tables were strewn about on the edges of the walkways.

"It's summer vacation. And all of this is a ghost town. I doubt if there were ever a hundred students in this school. I remember when I was in high school in Bakersfield and I thought about what it would have been like if I had stayed here. So small, so intimate. There was at least one fatal car accident a year involving high school students. There is nothing to do here, so the kids would get a car and go off to Taft to find entertainment. Mostly of the alcoholic kind. And then they'd drive home. That road, the curves and then add wet surfaces or worse, ice. The kids would either die on that road, or drop out."

"More than other places?" Brad asked.

"Nothing to do in Cuyama. The boys got the girls pregnant, and then they'd have to drop out, get married, get a job. Or get in trouble with the law. Oh, I'm not saying all of them did that, but it is hard to finish school when your classmates aren't there with you."

"So, what you're saying is that the idyllic valley wasn't such a paradise after all?"

"It never was, never. The wind was bad, but the water was worse." A shiver took hold of Very and she shuddered. "Just thinking of it makes me queasy. So many minerals in it that it's impossible to get them out. Boiling, letting it sit, sending it through a water softener, none of those things work."

"What do people do, drink bottled water?"

"Yeah, the water company sent a truck with big containers of water. They would come into the house and change them for my mother on the stand that the company provided. It was the only way that you could have a glass of water to drink. My mother used it even for making coffee and boiling pasta. If someone, a guest, tried to run the kitchen tap and get a glass of water, my mother would screech and take it out of their hands. I thought it weird that when we moved to Bakersfield, it was okay to drink out of the tap. But then, I don't do that anymore. Filtered water for me."

They headed into the office. A woman sat behind the front desk. Startled, she looked up. "Hello, how can I help you?"

Brad explained that they wanted to see the attendance records having to do with a cold case they were working on, from fifty years before. The woman's eyes went wide. "AnnaRose Bullitt?" she asked.

"You were here," Very said.

"No, but I was told about it. It's a legend around here." Her voice dropped to a conspiratorial whisper. "You know that Cindy Bullitt still lives here? The sister."

"Yes, we know that. We have permission to do this investigation, we have papers." Brad offered.

"No, I believe you. You look honest. So, what day is it that you want to check?" she asked.

Brad and Very looked at her.

"Oh, that day, gotcha. You are in luck. We have all the records like that of the school, going back to the founding. The only problem is, you have to dig a bit. And you'll have to do it yourself, I'm busy here. But, if you follow me, I'll show you where they all are." She stood and motioned them to follow her.

They followed the woman down a short, narrow, corridor, deep into the building. They passed a door that said 'Principal' and another that said, 'Teacher's Room.' Very slowed down and peeked in. Although there was room for many desks, only six were set out. And of those, only four looked occupied.

At the end of the hallway, they exited and then immediately the clerk took out a set of keys and unlocked another door. A janitor's room with supplies packed to the ceiling greeted them. Yet another door opened into a stuffy room with shelving.

Very sneezed. And then again. "Oh, sorry, the dust."

"No, I'm sorry. We only open this room a few times a year, to add more to the stacks. So, I don't even know who is responsible for the dust, getting rid of it, I mean. But then again, how do you do that? Anyway, we are lucky we are a small school." She waved her hand around the shelves. "Everything is here. And it's all labeled. I would ask you to just pull the door closed when you leave."

She left them, standing amidst the history of the sixty-year-old school, sorted, lined up and labeled.

"What are we really looking for?" Very asked. Overwhelming was a word that barely described the overpowering intensity of the mini Hall of Records.

"The day of and maybe the day before and afterwards, or maybe better, make that two days. We are looking for Mickey Kenton's attendance and possibly notes of punishment for wrongdoing? Anything around that time."

"Any other names we need to look for?" Very began scanning the shelves.

"We don't have any others, so at the moment, no. But do look for someone else who may have been absent with him?"

Very was picking her way down the aisle, checking the boxes, trying to discern the filing system. It appeared that it was in order by year, but that previous decades had been shoved to the back of the topmost shelves. Finally, she yelled, "Found it."

The box had a label that was beginning to peel off, but clearly indicated the year. Inside were folders. The light coming from overhead was too dim, so Very carried the box to the door where there was light.

Brad spied a folding chair and reached for it. He laughed. "I haven't seen one of these forever! It's so out of date, like from an ancient church hall." He opened the tiny chair made from wooden slats. It wobbled. Very stared and then carefully lowered the box. The seat was in the 'spill' position and Very used her leg to keep the whole box and folders on the seat. "Will it hold that box?"

"I'll catch it if it slips," Very said, opening the top. She extracted a few folders and checked the dates. She found the semester and pulled out a folder marked 'Grades.' She let the box gently down onto the floor, while she sifted through the folder. There were carbon copies of grades from all the students, all the classes. She checked for 'Michael Kenton' and glanced at his grades, C+, C-, D+. Not exactly a model student.

In the meantime, Brad had been screening and inspecting the other folders. "Attendance records here, I guess for the semester. It seems like a lot." He pulled out a stack.

They consisted of the teachers' handwritten day-to-day attendance records. At the top was the class and the period. Along the left side were the names, neatly printed by each teacher. They were in alphabetical order with additions to the class written at the bottom of the list. To the left were blocks of dates to be filled in with checks or zeros and an occasional 'E' for excused. "What was the date we were looking for?"

They looked at a few more files until they found the exact semester. Brad commandeered the file and tried to figure out the system. "What's this? And this?" he asked pointing to the headings.

"Okay, here is 'HR' and then they are divided up into F, S, J and Se." Very took the file and began flipping through pages.

"HR," Brad whined. "What does Human Resources have to do with it?"

"Home Room, silly. Okay, here is HR, F for kids in the semester. Now, what is the date?" Very began with finding Michael Kenton, then ran her finger over to the correct date. "A check for that date, and the day before and the day after. So, we know he made it to school."

"That's it, then, he was here. Are we sure those records are accurate?" Brad looked over Very's shoulder.

"We can be fairly certain these are correct. They would have been done by the teacher in the classroom, and he or she would be accurate. If a student came in late, they would have gone back and amended the record. It's what teachers do. But this is only for Home Room. Here are all the rest." Very took the folder and began to look for the other records.

The HR records were on top for the semester, but the others were scattered and Very had to check the top of every form. And she had to check if Mickey's name was on the list. "This is so much easier than checking records for a high school of a thousand students. Can you imagine trying to find one kid's name among all those names? There are only about eighty or ninety names all together. Okay, here we go. Mr. Smith. Math 1P. There are ten students on this list and here is Michael." She ran her hand across the sheet, looking for the day. "Here, a check mark."

"What are we looking at here? When is this?"

"First period, so about nine to ten or maybe eight-thirty to nine-twenty? Not sure. But he was here. He was in Home Room and now in first period. But let's look further." Very shuffled the papers until she found the stack for 2P. She looked through all of them. "I can't find his name anywhere. None of these classes have him as being enrolled. Oh, maybe Study Hall?" She looked again. "I can't find anything that indicates a Study Hall period. Even if they were assigned that, they should have taken attendance." She looked some more.

"Third period," Brad suggested.

Very found the stack of records that had 3P at the top. She searched for Mickey's name and found it. Running her finger over to the date, she stopped. "Third period, and Mickey has a '0'. He wasn't there."

Brad grabbed a batch that indicated 4P. "Check these," he said. He looked for 5P.

Very quickly found the English class that Mickey was enrolled in for fourth period. She carefully ran her finger over the dates. '0' for fourth period. "Not here, how about fifth period?"

Brad was running his finger over dates on another old, yellowed and delicate file. "Fifth period, History. Mr. Smith, again. I guess all the teachers here had to do double or triple duty. 'Michel Kenton' and again '0'."

"Sixth period, the same. '0' for Michael Kenton. Our innocent fourteen-year-old has no alibi. He came to school and sometime after first period, middle of the morning, he disappeared. And didn't return." Very stated.

"Where was he?" Brad asked.

Chapter Twenty-three: Mickey Kenton Comes Clean

Brad and Very drove back to Bakersfield with little communication. Brad turned on the radio and they listened to country music for a while. Very turned the volume down, but let it play. Country music defined the Southern San Joaquin. Bakersfield had been called 'Nashville West' back in the day. So, let the music play. If Brad wanted to listen, then Very could tolerate it.

When they arrived at the office, it was empty. Very called Darrell and found out they got hungry and went to Bill Lee's Bamboo Chopsticks. Very checked with Brad and then asked Darrell to pick up some Sweet and Sour Pork and Spicy Chicken and rice. The sandwich at the Buckhorn seemed hours ago.

Brad sat at the computer and started a new document. He reported on the visit with Cindy and mentioned the red dress. He transferred the photos he had taken of Cindy's two pictures of AnnaRose with the doll and included them in the document. Then he opened a new document and started on Michael Kenton.

"Just because he wasn't there at school doesn't mean he had anything to do with AnnaRose and her death," Very said.

"I know, but it's important to get all of this down."

"Remember, he couldn't drive and besides, he didn't have a car. What does all of this tell us, in the end." Very protested.

"It tells us he lied. If he lied about this, what else did he lie about? What untruths are still out there?"

"He was at school the next day. We checked on that, remember?"

Brad scowled. "He needs to come clean. He must tell us the truth, no more hiding."

Darrell and Olivia burst in the door, and all were enveloped by the smell of Chinese food.

"We had the rest of ours packed up to go as well as yours, so we have lots to choose from," Darrell said.

Olivia ducked under a desk and reappeared with plates and fresh chopsticks. She handed them around. Brad's dubious look was met with a burst of laughter. "If you want to know how to use them, check with Very; she's the master of chopsticks."

Brad grabbed a pair and with dignity fitted them to his right hand. "I'll manage."

Brad and Very filled in the newcomers on their investigations of the morning. Darrell repeated the same arguments that had already come up about Mickey. The fact that even if he had lied about being at school, it didn't mean that everything else he said was untrue as well.

Olivia burst out, "Once a liar, always a liar. I agree with Brad. Not that he told lies about everything, but how can we manage to distinguish between truth and fiction? He's out to cover his tracks, so what else has he not told us, or told us with devious intent?"

"I agree. But this kidnap and murder, doesn't seem like him. Somehow it is out of character." Very sat tapping her chopsticks.

"Do we even know his character?" Darrell asked.

"Could it be the unknown person?" Olivia said, pointing to the blank page on the board.

Very sighed. "What about DNA? How are we progressing on that?"

Brad's phone rang and he answered it.

Very continued, "What about Santa Barbara County? Have we gotten any answer from them, about having evidence that we might not have?"

Brad continued talking on the phone; Darrell and Olivia had finished their lunch and turned to their computers.

Very sighed. She waved goodbye as she headed out the door. They didn't want to answer her questions, they all had their own concerns and lines of inquiry. Darrell and Olivia were being close-mouthed about what they were working on, maybe a new case. No one cared about the fact that she had changed her plans to involve herself in this case. They had turned their backs on her.

Mickey Kenton needed to answer for his lies. He and his dad were both still suspects, especially Mickey, or maybe both together. There were questions she or someone needed to ask. She would do it. She got into her car and headed to Taft.

When she was growing up, there was nothing out this way. Everything west of Oak Street was country. In the southwest, Larson's Dairy, a real dairy with cows, and who delivered milk to their house, was the end of 'civilization'. The rest wasn't even farmland, but scrub. Now, Bakersfield had sprawled. The land had become saturated with huge dairies that duplicated the smells of the smaller Larson's, and orchards. Pistachio, almonds, and citrus in straight rows marched up and down the former salty desert. Progress had come to the west lands of Kern County. Before, the citizens had desert and further west, oil. Now they had jobs, food was being produced and the rich men who lived in Beverly Hills were getting richer.

Very drove into Taft and immediately felt stupid. She had been to the Kenton house, but Brad had been driving. She drove around town, passed the college, a landmark she remembered. Then, she passed the street, also with a name she remembered. Now, what was the house number?

She pulled over to the side of the road and dialed Brad.

"Hey, Very! Did you go home early? You never even said goodbye." Brad said.

"Yeah, yeah. Hey, what was the street number of the Kenton's house?"

She listened to Brad flipping pages. So, he had forgotten, too. Old age does that. Then he rattled off a number.

"Thanks," Very replied.

"What…?"

Very hung up. Repeating the number so she wouldn't forget, Very glided slowly down the street, checking houses in each block. There, there it was, just as she remembered it. They were tract homes, all looked alike, but each seemed to have a different combination of trees and bushes. Some had spacious lawns, dog runs in the backyard, and some had multiple garages or outbuildings. Some had all three.

She parked in front of the house next door and got out. A stiff breeze came up suddenly and blew dust into her face. "Yuck," she said. She wiped her eyes and then took a deep breath. As she walked slowly up the front walk, another gust of air caused her to turn and close her eyes again. She listened. Was that a front door lock twitching? She stopped and pinched her eyes shut in an attempt to clear her eyes of the dust.

Wow, wouldn't it have been better to call first? Find out if this was a good time to come by? She hesitated on the front stoop and waited, then rang.

The door was pulled open and a shout emerged, "You're late, you were supposed to be here at one."

Through the screen door, Very saw an angry Mickey Kenton. He pushed out the door, causing Very to step back and down onto the walkway. "Oh, it's you," he said, huffing his disgust.

Very stood outside, waiting for an explanation, an apology, or perhaps more of an acknowledgement than 'you.'

"I thought you were that nurse woman. She was supposed to help with my dad. And she didn't come." Mickey said.

"Oh, I can help if you'd like," Very said hesitantly. Changing diapers and bedding was not out of her experience, but would Ray Kenton appreciate the substitute nurse? "I did all that kind of stuff when my mother was…"

"Dying? Yeah, the old man is dying." Mickey held the door open for Very to enter.

The smell of unchanged diaper filled the room. Very opened her mouth and began to breathe shallowly.

"The stuff's all here," he said, leading the way into the bedroom, pointing to stacks of diapers, plastic bags, lotions, boxes of plastic gloves and fresh sheets and pillowcases.

Very bent to the emaciated figure in the bed. "Hi, we're here now. We'll get this cleaned up." She took his hand and stroked it gently.

She looked up at Mickey, and saw the aged man, not the fourteen-year-old whose records they had checked. "I am assuming you know how to do this? It's so much easier and faster together."

Mickey grunted and took directions from Very, but it was obvious that he had done this before. Together they changed the old man, giving him a quick sponge bath and changed the bedding. Very put the disposable things into a plastic bag and asked, "Where does this go?"

"Outside in the big garbage can. Through the kitchen." He jerked his head in the direction of the back of the house.

Very followed the direction of the head jerk and found herself in a kitchen, a bachelor's kitchen. Not unclean, but not as tidy, nor the surfaces as clean, as she would have wanted. She went out the back door and spied the garbage can. It was almost full of similar plastic bags. Hope that the collection was soon, and not delayed by holidays or forgetfulness of putting the can by the curb. She shoved her bag into the can.

She surveyed the back yard. A few fruit trees, in need of pruning, and a sad, un-watered lawn. Most of the yard was taken up by two Quonset huts put together. Cars, Very guessed. Room to store and work on. Classic cars, old cars, favorite cars, many cars. The front door was closed, but Very gave a quick measure and thought it might hold at least six cars, or four with a work area.

She went back inside, and used the kitchen sink to give her hands a very thorough wash. When she reentered the living room, she found the door to the front bedroom closed. Mickey sat on the couch and indicated the lounge chair beside it. "Wanna beer?"

Very declined, but Mickey got himself one from the fridge. He popped it and took a long guzzle. "Thanks. I mean it."

"I take it your father has gotten worse in the last few days?"

"Yeah, the hospital bed, the commode, the stack of diapers. All delivered on Friday. Someone came every day, but today, no one. I'm supposed to do this all alone?"

"No one should have to do this all alone."

"I've spent the last fifteen years on this old man. At first it wasn't so bad. He was able to do a lot for himself. But more and more, he has just given up, can't do anything on his own anymore. It's time for him to go." Mickey took another long drink of his beer. "You sure you don't want anything, water maybe?"

"Water would be fine."

"Taft water isn't very good, but it's drinkable, just barely." He went to the kitchen.

Very could hear the tap filling a glass. Maybe she could sip at it, she didn't have to drink it all.

Mickey sat with his beer, slowly sipping, as did Very.

"We checked attendance records at Cuyama High School," Very said.

Mickey looked up, startled. "What? You checked what?"

"You weren't there that day, not past first period."

"You checked records? How did you do that?"

"The school kept everything."

"I got sick," Mickey said. "I went home early."

"It didn't say 'E' for excused, the records, all of them, said '0' for not there."

Mickey face hardened, even as noises came from the bedroom. "Oh, shut up, Old Man."

"You'd better go and take care of whatever he needs."

With a stubborn face, Mickey got up and went into the bedroom. He didn't close the door. Very heard water being poured into a glass, and soothing murmurs.

Mickey returned and sat heavily. He picked up his beer and threw a deep gurgle down his throat. "Okay, you got me. I met my friend, outside the school. He was supposed to be at work or something, but instead he had come to school. He saw me going back to class after I went to the bathroom and whistled at me. I was alone and I don't know that anyone else saw us. Anyway, he got me to come around the corner of the building and sweet-talked me into going with him. I was bored with school, didn't know why I was there other than it was expected of me. He said he had beer. Stupid kid. I said yes. We walked back to my house. He had two bottles in a bag. We drank and then he said he wanted more. And he wanted to go driving. So, we, he, got the keys to my dad's car. We stopped by his house, got more beer and he drove out towards Aliso Canyon. We drove off the road and sat there and drank some more. Then he said we needed some food, lunch. But I wanted to go back to school. I wasn't happy. Anyway, we headed back to town and he drove into the driveway and let me out. I went into the house and immediately got sick. I was feeling really bad by then. It was too late to go back to school."

"What time was this? In the afternoon?"

"I was sick, I'd never had beer before. I'd seen my dad and other grown-ups drinking it and they could drink a lot." Mickey looked at the can of beer in front of him. He set it back down on the coffee table, joining Very's glass of tap water.

"What did you do after getting sick?"

"Gosh, it was awful. I hate vomiting. Anyway, after I got sick, I went to bed. I fell asleep. I wasn't feeling all that well in the morning, but there was no arguing with my dad about going to school."

"What time?" Very pressed.

"When I woke up, all hell had broken loose. Everyone was outside in the street, looking for AnnaRose. And I lied to my dad about school, didn't say anything about the beer, the car, the friend. I lied. And then, after that, it was just repeating that lie. If you say it enough, it becomes true, or at least in your mind."

"Your dad said something about the car." Very said.

Before she could continue, there was a pounding on the front door.

"Oh, your home help is finally here. I'll get it."

Very rose and headed for the door as the banging continued.

"I'm coming, hold your horses!" she said.

She jerked open the door and was about to push open the screen door, when she saw something.

The late afternoon sun shone in her eyes and she couldn't see who was on the front step. She blinked and put her hand up to shade her eyes, when she realized a small black hole was pointing directly at her.

It wasn't a large black hole, not a cannon, or even a big weapon, but a gun.

It pointed directly at her forehead.

She shook. She opened her mouth and tried to say something.

She looked at the large strong hands that held the lethal weapon.

And just over the top of the gun, she saw the white Stetson.

Chapter Twenty-four: The Car

Very's mouth fell open, but she was frozen at the sight of the gun.

"Is he here? Did he hurt you?" Brad's voice came out sharp and gravelly.

Behind the gun, still pointed at her forehead, she noticed another figure, also holding a gun, this one much smaller than the old-fashioned six-shooter Brad held.

"Darrell, what are you doing?" Very asked. "I hope that isn't loaded or cocked and that we will not have any gun battles today."

Darrell lowered his weapon, but Brad kept his at the ready. However, he deflected the trajectory to the side, not at Very's head.

"What are you doing here?" she asked again.

Mickey appeared at Very's shoulder and took in the situation. "You might as well come in." He snorted at the two would-be assassins.

"What's this all about?" Very asked again.

Darrell inched forward. "We couldn't find you. And we…"

"We checked this one's background," Brad nodded at Mickey.

Mickey stepped back, eyeing Brad's gun which was still being held at the ready. "That was a long time ago. What do you expect of me now?" He threw out his hands.

Very looked back at him. Thinning gray hair, his clothes hung loosely on his frame as if he had recently lost weight. Unshaved, rheumy eyes. Not in the pink of health, physically or mentally. "You didn't need to rescue me," she pointed her remarks at Brad.

"We were concerned," Brad said. "I tried to call you back. Why did you need this address?"

Very was silent.

"You should have waited." Brad leaned forward, concern on his face.

"Come in, all of you," Mickey said, holding the door open.

They silently began to enter the house.

"Beer anyone?" Mickey asked.

Brad shook his head and mumbled, "No, thanks."

Mickey muttered to himself, "Downfall, the booze."

As they gathered in the living room, Very turned to Mickey, "Do you have ice?"

"Yeah, yeah, in the freezer."

Very headed to the kitchen with her glass.

The three men stood in a small triangle and waited for Very. She soon came back with a tray full of glasses of ice and water. "We all need to cool off."

They all took a glass and sat down. They sipped. The silence was only broken by the clinking of ice.

Finally, Brad turned to Very, "So what did he say?" He nodded towards Mickey.

With sidelong looks at Mickey, to make sure she got the story straight, she retold Brad and Darrell about the day at school, meeting a friend, going out to drink beer, getting sick, falling asleep and then lying about it for the last fifty plus years. "Is that about it?" she concluded, asking Mickey.

"Yeah, that's about it. I would've told the truth, but I lied to my dad. I told him some story about getting sick and walking home from school, so I thought it best to just stick with it."

"Even to the police?" Darrell asked.

"I think I feared my dad more than the police. They wouldn't have beat me, my dad would have."

Brad sipped at his water, "Your dad said something about the car."

"Yes, he did. He knew something was wrong. He could tell that the car had been gone. He got mad at me. I told him I was just trying out the car. Just trying to drive it, just in the driveway. But he knew. Maybe he looked at the odometer. But I just kept lying. You see, he always parked it in the garage, but with the garage door open. When we got back, the car was in the driveway. I knew he was going to get mad at me for even moving the car. Think what he would have done if he knew that Wayne had driven the car."

This statement was met with silence.

Mickey started muttering again. "Stupid old man. He never wanted to get rid of the car. He drove it for years, but then he parked it. Wouldn't let me drive it, or even sell it. Even when it got too old, we could have gotten money for parts. Parked and rusting."

"Is it still parked and rusting?" Very asked.

"Yeah, you wanna see it? Wanna ask it some questions? What kind of stories would it tell you?" Mickey looked at Very with disdain.

"Well, I guess we don't need to see it, exactly." Very said quietly.

"No, you are going to see it. I want you to see it. I want you to see what I have been putting up with for years. The car. The old beat-up car."

Mickey jumped up, spilling his glass of water down the front of his shirt. He let out an expletive and Very flinched. Had a record, Brad said. She felt a creeping band of cold sweat break out on her back which leaned against the couch back. She stood, careful not to spill her water. "Okay, we'll see the car," Very said softly.

Mickey strode into the kitchen and the three detectives followed him. He reached up to a cabinet and flung it open. A tinkling sound emanated from the door. On the back were about fifteen hooks, all loaded with multiple rings of keys. Some were rusted, some were so old-fashioned that Very doubted they would open any lock anymore. None had labels on them.

Mickey reached up and pulled a ring of keys off. He looked at them. Then he took another set of keys, and then another. "It's got to be one of these, to the door. And do you want to drive the car, I've probably got that key too. He never threw away anything. He would never have thrown away that key."

"What kind of car is it?" Brad asked.

"A Ford, Ford Fairlane." Came the answer.

Brad leaned forward. "This key," he pulled one off a hook, "says 'Ford' on the key chain. Could this be it?" He held it out to Mickey to look at.

Mickey shrugged. "Maybe." He looked at the key bank and then slammed it shut, with a jingle chasing the sound of the cupboard door closing.

Mickey led them out to the back yard. The view of the long Quonset hut drew a whistle from Brad and a long inhale from Darrell. Mickey went to a small door in the side of the building that Very had missed before. He poked one key into the padlock, then another. Finally, one slipped into the hole, but resisted turning. He tried another, this one turning halfway. He thrust and pushed again and again, each time, the key went a bit farther than before. Finally, with a 'click' the padlock opened. He jerked the padlock off the door, banging his fingers in the process. "Damnit!"

He gingerly pushed the door and it squealed in protest as it opened. They peered inside, but it was too dark to make out anything but lumps and distorted shapes. Mickey put his hand inside and fumbled for a switch. He clicked it on, and a few sad lights lit up the interior. Very noticed a window next to the door, but it was so encrusted with dust and cobwebs, that little light could get into the interior.

Mickey entered and the other three followed. Mickey stumbled on something, a tool, a box, or maybe his own feet as he moved further into the large space. Old lawnmowers, stacks of hand tools and chain link fence pieces littered one section.

"It's back here," Mickey said, carefully maneuvering through the detritus. Very deferred to the men, but made sure to prop the door open to let more light in.

At one point, Mickey moved to the wall and felt around. Soon, an overhead light blinked on. And continued to blink. They needed to be quick, before it all went bad, all the lights went out and they were left in the dark.

Mickey led the way towards the darkest end of the hut and then stopped. Brad took out his phone and turned on the flashlight. They squeezed in beside Mickey as he stood before the car.

Brad whispered, "1956 Ford Fairlane sedan. Two toned."

Very stood close to Brad and asked, "How do you know?"

"You see the 'V' shaped chrome along the side. Two tones, one above, one below the chrome stripe. Blue and a darker color, with tones of green in it. Dusty, but you can still see it. Classic."

Mickey nodded and said, "Here it is. The car. Now ask your questions."

Brad asked, "Does it run?"

"I don't know, I shouldn't think so. I helped the old man push it in here. He said he was going to get the battery going. But he never did. It's been sitting here for, gosh, thirty, forty or maybe even forty-five years. I don't remember. When he's gone, do you think I could sell it for something?"

"It's a Classic Car," Darrell said. "Sure, maybe worth a bit."

"Why did he just park and leave it?" Very asked.

"He was upset. My mother had just died. I asked him then if they were divorced. He said he couldn't remember, papers or something. He hadn't seen her for years, so why that would upset him, I don't know. She didn't have any money, so he wasn't going to get anything. Why would he be upset then, I don't get it."

"Maybe they were together when he bought it? Maybe it had some memories or carried meaning from the past? Maybe connotations of…better times?" Very tried to construct a story that she herself didn't believe in.

Brad moved forward and opened the driver's door. It squealed and protested, but eventually gave way. He bent over and looked inside. Then he slid into the driver's seat, reaching his hands up to grip the steering wheel. He looked over at the glove compartment and reached to open it. It clicked open on the first try, flopping forward. Brad reached his hand into the dark interior. He pulled out a sheaf of papers. A few crumpled in his hand, old insurance papers, receipts for service.

Paper that was never meant to be kept in a glove compartment for forty or fifty years.

He reached again and this time was rewarded with a yellowed plastic sleeve. It was discolored on the top, but it could be easily read. "How to Operate your Ford Fairlane."

Very looked over his shoulder. "The dry air mummifies everything."

"Luckily for us. We could probably read these papers if we needed. Here," Brad said to Very, "take them. Carefully."

"Fingerprints?" Very asked.

"Not likely, but there may be something there." Brad slid out of the seat, gently closing the door with a 'clunk'.

He peered through the back window into the back seat. He tried to clean it with his hand, then snorted. "Too much dust." He then went around to the passenger side and opened the door. This time the door protested more vehemently and refused to open all the way. He again used his phone to light the interior.

"Empty, but something's wrong here." Brad began to pull on the back seat.

"What are you doing?" Very asked.

"What's wrong?" Mickey said, trying to peer over Brad's shoulder into the back.

"The seat isn't flat," Brad said, "it's been pulled up at some point."

"What, what are you doing?" Mickey said, trying to get into the back seat.

Brad took two hands and reached into the space between the seat and the back. He gripped the seat and pulled.

A cloud of dust spurted up as the seat bent and came up slightly. Brad reached into the breach. Then he sputtered and blew out dust. He sneezed.

He backed up, bumping into Very and Mickey who had crowded in behind him, trying to watch the messy operation. He brought the object out that had been stuffed down the back seat.

Brad held it up so all could see it.

Very looked at the dusty thing. She could barely make out the red faded fluffs of fabric, and the small arm that hung limply, hanging only by a thin string or wire.

"The doll. AnnaRose's doll," she squeaked.

Chapter Twenty-five: The Doll with the Red Dress II

Mickey stepped forward and reached for the doll. Brad pulled it out of his reach. "Don't touch," Brad said sternly. He held it by one edge, by the frilly red lacy dress edge.

"Where was this? I don't get it. This is AnnaRose's doll. What? Where?" said Mickey.

Brad looked at him sternly, "In the seat, stuffed down in the back seat."

Mickey fell back, confusion causing him to lose his balance as he gripped the side of the car to stay upright.

Brad turned to Mickey. "Yes, AnnaRose's doll. It went missing the same day she did. Now, the big question, how did it get here?"

"I don't understand. How did it get here? This is my dad's car. He didn't want me to drive it ever. I never did. When we pushed it in here, he hid the keys, well, he didn't let me know those were the keys. In fact, are they the keys? This car wasn't locked. Are you sure those are the keys? I mean, my dad had a series of Fords. That set could belong to any of his cars. When I asked about this car, he just told me to go get my own car. This was his. He even gave me some money to help buy a car. But this was years later. This had nothing to do with AnnaRose.

We lived in Cuyama then. It was later, when we moved here. Why, how?"

"Lots of questions," Brad said. "No answers."

"That old man," Mickey said. "It was stuffed into the seat of his car."

Very watched Mickey's face turn red, then saw it pale, and she could almost hear the brain wheels turning in his head.

"That old man, he needs to start giving some answers. He's been hiding this, all these years. Hiding this car and hiding this, this, little doll. Why? What's he doing with it?" Mickey turned and pushed his way out of the garage and stomped towards the house.

Brad turned to Darrell, handing him the doll by the edge, and whispered something about 'evidence' and 'bag it.'

Brad and Very followed Mickey into the house, leaving the car door and the garage door open.

When they entered the kitchen, they could hear shouts coming from the bedroom. They quickly headed in that direction. They found Mickey standing over the bed.

He shouted at his father, "You, you, you monster! You've been hiding things all these years. Pretending. Holier than thou. When I got into trouble, you just blamed me, blamed my poor absent mother. God knows why she wasn't around. But you, you acted like I was the bad seed, that it was my mother's fault. If there ever was a bad seed, you are it, not me. I'm not bad, I just got in trouble like all teenagers do. But you, you treated me like dirt. When other fathers would go down and pick up their kids from juvie, you just let me sit there. You'd tell me what a bad kid I was, wasn't worth springing.

"And this whole time," Mickey continued his rant. "It was you, you are the one who did that to her. You murdered little AnnaRose. You, You." Mickey raised both his arms and shook them at his father, lying quietly in his death bed.

Brad stood by Mickey's side, ready to dampen anything more than shouting. "Careful," he said to Mickey.

Ray lay in the bed, his eyes wide open, but seemingly unable to respond to Mickey's bellows of rage.

Darrell had bagged the doll. He now held it up so that Ray could see it.

"Do you remember this?" Very asked in a soft voice.

"I, I, I," Ray stopped and swallowed. "I gave it…"

"We found it stuffed into the back seat of your car," Mickey shouted again, "the car that's been sitting there for forty years. Forty-five years. Can you answer that one?"

Ray's eyes opened wide. He looked around at the gathering. He seemed puzzled to see them all here, surrounding his bed. "It's not been there for fifty years. It wasn't until that time, when the police came snooping. Cold case they called it." He stopped, his breath came with wheezing gasps.

Ray smacked his lips and tried to wet them. Very interpreted this gesture as one meant to ask for water. She pushed her way to the front and found the water glass. She checked the water and the straw. She looked around for Mickey. It was his job to do this. But she looked at Mickey's stormy face and then gently lifted the glass. She placed the straw on Ray's lips. He sucked, and stopped. Very let him take his time, she offered the liquid again. He used his tongue to position the straw and tried to ingest more. Very waited. Oh, this was a game little kids play, stall, ask for water, for food, for entertainment. She took the glass away.

Brad leaned over the bed, looking directly at Ray. "The cold case investigation. That was eleven years after it happened. We came here, to this house, to talk with you again."

"Then, then I started thinking. Not before, it was then. I knew he had lied to me." Ray looked at Mickey and said quietly. "It was the car in the driveway. I always left it in the garage, but it was in the driveway. I knew he had lied."

The three detectives looked at Mickey.

"Yeah, I lied," Mickey said through clenched teeth, "but I didn't have anything to do with AnnaRose. It was just having fun, I was just doing something fun, for a change. But I got sick, you know. In the end, not so fun. It was the beer. You know, when you're not used to it, and you drink it for the first time? You don't know how much to drink. I just threw up, then I went to bed. I was asleep when they all came looking. I wasn't driving the car, I couldn't drive, I didn't know how."

Silence settled.

"Tell us again about your friend, Wayne, was it?" Very said.

"Yeah, yeah. He knew where the keys were. He could drive, he even had a license. He drove the car."

Ray lay in the bed, his eyes half open. It wasn't clear if he understood what was being said or not.

Very looked at Ray and then went on. "Okay, Mickey, from the beginning. You told me, but one more time. Tell us everything that happened."

Mickey's shoulders slumped. He took a deep breath. "Truth, tell the truth," he said to himself.

Very said, filling in what she knew. "From the beginning. You went to school. That we know. You were marked in for Home Room and first period. Not the rest of the day. So, when did you leave school?"

Mickey's head went lower. His voice became softer. "He was there in the parking lot. I told you that."

"Did anyone see you? Did you try to hide? Did he try to hide? Why weren't other people there to see you?" Very pressed.

"I think I asked to be excused to go to the bathroom. I was outside, on my way, when I saw him. He waved to me. I think maybe he was hiding a little because I don't think anyone saw him, he was just around the corner. Just beyond the office part. He motioned to me and I went to talk with him. Then we walked home. You know, it's just a really short walk. We even took the short cut, across the pipe over the river. So we didn't even go out to the highway. It was easy for no one to see us."

"Who's Wayne?" Brad asked.

"Wayne Gordon, Gordon was his last name. He lived on the next street. He was older than me, he had a driver's license, so he was at least sixteen, maybe seventeen." Mickey said.

"Were you friends? See each other a lot?" Very asked.

"Well, not really. He was older, so he should have had some friends his own age. And I think he had dropped out of school. You know, you don't go to school, and bingo, no one to hang around with."

"What time was this?" Very asked again.

"Maybe ten in the morning. I don't know. I didn't have a watch, it didn't matter what time."

"And then you walked back to your house?" Very pressed. "You stole the car keys to your dad's car. You drank beer. Where'd you get the beer?"

Mickey licked his lips. He knew what had happened. Always knew. If he had tried to put it out of his mind, it had failed. But he had never had someone ask him like this. Time to tell it all. "Wayne stole it from his folk's fridge. It was only a couple of cans; he said they wouldn't miss it."

"And you drank at his house?" Very asked.

"No, no we drove. He drove."

"Drove where?"

"Up into the hills, up towards Aliso Canyon. Somewhere up there. There was no one there. No one was camping, wrong time of year. Everything seemed deserted."

"How long were you there?"

"Long enough." Mickey hung his head and dropped his voice. "I got sick. I insisted that we go back home. He laughed at me, but he drove me home."

"What time was this? What happened then?" Very's voice rose in frustration.

"I told you, I got sick, I went to bed."

"Where did Wayne go?"

"I don't know."

"What time did you wake up?"

"I don't know. My dad had come home from work. But now, I think he came home early. He took AnnaRose and murdered her and then he came back. He thought I was at school, so he just took the car and snatched her." Mickey looked at his dad, at the old man lying in the bed.

"No, no, not me. You took the car, you took the car and you stuffed that doll into the space in the back seat." Ray said, his voice weakening as he went on.

"What made you think that?" Mickey stood over the bed, shouting again.

"That cold case. They were asking. Asking about where I was. And I remembered about your lie. You lied about the car. So, I went looking. In the car." Ray stopped, heaving for breath. His color, which had heightened while he was talking, now faded. His face turned gray and pasty. Very hastily grabbed his glass and tried to get him to sip some more water. They all waited. Ray's lips moved. "I found the doll. I thought you had done it. I didn't want to tell anyone. My boy, my son. It was a long time ago. I couldn't tell anyone."

"So, you put the car in that garage," Mickey said. "You made me help you push it in there. And you thought I had done it? You hid it from everyone. And you told me that you had lost the key. You wouldn't let me drive it, wouldn't even let me sell it."

"I got you another car, didn't I? I tried…I tried to keep them away. I tried to keep your secret."

"You thought I had done it? Killed AnnaRose? So you lied for me?" Mickey stared at his father.

Ray turned his eyes on Mickey, blinking them. His mouth moved. Was this an apology? An explanation?

Silence spread over the room. They waited. Was there more to be said?

Brad looked at Mickey, "We need to know more about Wayne Gordon."

Mickey turned to Brad. "He lived around the corner. By the time I met him, he had dropped out of school. He had odd jobs, I think. He had some money, but not a lot. I didn't really know much about him. You know, guys, they don't say much to each other. They just talk about sports, and girls, and drinking. I didn't keep in touch with him. I don't know that I ever spoke to him after that day. Maybe. Maybe just to say that I wouldn't drink with him again. Or he asked me how I was that day and I said I got sick and… I don't really remember the conversation. I had no idea I was supposed to remember it. I never thought. He left, his whole family left in the next few weeks or maybe a month later. There was no need to keep in touch. Why?"

"And I venture to guess you weren't drinking more beer and playing hooky from school? We did notice that you had gone to school the next day and the day after. Did you get better about going to school after that day?" Very asked, an edge to her voice.

Mickey hung his head and shook it.

"Where is this Wayne now? Where can we find him?" Brad demanded.

Mickey shrugged. "He wasn't one of the good guys. I heard that he was in trouble with the law."

Very squared her shoulders. "We need to find him. We need answers."

Chapter Twenty-six: A Race with the Grim Reaper

Darrell's phone rang. He held up his hand for silence and then said, "Yes, yes. We are on our way."

Darrell beckoned Brad and Very outside into the living room. "That was Glen Bullitt. His dad is in the Emergency Room at Mercy. Stroke, heart attack, episode, something. Eugene is really upset. We need to get there."

Brad said, "Okay. I think we are done here. No more information, or misinformation, needed from those two."

They went back inside to say goodbye, and heard more of the tirade.

"Pop, you didn't need to lie for me. I didn't do it." Mickey stood over his father.

Ray looked up at Mickey. "You're a good boy. Not all boys would have stayed with their old man like you did. I'm sorry about suspecting you. I…"

Brad said loudly, "Don't go anywhere."

"I'm not going anywhere, I'll be right here. But I'm not so sure about him." Mickey gestured at his father, whose color had gone pale and whose breathing had become more labored.

Very entered the bedroom, "Look out for him." The old woman, her mother, lying in her bed, fading away, mirrored in the old man now lying in his death bed. "Hold his hand," she said to Mickey.

Brad's truck sped down the road towards Bakersfield. Very followed as closely as she dared. The sun set in a brilliant display in her rear-view mirror. The dust of the valley, carrying Valley Fever spores, pesticides and soft, fine dirt, also made for brilliant sunsets. A few wispy clouds caught and dispersed the sunlight, creating heavenly shafts of light onto the barren hills of Taft. Soon, the entire sky shimmered and shone like fire.

They drove down Truxtun Avenue to Mercy Hospital. She hadn't been inside for years. Her father was born here, and died here as well. She was born here, too.

Brad's phone call to Glen had summoned him to the lobby. He looked glum.

Very took his arm and talked quietly to him as they took the elevator upstairs. They found Eugene lying in a bed, a feeding tube stuck into his arm, an oxygen hose stuck up his nose. The brown spots on his skin showed browner against the gray of his flesh. Glen approached the bed.

Brad, Very and Darrell huddled in the doorway. Brad said, "Darrell, can you get to the office quickly? We need to find out about Wayne Gordon. Birthdate, about 1945. We need to find him."

"Oh, he's probably dead." Darrell said.

"What makes you say that?" Very asked.

"He'd be so old. You know, like over 70."

Brad and Very looked at Darrell with wide, incredulous eyes.

"Darrell, the average, AVERAGE, life expectancy for American males is way over 70. Now, he could easily be dead, but chances are, he is still around somewhere,"

Very said, turning her back to look again at Eugene and Glen.

Very approached softly, "How is he?"

Glen turned to look at Very. "I think this is the end. I don't quite understand. This morning, he was okay, but then…"

Brad intervened, "He got tired of waiting."

Very said, "Can we talk with him? I think we can give him some news."

"I think he would like to hear anything you have to say. I'm not sure how much he will understand, but…" Glen approached the bed, followed by Brad and Very. They gathered around Eugene's bedside, watching his chest heave up and down.

He opened his eyes. "Oh, the ghouls have arrived."

Very stepped back. Did he think they were here to gloat? To carry him off? Grim Reapers en masse?

Brad stepped forward and looked down at Eugene's shriveled body which hardly made a lump in the bed, just a slight mound under the sheets.

Very went around to the other side of the bed and took his hand, "Eugene," she said. "We've come to talk with you. Are you sure you're up to it?"

Glen leaned over him from the other side of the bed.

Eugene turned to look at Very, "You're too old to be an angel."

"Yeah," Very laughed. "I'm no angel."

When the silence around the bed grew long, Very said, "We've come to tell you we know you had nothing to do with AnnaRose's death. You know that, you've always known that. And now, everyone will know that. You don't have to worry. You can carry on and your legacy will be that you were a good father to your daughter."

Eugene struggled to speak. "She was a high-spirited girl, that one. Always getting into trouble. But she didn't deserve that, no one does." He turned his head as tears seeped from his eyes. The oxygen tube prevented him from hiding his turmoil.

Very plucked a tissue from a box on the side table. She bent to carefully wipe his eyes, gently smoothing the tears from inside to outside. "We'll carry on from here. You rest."

Eugene sighed and closed his eyes.

A hospital person arrived at the doorway and frowned on them, clustering around the bed. Very motioned the other two to leave, they could talk in the corridor.

Glen was distracted, but curious. "What have you found out? Something new? Something different?"

"Let's go to a coffee shop or somewhere. I could use something to eat. And drink."

They stopped at the nurses' station and Glen made sure they had his phone number. Then they headed out.

Seated at the Sugar Mill on North Chester, they ordered some food. Very thirstily drank a large glass of water. Brad looked at her strangely.

Very stared back, "What? Anxiety makes me really thirsty. And the last few hours have been full of anxiety. And now, food is a different thing. I was hungry, but now I'm not. I'll just take it home with me, I guess."

She phoned Darrell. He had walked back to the office, which was only a few blocks from the hospital. He and Olivia had ordered pizza. They were working on finding Wayne Gordon.

As they waited for food, Brad and Very talked about the coming summer and the heat wave predicted for the next week.

"Heat wave in Bakersfield. So what else is new? A hot, dry summer? Aren't they all?" Brad's words dripped with sarcasm.

Glen stared at his phone, as if waiting for a call from someone. He set it down and looked at his newly arrived hamburger. "I don't know whether to be happy, and grateful, that you have figured out he didn't do it. And that now he can go to his grave in peace. Or maybe I should feel sad because he's dying."

"Does he have any other unfinished business. Something else he needs to do?" Very asked.

"I don't think so. This was it. I haven't called Cindy, to let her know he's in a bad way. Maybe she wants to say her goodbyes?"

"I think that would be nice," Very said as a plateful of food was set in front of her.

Glen looked at his plate, but he needed to ask one last thing. "Can you tell me? Do you know what happened?"

Brad's phone rang. He pulled it out of his pocket and looked at the caller ID. He held up his hand, indicating a pause in conversation. The tinny voice came through, "I think he's gone, he just went. He's unconscious. I'm calling 911."

Very took the phone from Brad's hand. "Mickey, open the window. Let his spirit out. It's all over now."

Chapter Twenty-seven: What Happened that Day

"Ray Kenton just had a turn for the worse," Brad said to the table. He whispered a few more words to Mickey and then hung up.

Great plates of food had arrived. Large white platters of brown meat, smothered in gravy and accompanied by shiny orange bullets of baby carrots. The French fries lay in comfortable masses of long golden spears. Green florets of broccoli snuggled together. Another plate held fluffy white slabs of bread gleaming with yellow butter. The cheerful waitress refilled the water glasses.

Very found hunger lurking somewhere and attempted to satiate it. The table was quiet for five minutes while they ate.

Brad stopped, took a long drink of water and sighed. He looked at Glen. "We're not exactly sure what happened that day, but here is a probable scenario." He glanced at Very.

"Betty Jean went out with Cindy in the stroller; they met her friend." Very continued the story. "AnnaRose had complained about not feeling well and she didn't want to go to school. We found a baby tooth in the pocket of the jacket she wore that day. She was only six, so this was in all probability the first tooth she had lost. You can imagine what you feel like when it starts getting loose. You use your tongue to worry it and it wiggles and it doesn't feel good. And if it's the first one you've lost, you really don't know what to expect. You can taste blood, and maybe you're afraid it will bleed more or whatever. She might have been frightened, curious, in pain, who knows? But what a good opportunity to not go to school! Just say you don't feel well, don't really have to say why, just 'don't want to go to school.' AnnaRose, that was her."

Brad took up the story. "Betty Jean was rather cavalier about AnnaRose. You said, didn't you Very, that your mother let you wander around alone, even at an early age. Cuyama was such a safe place. Friendly, everyone knew everyone else. If a little girl, a very friendly little girl, somehow got lost, well someone would surely bring her home. Betty Jean was never a bad mother. But she was a single mother and she had lots to do. You remember, she was off to the grocery store that day, and on foot. She couldn't buy too much in one trip, she only had the stroller to carry things in, so you can imagine that shopping was a big problem for her. I suspect your dad would help take her to the store and to buy things. And maybe Ray would too.

"In her statement, she said she looked in on AnnaRose. She said she was asleep; she was fine. It was safe to leave her. In fact, she said she looked in on her twice. Once before and once after going to the store. The last time was about eleven. AnnaRose was safe in bed."

"But AnnaRose could have made a 'fake' and slipped out. I taught her how to do that," Very said. "You know, use pillows and extra blankets to make a body in the bed. She thought that was a great joke. We practiced it a few times, but I don't think her mother ever figured it out. She could have done that, and then slipped out. If the curtains in the room were pulled, it would have been dark in that room. That side of the house faced north, so there never was any sunlight; it was always a bit dim in the rooms on that side of the house. Maybe Betty Jean did look in on her, I have no doubt she did, but what she saw was most likely not her little girl, tucked up in her bed, asleep."

"So, we're not sure when AnnaRose left, or whether she went by herself," Brad said.

"I think she went by herself. That's what she would do," Very said. "Sassy, independent. She did what she wanted to do – always."

"How she got out, or whether she was kidnapped, is also not known yet." Brad said. "but she could have walked out the front door. It was unlocked. Apparently, all the doors in Cuyama were unlocked. She could have done that easily enough. She was certainly tall enough to reach up and turn the handle and she had obviously seen others do it, and she might have done it herself a few times. I'm sure I did by the time I was six. And she wouldn't have had to fiddle with a lock, just grab the handle."

"No one locked their doors, but after AnnaRose went, everyone did," Glen said. My dad told me that once, when I came in late and didn't lock the door. He told me that it was my half-sister that made everyone realize how easy it was for someone to get in, kidnap the little ones and murder them. I think that was the first time he ever really talked to me about AnnaRose. I mean, I knew, I always knew, but he talked more that day, that evening. And he made me promise to always be careful about locking the doors. In her name."

"I remember too. My parents started locking doors, especially in the evening," Very said. "When everyone was home for the day, my dad would go around making sure all the doors were locked. I had never really thought about it much, but it was about that time. AnnaRose being killed was one of the horrors of my childhood. And because I had known her, it seemed so close. And I never thought about locking the doors before. Even now, if I forget to lock a door at night, I feel panicky, like I've let someone down. Or someone will know I have been remiss and take advantage of me." Very shivered at the memory.

"What we are not sure about is when AnnaRose left, whether she went by herself or was taken." Brad stated.

"I think she went by herself," Very said.

"And how she got out," Brad continued. "We don't know if she was kidnapped from her house, or… But she could have walked out the front door."

"Or she could have gone out the back door, the door in her bedroom. And then she could have gone over the fence. We know that it wasn't as high then as now. And then she would have been on the walkway," Very continued.

"From there," Brad said, "it was easy to get to the edge of town, to the highway. And remember, we don't know what time any of this happened, exactly. When questioned, no one said they had seen her."

"But AnnaRose could have sneaked around. She knew she shouldn't be outside, so she might have hidden in the bushes or behind the fence. She was an excellent 'Hide and Go Seek' player. And now, we have new information about lies," Very said.

"Lies, lies, lies," Brad continued. "Mickey Kenton lied about being at school, but what he is telling us now is that between ten in the morning, he thinks, and early in the afternoon, no specific times, he was with a friend.

They took his dad's car, drove out of town and drank beer."

"And Mickey was only fourteen, never had beer in his life. It made him sick. He wanted to go home. So, they went back to Mickey's house where he threw up and then went to bed and to sleep. He woke up late in the afternoon when they all began to search for AnnaRose."

Brad said, "And his dad knew the car had been driven, or at least moved, how far he might not have known. Even if he had checked the odometer or the gas gauge, who remembers that sort of thing? But he had always parked it in the garage, and now it was in the driveway. He asked Mickey, but Mickey lied to his dad and said he didn't know anything about it. He couldn't drive, remember? And once he had lied, he continued to lie. But once Mickey had gone to sleep, what happened to the car? It was in the driveway when he woke up, but where had it been for the middle part of the afternoon?"

"We think his friend dropped him at the house and then drove the car some more. Joyriding when everyone was at work, or school or somewhere else. What an opportunity to take a car and go…wherever," Very said.

"Like out on the highway," Brad said. "Giving a ride to a vivacious little girl that he probably recognized and she, him. Everyone knew everyone in town and if he had stopped and asked if she wanted a ride, she could have gotten in with him. No fear. He lived in the next block, he was part of the community. He was a 'friend.' Maybe he offered to take her home, or to the library or somewhere fun."

"And instead of taking her home or somewhere else, he drove up the valley, it only takes ten minutes on the highway."

"And then off the road," Brad said. "He found a hidden spot, not far off the road and…"

"She took her doll with the red dress everywhere she went. She must have had it that day. And then it disappeared." Very looked away, somewhere into the distance, into the past.

"But we found it today. Or rather, we found it again today. Those two, father and son, secrets from each other. So many secrets, so many lies."

Very said, "This friend, when he returned, must have realized that the doll was still in the car. He parked in the driveway and did what must have been the easiest thing to do. He hid the doll in the car. You know, the old cars with their seats weren't really solid. There's a weird space in the back seat. Actually, it gives some access to the trunk. But in this case, that doll was shoved into the weird little space that couldn't be seen from the trunk, or rather in any casual perusal of the trunk. It could have, actually it did, go unnoticed for years."

Brad interrupted, "That is, eleven years to be precise. When we started nosing around during the cold case investigation, someone found it. We sniffed too close. But we weren't thorough enough, we just did some repeat questioning. But for two people, it was traumatic. Ray Kenton, when questioned again, stuck to his alibi. We checked it out, again, so that was that. Mickey wasn't around, so he was never asked to repeat his alibi or anything else. But Ray remembered the car. He knew his son had lied about the car, he was sure his son had taken it out driving and parked it in the driveway, instead of the garage. So, he searched the car again, looking for anything that might be a clue as to why his son had lied. He practically tore it apart. He found the doll stuffed down in the back seat. Actually, it was easy for me to see because the light was so dim, I was only glimpsing shapes and shadows. The slight bump came up more readily as an anomaly in the smoothness of the seat. And

Ray must have found it the same way. He must have seen that the back seat wasn't smooth, a bit askew, like someone had taken it out and not gotten it back in the same condition, the same smoothness. So, when he found the seat not quite right, he pulled it up. Ray found the doll. He knew exactly what it was because, apparently, it was he who had given it to AnnaRose."

"We got Mickey to be straight with us. When it all came out, he admitted that he had lied. But he was at home sick, and seemingly had never thought about his friend." Very said. "His friend had the car, but Mickey didn't think about that?"

"I think the psychologists have a name for that. When you don't want to think about something bad, there are ways to conveniently forget about it. Compartmentalized and forgotten." Brad sighed.

"But when we found the doll, Mickey accused his father of killing AnnaRose, so he hadn't forgotten everything." Very said.

"And his father accused Mickey of murdering AnnaRose. Told him that he had found the doll in the car and knew his son had done the evil deed. And then he covered up for him. Oh, so many years of secrets, of bad blood, of fearing the worst of your own kin. And then, Ray hid the car from everyone. He even made Mickey help him push it into the Quonset hut, and then told him he couldn't sell it. Oh, suspicions and lies, and unnecessary hatred of the other. And yet…"

"There they are, in the same house, son by his father's bedside as he lay dying. That's devotion, that's caring for family." Very leaned back.

Glen sat there. "Those two weren't the only ones lying. My dad hid where he'd been for over fifty years. The follies of our youth. He thought someone would care too much."

They ate a few more bites, but then asked for boxes. They decided that coffee was in order and asked for that. Glen paid the bill.

Brad looked at his coffee and then out the window. Night had well and truly come, the crickets could be heard and the restaurant was closing up.

Glen turned to Brad, "You said that there were two people traumatized by the cold case. One was Ray, who found that dress, and then hid what he thought was an evil secret for years. He suspected his son of being a murderer. He hid the doll and the car, and then lived with the pain for all those years. But who else was traumatized by the cold case investigation?"

Very answered, "Betty Jean Bullitt. She committed suicide."

Chapter Twenty-eight: A Long Night

Glen opened his mouth, "No, that was an accident." His phone rang.

He turned his face aside and spoke quietly. Very heard the number of the hospital room where Eugene Bullitt lay.

"Cindy is coming. I'll meet her at the hospital. Let me just finish my coffee." Glen sighed heavily.

Brad and Very sat quietly while Glen looked deep into his coffee cup.

"So," Glen said, "what you're telling me is that Betty Jean committed suicide by driving off the road, deliberately?"

Very said, "I believe that Cindy wasn't old enough to understand at the time. Betty Jean had been traumatized by the cold case investigation, by digging up everything from the past. She had never gotten over the initial trauma in any case, but when the police came around, sniffing, questioning her again, she just lost it."

Brad said, "Think of it this way, Betty Jean was once more doubted. Cindy was still too young, and of course, she was only a baby at the time, but they interviewed her mother. I did. I was there. It was not gentle. There were hard questions that Betty Jean found hard to answer. Things like why she had left her daughter alone, why would any mother leave a six-year-old by herself? Wasn't that the act of a bad mother? She was never accused directly, but the implication was that if she had been a better mother, her little girl would still be alive. It was somehow her fault that AnnaRose had been kidnapped and murdered."

"It's hard to say what Betty Jean felt that day," Very said, "whether she left Cuyama and really meant to drive off the road or whether it was a spur-of-the-moment thing. Something like, 'I've had enough' and that she couldn't stand any more questions. I am sure that Cindy had no idea if her mother had planned that or not. Cindy knew that her mother was distressed. You don't talk to a thirteen-year-old about things like this. She couldn't say to her daughter, 'I feel suicidal.' Could you? Cindy, although she knew that her mother was not happy, couldn't have known that she would take her car out and run it over the railings on that road. I think Betty Jean felt alone, that no one was there for her."

Glen sighed, "She didn't think about Cindy, did she? She left that kid all alone."

"And Cindy has paid for it. Again and again. I hope you can be a good brother to her." Very sighed with him.

"Yeah, you're right, we're victims too. And maybe it's okay that there isn't another generation to suffer from this too." Glen sipped at his coffee. "So, who did it? Who killed AnnaRose?"

Brad leaned forward and said quietly, "Wayne Gordon. Do you know him?"

Glen's eyes widened. "No, the name isn't familiar. Should I know him?"

"Not really. No, he lived around the corner, in Cuyama. His family moved away shortly afterwards. He was about sixteen or seventeen at the time, so you probably would never have run into him at school, or sports or anything. We think, we have good information, that's who it was."

"It's as though he killed more than one little girl. Betty Jean, and my dad, it ruined his life. And Cindy? All her life she has lived under the shadow of that crime. And Mickey and Ray Kenton, it sounds like it cast a deep shadow over their lives as well. What a life of lies and resentments the two of them had." Glen slumped in his seat. "Is it over?"

Very sat up. "Crime does that. It touches and changes lives. And for many, they are never able to live a 'normal' life. They are repeatedly haunted, followed, and eventually twisted by awful things. I hope that everyone can find some closure on this one."

Glen stood. "I'd better go. I need to meet Cindy. Please keep in touch with me. Tell me when you find the monster."

Very and Brad sat for a few more minutes. Brad called Darrell. There was no answer. Brad then sent a text.

Very declined more coffee and listened to the sounds of the restaurant closing up. The pots banged in the kitchen, the waitress filled a small bucket and came to swipe down all the tables, while another hauled a vacuum out of the closet and started the whine of clean-up.

"Nine o'clock, and Bakersfield rolls up the sidewalks." Brad smiled.

"To the office?" Very asked. "Where could Darrell be this time of day?"

They drove the few minutes down Chester Avenue, across the dry river bed and then past the large buildings that once housed premier department stores, upscale offices and familiar restaurants. Except for the bus station, the city center was deserted. A few cars were parked along the street. Homeless denizens gathered on street corners, surrounded by their belongings in shopping carts, and their pets. Monday wasn't a big party night in Bako.

As Very and Brad entered the deserted office building, Brad whispered to Very, "Is there a witching hour around here? When do the cleaners come and go? Is there an alarm system?" He looked upwards to check CCTV cameras and found nothing.

Very shrugged. "I have no idea. I've never thought of being here this late. Where is Darrell? He might know. I'm sure there is some sort of security. And I'm sure that we are waaay too late to be here."

But all remained quiet as they let themselves into the office. Brad took the plastic bag that contained the doll and set it on the unused table. He sat at a desk and pulled out a pad of paper. Then, he proceeded to write. Very looked over his shoulder and saw the meticulous recreations of the conversations they had had today. Who said what, when. Who reacted with what. What time each encounter took place, who was there.

Very sat and communed with her own thoughts. Such an incredible day, so many things had happened. She glanced at the board, which now spread out over the entire windowless wall. She found the photos of the possible suspects and looked at the blank space. She took a marker and wrote 'Wayne Gordon' under the vacant place. No longer a gap in their knowledge, now a known entity. Brad asked Darrell to find Wayne, how long would that take? Finding Frankie Monroe had taken a long time. Maybe just using the internet search engines wasn't going to turn Wayne up. Maybe she could try doing that. She swiveled to the computer and turned on the power.

While Very waited, for a very, very long time for the computer to boot up, she looked at the doll in the red dress. "DNA?" she said.

Brad turned from his notetaking and followed her gaze. "DNA on that? Look at it, disintegrating before our eyes. Look, that red stuff has fluffed out and I swear it's taken on a mind of its own. And if you think we are going to find Wayne's DNA on that, think again. Yeah, if we are lucky, they can find his, but they will also find lots and lots of AnnaRose's."

"Well, we have the tooth to check for verification with that," Very said.

"And also her mother's DNA, and as of today, mine, as well as Ray's. Don't think that will be the end of the story, to find Wayne's DNA among all the others."

"And the cigarette butt?" Very said.

"Hmmmm," Brad said. "Okay, if we can get DNA from both of those, then we might have a case. But we need to find Mr. Gordon. What if he has disappeared?"

"Or is dead?" Very said. "Oh good, the computer has finally booted up. This thing is getting really old and slow. I guess if I need to, I can use my own computer. Well, that is, if I am still part of this enterprise. I'm going to look up Wayne Gordon, see what the internet has to say about him."

Before she could type in the name, her phone rang. "Yes, yes, slow down Mickey. I'm putting you on speaker."

"They've come. And they hooked him up to breathing tubes and stuff. But he's going. They're taking him away. To the hospital. Or the morgue. He looks awful and he can't breathe on his own. I couldn't find a pulse."

"Mickey, I'm sorry. I hope you made your peace with him." Very said.

"I think we were good, in the end. I just didn't know what to do today, this evening. I didn't know what to do at the end, it came so suddenly. You were there, this afternoon, he was talking, he was okay, wasn't he? So what happened?"

"Mickey," Very said. "Did you open the window?"

"To get rid of the smell? It's not bad, really, it's okay," Mickey answered.

"No, it's to let his spirit free. Let his soul go wherever he needs to go."

"Oh, one more thing, not to confuse matters, but I talked to a friend later this afternoon. He knew of Wayne. A little. And he said that the last he heard Wayne was in prison. It makes me sad to think of that, someone I knew. But it makes sense, doesn't it?"

Very was speechless. "Oh," she said finally. "Thanks for letting us know. Please, do keep in touch, let us know how it all plays out. And good luck to you."

Mickey hung up without saying anything more. Very felt relieved. How many more platitudes could she spew? 'Open the window.' 'Good luck'. Really?

Suddenly, the door flew open. Darrell, followed swiftly by Olivia, tumbled in. "You are here!" he exclaimed. "Good."

Brad left off his note-taking and stood to greet them. "Well, what?"

"I know what happened to Wayne Gordon," Darrell declared. He looked at the board and the empty space that had been left for the 'mystery man'. Mystery no longer. "I see the name has been filled in, and I can get a photo if you like."

"I think the name should suffice. So, where is he?" Very asked.

"Six feet under. Or perhaps in an urn somewhere. He died in San Quentin prison in 1998. Had a record as long as both my arms. And, the murder of AnnaRose may have been the first, but not the last. You want to know what happened to him? Murdered. Perhaps being stabbed to death by his cellmate was a fitting end to a misspent life."

There was a moment of silence, perhaps not for Wayne Gordon, but for all his victims, not the least of whom was AnnaRose Bullitt.

"And there were also rumors of sexual…"

"Darrell. Enough," said Very. "I don't want to hear."

"Justice? Maybe?" Olivia said. "What about DNA? Can we try to get him for this, this murder?"

"I doubt it. I doubt that anyone, including the state or the FBI, would care to spend any more money on this. I think maybe, this will be the end." Brad sighed. "I will file these notes with the rest of the file, but I don't think anyone cares at this point. And the one who does care, Eugene Bullitt, is lying in a coma in the hospital, not likely to live much longer."

"Glen will care," Very said. "He will know. And maybe Mickey will have some interest. And I care. I can have a different relationship to Cuyama now. I no longer have to fear going there. It's closure for me. And yes, justice."

Two weeks later, Brad was at Very's house at eight in the morning. She answered the knock and said to Brad, "I'll be ready in a minute. I need to get my purse and then we can go. Imagine, two funerals in one day. And then, tomorrow, I am off. I'm going to Canada. And that's that. And no, I don't want to talk about it."

At nine, they joined a small gathering in Taft. Mickey was not the only mourner, but there were none of Ray's contemporaries. They were all dead or incapacitated, soon to follow Ray to the marble forest. The graveside service was short. Brad and Very hung back, respectfully watching the proceedings.

They saw Mickey near the gravesite, black suit, respectfully hanging his head. A man, only slightly younger than Mickey, approached, slapped him on the back and spoke. Brad and Very inched closer to hear the conversation.

"Saw that great classic car sitting in the front yard," the man said.

"Yeah, I guess it's time to let it go," Mickey answered.

"Whoa, that's what I wanted to hear. How much are you asking for it?"

"More than you can afford."

"Well," the man said, "I've got contacts, maybe you'll give me a commission? How much for a classic 1956 Ford Fairlane, huh?"

Very shivered as she thought about the history of the car. When a murder has been committed in a house, you have to notify the prospective buyers. What about cars that have had murders committed in them? Or associated with them? Is there a time limit? Who would want a car like that? Would Mickey ever tell anyone?

Very turned to Brad and whispered. "Do you think that's a good idea? Do you think we should say something?"

Brad hung his head, hiding his face under his Stetson. "No, none of our business."

Less than an hour later, they quietly entered at the back of the room at Greenlawn. Darrell was already there with Olivia. They had saved seats for them. Glen and Cindy stood in front, side by side, the chief mourners. There were a few more than at the last ceremony, but not many. When the deceased is ninety or older, there aren't many of their own generation to mourn them.

After the short service, Very and Brad went forward to speak with Glen and Cindy. Glen was introducing Cindy to a few friends.

Very overheard one say, "I didn't know he had a daughter?"

Cindy turned to the nosy questioner and answered, "I'm not his biological daughter, but he was generous enough to give me his name and I have always been proud to call him 'dad'. But as you know, it wasn't a close relationship." She smiled, a slight viciousness to the grin that Very recognized. An AnnaRose snarky riposte.

Cindy peeled away from the group and came to Very. "Thank you so much for coming. I just have to tell you that I have chosen two of the afghans to keep and have packed all the others away. I think I know where I want to give them. And I need them out of the way. I'm getting new furniture and the whole place painted. I am going to redo the kitchen and the bathroom too. Dad left me some money, so I might as well put it to good use. And it makes the property more valuable. Some of my friends say I should get out of there, but I feel close to my mom and my sister there. I am not haunted by ghosts, I just feel like it is my home and theirs, too."

Very smiled at Cindy. Resilience, what it can be. More people could look to Cindy for how to overcome adversity. Not that she would ever forget or be totally free of the sadness of losing her family, but she could be a willing participant in life.

This was a woman to emulate. Face the past and live for the future. Maybe Very could use some of Cindy's outlook. She needed to deal with her own past.

Chapter Twenty-nine: What Happened to Frankie Monroe

It was uncharacteristically cloudy; not cold, but cooler than usual and the sky was leaden. Gray dirty clouds, not puffy white ones, dulled and hid the sun.

Joey stopped her SUV in front of the Meadows Field Airport terminal, and Very unbuckled her seat belt. She leapt out. She snatched at the handle to the back and then reached into the seat to snag her carry-on bag. She hauled it out and stood on the sidewalk.

"Very, I can help you," said Joey.

Very stuck her head into the open window. "It's just a small bag, I can do it myself. See you."

"In a week?" Joey called after her.

Very stopped and turned, "I'll let you know."

Very walked quickly towards the terminal. Now was not the time for Joey to demand a rehash of all the ins and outs of looking for Frankie Monroe. Did anyone understand why she had to go to Canada herself? No more phone calls, no letters, no hiring some other PI in another country to check this one out. This was Very and her ghost. No more conversations with anyone about this. It was a personal journey. In fact, she hadn't told anyone but Joey and Darrell where she was going and when. The last few weeks, working so hard on the

AnnaRose case, trying to tie it all up, had been tiring. As soon as she knew the dates of the two funerals, she had rebooked her flight for the next day.

The pressure of trying to get anyone to care, about DNA testing for the doll, for the tooth, for the cigarette butt, had fallen through. No one was concerned about the change in the story of some fourteen-year-old boy, now in his late sixties, about what might have happened. There was no confession, no jailbird who had snitched and said that his cellmate had confessed to some long-ago crime. Law enforcement was not going to pay for any testing, or any help whatsoever. The case had gone from a cold case, to a dead case. Brad had tried to file new evidence, but his notes about interviews, change of story and possible scenarios, was taken, but as everyone feared, had been filed in the proverbial 'round' file.

Brad had quipped, "Someday, someone may want to write a book about this. You know, true crime stories are big these days. Anyone have a fancy to become a writer in their retirement?" Very had quashed any more flippancy with a withering look.

Very asked Cindy if she wanted the 'artifacts,' the jacket, the tooth, the doll. Cindy had refused. "I have photos," she said, "that's all I need. And my DNA, half of which we share. I will remember her from my mother's words. 'She was a smart, happy, lively girl. Always laughing, always having fun.' Those are my memories. I don't want things that will remind me of that day." She had seen Glen and Cindy at the funeral, heads together. Brother and sister.

Very spent the day in airports and on planes. That's what happened when you flew from Bakersfield. There were few places where planes went to, so it was a series of hops around the country. She arrived in the evening, picked up her rental car and found her modest hotel. There was one of those fast food places across the street. Did they have vegetables or salad on the menu? Or only meat, potatoes and white bread? She walked there and chose the healthiest thing she could find on the menu. The waitress said she had to have it as take out, as the restaurant was closing. Fine, eating soggy fast food in her hotel room, from a paper carton with plastic utensils; that was just fine.

She sat on the bed in her small hotel room and ate her limp lettuce and soggy veggie burger. She turned on the TV and found only commercials and sports. She turned it off. She showered and crawled into bed. The room was cool and it felt good to burrow into the blankets. She set her phone alarm for the next morning. Maybe the restaurant across the street would be serving hot food at a table in the morning.

The night passed with dreams, nightmares, waking up and trips to the bathroom. The buzz of her phone came too early. But the eggs and toast, a decent cup of coffee and fruit cup of canned fruit made the day start right.

She dragged out the map that she printed off her computer, pinpointing the address in a suburb of Sudbury. She got in the car and headed out. Less than fifteen minutes later, she found herself in a section of the city with rolling hills, winding roads and houses set back from the street. There were no sidewalks, but mailboxes mounted on posts with numbers painted on the sides. She found the number and pulled up across the street, one house down. She checked her watch. If he had gone to work, if he still worked instead of being retired, then he was probably not at home. But if he had retired from whatever job, he would be at home, not gone on errands yet.

She walked slowly up the driveway, mounted the steps to the front porch and stared at the knocker on the door. She watched as her hand reached up and tapped the brass knob twice. She stepped back and waited.

From inside, she heard footsteps and the lock snick open. The door opened slowly. Very peered and blinked into the darkness. Then the man stepped forward.

He was sixty-five or so. His graying hairline framed wide-set eyes. A two days-worth of growth grizzled his chin and cheeks.

Very's mouth fell open, stunned. Her lips were frozen as she stared, looking deep into the man's eyes.

She licked her lips, "You're not Frankie."

The man relaxed his shoulders, sighed and looked beyond Very into the street. "No, I'm not. You'd better come in."

Very stood, rooted to the spot on the front step. "But, if you're not…"

"It's a long story. Come in."

Ten minutes later, after numerous exchanges about how Very liked her coffee, whether she had had breakfast, and Very had admired the view out of the living room window, they sat on the couch. The floor to ceiling window looked out over the rolling hills on the edge of the city. It was green, full of trees and the blue sky arched over it all.

Very sipped her coffee, better than that in the restaurant, and felt as though she needed to make the first move. "If you're not Frankie Monroe, who are you?"

"I'm not even Marvin Franks, but that's the name I inherited, bought, stole, whatever. It's on my ID. Do you remember the draft? The Vietnam war and men being called up to join our brave soldiers in Vietnam, fighting the communists? Well, I was young, stupid and scared. And I ran away. To here, to Canada. I tried to hide for years, bummed around, didn't let on that I was a draft dodger, but I think everyone knew. Well, by the time the Amnesty came, my folks had died, my sister got religion and didn't want to know me. So, why not stay here?

"But it was just before then that I met Marvin, I guess you knew him as Frank."

"Yeah, I knew him as Frankie, Frankie Monroe. When people change their identity, they often don't want to change it too far. They don't want to erase themselves completely. So, in some ways, I'm not surprised that he chose something not totally unlike his name. So, how did you meet?"

"In a bar, one cold day. We sat at the bar, and then someone asked if we were brothers. We both laughed, but when we looked again, we realized that we could be. You know the idea of the doppelganger? The concept that each of us has a twin, someone who looks like us, somewhere out there. We could have been doppelgangers; we were doppelgangers. I'm an inch shorter, but we were about the same weight, our bodies were similar build, our face, well, what do you think?" He smiled at Very.

"I see, I see how someone might think you were brothers, or even twins. It's the hairline, and the eyes, and that smile. I can guess that he looks like this now. So, what??"

"Well, after that, we found a table in a corner and talked some more. He guessed I was hiding out from the army recruiters and I sort of figured out he was hiding too. He hemmed and hawed and tried to get me to tell him about myself. You know, if I tell you something, you need to tell me something. Later, I realized he was trying to establish trust. Because he had secrets. I didn't have many.

"He just called them 'the bad guys,' although you might know more about who they were?"

"Yeah, I met up with a couple of them a few years ago. But no one was able to tell me what happened to Frankie. They were not good guys. But gone now, so I guess Frankie could go back, if he wanted."

"You'd have to find him first to tell him that. You see, at the time I met him, he was Marvin Franks, that was his name, mine was something else. He had run here, hiding out from the bad guys, and created a new identity for himself. But I think he felt as though he needed to move on. So, he suggested that I could 'buy' his identity. He needed to go elsewhere and establish a new, or newer identity, but he said that if I wanted, he'd let me be Marvin Franks. He owned this house, or rather, this cabin as it was then, a mortgage on it, that he said I could assume. And he helped me get my 'new identity.' He had cut his thumb, so his thumbprint was real distinctive. He held me down and cut my thumb in the same place. And then he had me use some acid on the rest of my fingers, to obscure my prints. Look, even now, they are weird." He held out his hands to Very, who noted the disfigured finger pads and the heavy calluses.

"And then, what happened?" Very asked.

"Well, it only took a few days, and we stayed here, keeping away from anyone he knew, which wasn't very many people. He was a recluse of sorts. He helped me assume his work history and I got a new job. Thank goodness I knew a bit about carpentry and plumbing and building, so I could pass as the Marvin that anyone knew, or had heard of. And this house, this shed as it was; he passed on all the plans he had made and gave me the materials he had bought. I was set."

"What about me, did he say anything about me? You knew my name, so he must have said something?" Very looked out over the forest.

"Yes, he told me some things. He did warn me that if some woman came looking for him, that it would probably be you. I had no idea it would take you so long. I'd almost forgotten. But he said that…" Marvin hesitated.

"Did he tell you about leaving me the day before we were to get married, that I was pregnant and that he never told me anything about the bad guys and…" Very fought back tears.

"Yes, he did tell me that. But he said that he had gotten word the drug dealing bastards were looking for him. That was the night before. And he couldn't tell you, or his mom, or anyone like that. He just needed to disappear, quick, and completely. It was his life. But he told me about you. He said that you would cope. That you were smart, really smart, and capable and strong. He knew that he wasn't really the right guy for you, but after he knew about the baby, he agreed to marry you and he thought that with you, things could go the other way. But the night he heard about being targeted, he lost it. He felt bad, but he knew that you would be all right. He left, that night, he didn't tell anyone where he was going. He left and said nothing because he was trying to protect you. If you knew nothing, you would be safe."

"Well, they didn't get him, but they got his friend, Danny. Did he tell you about Danny?"

"No, he didn't know. He worried, but what could he do, after the fact? He was scared, that's what he told me."

"And I guess I knew, when Danny's body was found buried in the orchard, that Frankie would have been dead too, if he hadn't gotten out. I guess I knew that Frankie was a bit of a long shot, for me. Maybe I would have been happier with some grey-suited corporate type. But I never found anyone." Very sat quietly.

"But your child?"

"No, I, he or she, never had a chance. Miscarriage. And, although I never let anyone say it to me, it was probably the best thing. I went on. I became an old-maid librarian, and a world-traveler. I had a wonderful job, friends. It was a different life from the one I think I had planned, but I am not sorry."

"Frankie knew that, he knew that you would go on, happier without, than with him. Gosh, that sounds weird. I knew what his name was, that was the last thing he whispered to me before he left that day. But I hadn't used it before, now. Wow, what a story."

"What happened to him, where did he go?"

"He packed a duffel bag, asked me for as much cash as I could spare, and just walked out. Literally, walked out that door, early one morning. He was protecting me, by not telling me anything more, and not saying anything. If someone figured out who Marvin Franks was, then they would come here, looking for me. So, the less I knew, the better.

"He was a good friend to me. He saved me from wandering and being lost. He basically gave me this house, and a job and an identity. Although I only knew him for a few days, I can truly say he had a great influence on my life. I mean, I got married and had kids. Divorced too, but that's not unusual. What I'm trying to say, is that he was a good guy, despite his past life."

Very sat quietly, thinking about all of this. Something she had not expected. "Where is he now?"

"No clue. Never heard from him again. He only had that duffel bag, maybe a tent, a sleeping bag. Or he could have bought something else. I can imagine him just wandering, coming to a new town. He was so friendly, so…"

"Chameleon-like. He could be whatever you wanted him to be. I guess that I knew that, I just didn't want to know. Easy to overlook in the heat of the moment." Very smiled. "So, this is your house now. What a wonderful place. Congratulations."

"It took a number of years. For a time, I had to rent a trailer and live outside, plumbing issues. But my kids liked it here. Lots of room to play and explore. My wife would have wanted to be closer to town, but this was close enough for me. Marvin Franks, huh?"

Suddenly, Very felt replete. With coffee, with revelations, with some sense of closure. "I'll go now. Here is a card, if you ever think of anything else."

"Or if he shows up?" Marvin laughed. "Good-bye. I wish you a happy life."

"Same here. Good-bye."

Very got into her car and drove it out the road until the houses disappeared. She found a place to pull off the road. Getting out, she breathed the fresh mountain air. She stood on the edge of the great valley that lay before her. She could see trees and mountains and the sky. Where did Frankie go? What did he do after he left here? Did he create a new name, make a new life? Did he find someone to share his life? Did he ever know about her lost child and his own biological child? It seems not. It seemed as if he walked away from everything in his past. Suddenly, she felt very tired, and her shoulders sagged.

She whispered, "Goodbye Frankie. I'm done looking for you."

At her hotel, she changed her return flight to the next day. She tried to call Joey, but there was no answer so she texted instead. She turned off her phone and got into bed.

All day, during the flight home, Very could feel the world tilt and change. She suddenly wanted to pet her cat, Cleopatra, and vowed to be nicer to the orphan. At the last layover, she texted Joey again. She said she hoped Joey could meet at the airport, although it was late. On the flight, she closed her eyes until she felt the plane bump and land at Meadows Field. She had to wait for her luggage, although it was only one small case, with a wad of unworn clean clothes.

Outside, the curb looked deserted. The flight had been a few minutes late, so most passengers had been met and carried away. In the dark, Very looked around, a small knot of fear beginning to build. She looked further and then she saw it.

Bradley Parker's truck. It was parked directly under a light, about two hundred yards down. A tall man in a white Stetson stood beside it. She turned and let her legs carry her towards the man, her suitcase bumping along behind her. When she reached the truck, she stopped and set her case upright.

She moved slowly into his orbit, under the light. His arms reached out to her, surrounding her shoulders. She leaned in, feeling his warmth through his shirt, his smell, the rough skin of his beard against her cheek. Her arm encircled his waist and she raised her face and her lips…

Chapter Thirty: Epilogue

The phone rang, but Very tried to ignore it. It rang again and again. Finally, Very got up, put on her summer robe and wandered into the office. The phone had stopped ringing. It was Gabby. She had better call her back. Anyone who called so early in the morning must have something going on.

When Gabby answered, she was out of breath, "Oh, Very. Good, it's you. I need your help. I have the stuff."

"What stuff?" Very said, blearily.

"You told me to collect evidence. I did. And now that I have it, what should I do with it?"

"Sit tight. Don't say anything to anyone, yet. I need to make some phone calls. Are you going in to work today? Are you scheduled?"

"No, I'm not on the roster. Not today. But…"

"Hold on. I'm going to arrange a meeting. In a neutral place." Very sighed. She needed her coffee. "Are you sure about all this? We don't want to accuse someone falsely, or accuse someone with no proof."

"No, Very, I've got this. I've had time to gather all the evidence."

"My great Watson! Wait for my phone call."

Very walked into the kitchen. The sink was full of dirty dishes; take out containers littered the countertops.

This was not what she had wanted to find this morning. At least the coffeepot was clean.

After Very had cleared and cleaned the dishes, drank two cups of coffee and eaten some breakfast, she called Joey. She arranged to use Joey's house for a meeting late that afternoon. She waited until later in the morning, and texted Father Sullivan. Who knew what a priest's schedule was on a Sunday? She knew that the Sanchez house was neutral ground in this instance.

She did laundry, cleaned the house, spent hours petting her cat. With a light heart, she fixed a large tray of olives, big black pitted olives that would fit on Clara's fingers. She boiled eggs to make deviled eggs, stuffed celery stalks with cream cheese. Sprinkled paprika on top. She lined up little pickles in rows. She covered the whole tray with cling wrap and took it to her car.

When she arrived at Joey's, far too early for Sunday family barbecue, she found cars in the street. She hesitated. It wasn't her business, she was only the one who had negotiated the meeting. When she entered the kitchen, she met Joey.

"Are they all here?" Very asked.

"Yes, in the den. The 'Inquisition Room' the boys always called it."

"Oh, I remember that room. Great name for it. I got my questioning there as well. I'm going to listen at the door, just to check. It's not my business. But Gabby and two grown men who can be rather intimidating, I don't want to leave her to the wolves."

As Very walked through the house, she could hear the voices from the den. The door was open already, so she stood to one side. She heard Gabby's voice.

"And this day, she checked this kid in here, see here, and took his money. But there is no indication that it was given back, no mark, no check. And then here, I've made a note. And two days later, his name has been erased. See?"

Very heard papers ruffling.

"These printouts are from my phone, photos printed out. And see here, another time."

Hmms, and uhhs accompanied the explanations.

"This last week, the kids have been complaining, a lot. I heard it. And now, she has threatened them; I've heard that too. Not good. And she has been cheating on the supplies too. The invoices. Here and here. And then, voila, boxes of pencils and pens, not there! Packages of TP, not there. Where?"

Very peeked in the room. Gabby sat on one side of the desk, Father Sullivan sat opposite her. Bobby Sanchez stood behind her, arms crossed, witnessing.

Father Sullivan said, "Well, you've been thorough. You have done an excellent job of collecting evidence. But of course, I need to hear what the other side has to say…"

Bobby leaned over Gabby and said, "You've been brave to do this. I'm impressed."

Very leaned in the door and smiled at Gabby.

Father Sullivan stood, "Let me just take these papers."

Gabby's eyes lit when she saw the stack of papers she had presented returned to the folders they had come in.

"I can take these, can't I?" asked Father Sullivan.

"I have the originals, and copies, don't worry." Gabby smiled broadly.

"Good work," Father Sullivan repeated. "But a sad business. Our Boys and Girls Club just opened. We want it to succeed and have a good reputation. Thanks." He stood and turned to leave.

Joey appeared at that moment as if she had been listening. "You will stay for dinner, won't you? We always have a potluck with lots of food. And you are most welcome. It's a Sunday tradition at our house."

"Thanks, but my flock's business calls." He stood and strode out the door, his large frame filling the doorway.

"Gabby," Joey said, "You are welcome to stay if you like. We'll make sure you get a ride home."

Gabby looked panicked. "Oh, a bunch of grown-ups. I don't know…"

Very put in, "There will be lots of kids as well."

At that moment, Very heard a squeal behind her.

"Aunt Berry, Aunt Berry." A whirl of pink and white threw itself into the room and stuck like a limpet onto Very's leg.

"Clara, how are you?" Very turned to Gabby, "This is Clara, my favorite Sanchez."

"I thought I was your favorite," Gabby said. A smile sneaked onto her face.

"Well, there you have it, my fan club. Clara, meet Gabby."

Gabby gave Clara a huge smile and took her arm. "Yes, I'll stay for dinner. What can I do to help?" She and Clara headed for the kitchen.

Joey turned to Very, "Someone is asking if you are here."

"Oh, I forgot. I meant to send a text, call, or something. I came early and…"

Very went to the backyard, now teeming with life and laughter. She spotted him at the same time he saw her. Their eyes locked onto each other's as they slowly closed the gap between them. Guests moved out of their way as the two of them met.

Very lifted her head back as their lips met in a warm, passionate kiss. A very public kiss.

The buzz around them fell silent until Very and Brad realized they were the center, the very heart of the party.

They turned to look as a sea of faces watched them. Joey, directly behind Very, whispered, "Oh my God."

Clara ran forward, "Oh Aunt Berry! Does this mean you're getting married? Can I be the flower girl?"

About the Author

Phyllis Wachob grew up in the Central Valley of California, loving to read and use her imagination. After college at UC Santa Cruz, she began a career of travel and adventure, studying for an MA in England, traveling by bicycle through France and Italy, and then busing through Greece and Turkey. While trying to settle to life in California, working at a desk in an office, she stretched even further during vacations to Asia and beyond. She then became a full-time traveler and writer, spending a year in India, followed by a year traveling in Africa. She has continued to travel throughout her life and has to date, traveled to 76 countries.

English teaching as a profession was embraced during a spell in China, where she fell in love with the wild scenery and peoples of Chinese Turkestan. She subsequently lived in Japan, Taiwan, Australia (where she earned a Doctorate of Education in Teaching English to Speakers of Other Languages), China, Singapore, Egypt and Turkey, teaching and traveling. These extensive experiences are reflected in her mystery novels in the Teachers Abroad Mystery series. She took her knowledge of the people, places, food and customs and wove fictional stories of mystery and murder.

She has been influenced by the great mystery writers, (although she started with the Nancy Drew mysteries), enjoying Sherlock Holmes and Agatha Christie's books among others. She believes that characters and their vicissitudes form the crux of mysteries and the motivation to solve the whodunit is the driver of the story. The colorful, exotic, and unfamiliar should draw the reader into the core of the mystery, while the mundane and conventional hold the keys to the solution.

Currently she resides in Bakersfield, California where she was born. Her newest series, the Kern Kapers Mysteries, is set in Bakersfield and environs and features the characters who live there. She is a member of Writers of Kern and benefits from the connections of this professional writing community.

More information and blog posts can be found on the webpage: phylliswachob.com.

Questions for Book Groups

1. This story entails Very going back to a childhood hometown. She has mixed feelings, but we soon see her wallowing in nostalgia for her remembered early days. How does revisiting childhood affect us, especially as we age and move away?

2. New Cuyama is described as small, with all that implies. Everyone knows everyone else, for good or evil. How does this play out in the scenario of AnnaRoses' murder?

3. Very mentions, more than once, how comfortable people felt in the 50s letting children roam freely. Is that the same today? What has changed?

4. Very keeps her 'directional dyslexia' to herself. Why? Do you, or someone you know, have a similar challenge?

5. Very encounters two old men who are on the brink of death. She recalls her own mother's death and imparts pieces of wisdom to the caretakers. Do you think this is a way to be helpful, or is Very being a busy-body?

6. Very still does not find Frankie Monroe, but she does learn more about him. In the end, she gives up her quest. Why?

7. Who is your favorite character and why?